BABY X

Rebecca Ann Smith

BABY X

by

Rebecca Ann Smith

Mother's Milk Books

Published in Great Britain in 2016 by Mother's Milk Books

Cover image illustration copyright © Emma Howitt 2016
Cover design copyright © Teika Bellamy 2016

Typeset in Georgia and Didot
by Teika Bellamy.

Printed and bound in Great Britain by The Russell Press, Nottingham,
on FSC paper and board sourced from sustainable forests.
www.russellpress.com

Published in 2016 by Mother's Milk Books
www.mothersmilkbooks.com

For Dexter and Euan

1

Alex

Now, Sussex

It's midmorning when we turn off the motorway, taking the road which leads to the sea. Still raining: January rain, shot through with sleet. It's been raining all night, raining since yesterday evening. Raining since —

Enough of that. I don't have the time to think about what I've done.

I keep glancing in the rear view mirror, checking to see who might to be tailing us. I have to stay one step ahead. I don't think we're being followed. Not yet, anyway.

The road leads up into the rain-drenched, grey-green sweep of the South Downs. As we reach the top, I turn the wipers up to full. Below us the slate-coloured sea is only distinguishable from the grey fields by its unnatural flatness. I know this road. We don't have far to travel now.

Another glance in the rear view mirror. There's an infant car seat, facing forward, plastic and stiff polystyrene, upholstered in faded red tartan. X seems so tiny in it; I have to remind myself he's barely twelve hours old. His eyes are open, wide pools of deep blue, and I could swear he's in on this. The plan, such as it is. Our mad dash for safety and freedom. I could swear he knows exactly what's going on, and wants this as much as I do.

But no, I'm being irrational again. Acting crazy. He's only a baby.

As we follow the road back downhill, we hit a stretch

which is partially flooded. A crowd of mournful sheep huddle by the fence. We cut through the grey pool, high arcs of dirty water rising up on either side of the car, splashing the sheep and causing X to startle. In my peripheral vision I catch the flicker as his limbs jerk into life and then relax again.

*

It's still raining as we turn onto the gravel path that leads to the house. No one's followed us, have they? No. No one knows we're here.

Grannie's house dates from the nineteen thirties. The white render and original metal windows have seen better days; it takes a lot of work to maintain a place like this on the edge of the sea, and Grannie could never be bothered with it. It's cosy and warm inside though, or at least I can make it cosy and warm. We can hide out here, if only for the night, until I come up with a better plan.

Behind the house is a short, terraced garden, and at the end of that, beyond a low fence, the shingle beach leads steeply to the water, even at low tide. The nearest house is over a mile away, and no one uses this stretch of shingle – neither dog walkers, nor visitors to the pub on the main road – because access is restricted by banks of rocks, segmenting the beach and marshalling the cold, sloshing sea.

It occurs to me to hide the car, just in case. There's a space alongside the house, overhung by trees, and if I drive in far enough the car won't be visible. By four o'clock this afternoon it will be dark, and no one would guess we were here.

I turn the key to kill the engine and squeeze out, grabbing my handbag from the front seat and fumbling inside for the keys. Then I pull our meagre luggage from the boot – my soft-sided beach bag, the sports holdall I took from Fiona's, a plastic carrier bag from the service station. The rain drums on my back as I dash for the front door, and the key is as stiff in the lock as I remember it. Holding the handle towards me I nudge the mechanism until the lock slides. I throw the bags through the open door and into the hallway before I go back for X.

For a moment I find myself standing in the rain under the trees, staring at him through the water-spattered window. Under glass.

My heart is filled with so much I can't say. I open his door, lean in and smile.

'We're here, little man. We made it.'

His eyes haven't yet learned to focus, but at the sound of my voice he lifts his chin. I unclip the heavy buckle at his belly, slide my hand under his body, and pull him to my chest. A deep breath and we dash inside, out of the rain.

*

The house has a musty smell, the scent of damp, uninhabited spaces. It's also cold. I cross my fingers the gas and electricity are still connected. Still, the house seems pleased to see us. The walls of the hallway are a welcoming pale yellow, my memory of the living room is of two old but comfortable sofas, and beyond that there is Grannie's kitchen.

X lies in the crook of my arm, his head resting on the inside of my elbow, his eyelids starting to droop. I hold him close to my body, enjoying the soft, slight weight of him. I'd like a cup of tea, but I should change his nappy first, make sure he's dry and comfortable before he falls asleep. Once he's down, I'll have a few minutes to get my bearings.

I'm a mother now. That changes a person's priorities.

I grab the beach bag and head upstairs. As I hoped, the master bedroom is still made up with Grannie's things. A satin quilt the colour of dried blood hangs heavily over the dark wooden frame. I place a towel in the centre of the bed and lay X on that, digging into the bag for the changing things. I fill a small plastic bowl with bottled water and set this on the bedside table, then locate a clean nappy, and a thin, plastic bag, sickly sweet-scented, for disposal of the dirty one. I unpop the buttons at X's groin and neck, shuck him out of his baby-grow and pull open the sticky fastenings on his nappy. His skinny buttocks are caked in green-black tar, meconium, and I wipe this off with cotton wool and water. I watched my sister, Fiona, do this, when her babies were newborn. I wash my hands in the bathroom, pleased to find the water running clear and soap in a dispenser bottle on the sink. I refresh the plastic bowl of water and go back into the bedroom to dab more clean water around the crusted stump of X's umbilicus, gently lifting off the dried blood and yellowed gunk.

I'm a mother now. This is what I do.

Then a flash of anxiety, and with it a sudden, violent mental image: a screeching rhesus monkey, teeth bared in aggression or terror, lifted from a lab cage by black gloved hands. I don't know where this image comes from, but it brings to mind those anti-vivisection protesters, the ones who "liberate" animals from labs, not knowing what diseases they might be carrying.

Is that me, then? Have I done something heroic? Or reckless?

I look down at the baby lying on the bedspread. My X. My beloved. His skinny legs flop open froggily from his hips; his eyes are half-closed. A sweeping back, a sucking in, and in a wave my love for him crashes over me, drowning my doubts. I did what I had to do. To keep him safe.

I did what I had to do.

2

Karen

Fifteen months earlier, Newcastle-upon-Tyne

We sat in the car for several minutes, not speaking, just looking up at the building. Our first view of the Centre for Reproductive Medicine. I was struck by how big it was, how brand spanking new it was, all those curves of glass and concrete.

Rob moved first, unbuckling his seatbelt and reaching for the door. 'Okay, love?'

It was a cold morning and the heaters had gone off with the engine. The inside of the glass started to mist.

'We're just going to find out,' Rob said. He was using what I'd come to think of as his "hospital appointments" voice, a mixture of let's-get-on-with-it common sense with a large pinch of optimism thrown in for good measure. 'We don't have to go through with anything if we don't want to.'

I looked at my husband of almost a decade, taking in his thin face, the lines around his eyes deepening, the hair greying at his temples.

'Come on then,' I said, giving him a small smile. 'We've made it this far.'

*

I was nineteen when I met Rob. My brother Ian had talked me into coming out with him and his mates; there was someone he wanted me to meet. Rob and I played pool together, and afterwards we got chatting. He was a bit lanky, but he had a nice smile, and I knew I could talk to him. Looking back, nineteen seems too young to meet the person you want to spend the rest of your life with. But still, when you know, you know.

We got married when I was twenty-four, and bought a new-build on a nice estate, a three-bedroom-semi on the kind of street where a kid could learn to ride a bike and the parents wouldn't have to worry too much about the traffic. We'd talked about children, and it was what we both wanted, though we didn't make a big song and dance about it. Not at the beginning. I suppose we just thought it would happen naturally.

Then one day, Rob and I had *the conversation*, and soon afterwards I came off the pill. It was almost a year before one of my periods didn't arrive, and yes, to be honest, I was starting to worry. But you tell yourself it's going to be okay. You have to. Anyway, I was young, I was fit and healthy. I had a good diet, didn't smoke, ran twice a week with my friend Claire, did Zumba at the leisure centre after school on a Tuesday. And as soon as I fell pregnant, those twelve months of waiting didn't seem so important anymore. I remember doing the test at home, and then another one straight after, just to check. And there it was, the second line.

We were going to have a baby.

Ten weeks in, I miscarried. I don't really like to talk about it, even now. It wasn't very dramatic, I just started bleeding. What more can I say?

The hospital patched me up, and sent me to see my GP. He asked me lots of questions, then he said, 'Don't worry, Mrs Frey, it's not significant. Just keep trying.'

Later on, I thought about those words. Not significant.

I know he meant well. He was trying to reassure me that there was nothing wrong with me. Nothing serious anyway. But you know. *Not significant*. I can still hear his voice saying it.

I got pregnant again. Not immediately; it took another eight or nine months. We'd been trying harder this time too, watching the calendar, paying attention to the signs, staying off the coffee. As soon as Rob and I had done the test I phoned my Mum and Dad, then Claire, and then my brother Ian, and then Rob phoned his mum. We left it at that. We swore everyone to secrecy too, despite all the excitement, all the hopping up and down we could hear coming over the phone line. I told my Head at school, so she'd know if I needed to go for any appointments, or have time off, because I did get sick in the mornings sometimes, and felt tired by the middle of the afternoon. We decided we'd let everyone else know after thirteen weeks, when the risk of miscarriage was less. We didn't exactly enjoy keeping it secret, but after what happened last time, we wanted to be careful.

When I was thirteen weeks pregnant we went to the hospital for an ultrasound scan. I lay on my back while they squirted gel on my belly, which had got a bit tight in my jeans by then but was still flat really. And we saw the baby, strange but perfect, lying on its back, kicking its legs. The sonographer reassured us: everything looked fine; the baby was healthy. I realised I'd been holding my breath the whole time, dreading another miscarriage. But here we were, seeing our baby kick its little legs. Everything was going to be okay.

When I got back to school it was lunchtime and the staffroom was busy. I showed my colleagues the grainy black and white photo we'd brought from the ultrasound, and I pinned one of my copies to the notice board.

Everyone squealed and squeezed my shoulder, and Gill Hardy who takes Year 3, broke out the box of high-quality chocolate biscuits.

'Well, done, Karen,' they all said. 'You're going to be such a lovely mum.'

I started to feel pregnant. My breasts hurt, my belly started to swell, the sickness got worse. I bought some maternity trousers to wear at work, and a couple of roomier tops. I started to think about names. I'd always noticed women with babies when I was out and about, but now, when I saw someone on the estate pushing a buggy I'd make a point of saying hello, and she'd ask about my due date and we'd chat for a bit, you know, like we were part of some special club.

The gnawing hunger ebbed away, and with it the sickness and aching tiredness. I started to worry again. Claire said it was normal. A different trimester, a different set of symptoms. 'Don't worry,' she'd laughed. 'You're bound to feel like shit again by the end.'

I didn't make it to the end. Fifteen weeks in, I miscarried again.

There's not a lot to say really; I can't see any point in dwelling on it. We picked ourselves up and carried on. Seven or eight months later I was pregnant again. This time my mum was a bit more subdued on the phone, although Claire was upbeat. She was pregnant herself by then, with her second one, and I know she'd been careful around me, not wanting to talk about it too much. Not that I'd've held it against her if she'd talked about it all the time, although I know I'd've been the same way if our roles were reversed. But yes, she was excited about the timing; this way we could be pregnant together.

Was I excited? I was. I'm sure I was. It's hard to get a handle on my feelings, looking back. I remember sitting very still with a hand on my belly, listening in for a sense of my baby swimming around. I do remember how hard it was to relax. You try to get into the swing of it, but it's difficult to know how to feel. You don't want to jinx anything by buying baby clothes, and at the same time you don't want to ruin that special time with too much worrying. And then you start worrying that all the worrying might be bad for the baby, and maybe even bring on another miscarriage.

By that time, the hospital were keeping a close eye on me. I had scan after scan, though I didn't take the photos into work that time round. When colleagues in the staff room asked me how I was, I caught the little flickers of anxiety in their eyes.

Turns out they were right to be nervous. At fourteen weeks it happened again. I phoned the hospital the moment I started bleeding, but there wasn't anything they could do.

That was when I was referred to see Mr Andrews at the University. He ordered a lot of tests, on me, and on Rob, and in the end they diagnosed me with Hughes' Syndrome. Mr Andrews explained it was a rare blood clotting disorder, and had caused all three of my miscarriages. But it was good news, he said, because it could be treated.

In the car on the way home, I was quiet. Rob said, 'At least we've got a proper chance now. Now we know what it is.'

I took the aspirin every day. And when, six months later, my period was late, the first thing I did was let Mr Andrews know. He prescribed something else – Heparin – to thin my blood. Every week, a new box of filled syringes arrived at the house, and I kept them in the fridge until I needed them. Then once a day, I lay on my back on the bed, my head propped up on three pillows, and pressed the needle into the fat of my hip, chucking the empties into the yellow sharps bucket.

And it worked, counteracting the effect of the Hughes' Syndrome.

Or at least, it worked for a while.

We lost that baby at twenty weeks. I have to say, the midwife at the hospital was very kind. It can't have been an easy day at work for her. After the labour was finished, she cleaned the baby's little face, and wrapped her up in a blanket. And then she laid our baby in my arms. She was a tiny thing, our daughter, just over a pound.

We called her Ellie. It was the first time we'd given any of them a name.

Everyone was lovely about it. Really lovely. Family, friends, people at school. They were so kind, sending cards, trying so hard to be supportive, being so careful to say the right thing. I appreciated it, I really did. Only, after the fourth time, it sort of gets so people don't know what to say anymore.

Most of the time I just kept breathing. I kept quiet, concentrated on holding it together. I ran a lot, put the hours in at school, worked hard to help the trickier kids, the ones everyone said I was good at getting through to, the ones who drove the rest of the teaching staff nuts. I smiled at my neighbours on the estate and asked after their children when I bumped into them on the street. When Claire gave birth to her son, Max, I went out shopping on my own into town, and bought him a couple of cute little outfits and a specially named bear, and when Claire asked Rob and me to be his godparents I talked Rob into accepting.

Most of the time I just kept breathing.

Rob and I had decided to hang on for a bit. Neither of

us was in a hurry to get pregnant again, not after Ellie. We hadn't given up on kids, not by a long shot, we just didn't know what to do next. So we waited. What for, I don't know exactly. Some sort of breakthrough, perhaps, or just for our bruises to heal. When the letter came from the Centre for Reproductive Medicine we read it over and over again, not knowing what to make of it. And then, eventually, we decided to go along. Not to go through with anything necessarily; just to find out.

So. Here we were. We'd made it this far.

I looked up at the glass and concrete of the new building, and took a deep breath, feeling the cold morning air filling my lungs. Then I breathed out, all the way out. And we made our way towards the entrance together.

3

Alex

Now, Sussex

I'm drinking tea in the kitchen. Next to me, X is asleep in his tartan car seat. It's still raining outside, but I've found controls for the central heating, the gas cooker is working, and the boiler is heating a tank of water. With this pocketful of small victories, I am ridiculously pleased with myself.

Perhaps it's just nostalgia brought on by being here in Grannie's house, the place my sister and I spent our childhood summer holidays, but I have a feeling that all will be well. I made a good decision, coming here.

Perhaps we don't need to move on straightaway. Perhaps we could stay for a while, rest up, catch our breath. The thought of hiding out, just me and X, is seductive.

Or perhaps we could stay here forever. I mean, what's to stop us? Come the spring, it'll get warmer, and then X will enjoy lying out on the grass, under the trees, listening to the sound of the sea. I'll take out a blanket for both of us, and a novel for me, and I'll lie next to him, ignoring my book while I gaze at his perfect face.

When he learns to toddle, I'll put up a small fence to separate the top section of the garden, keep him safe until he's steady enough to tackle the steps without tripping and banging his knees. He'll potter happily on that soft stretch of lawn while I watch him. Later, I'll teach him to catch, to kick a ball. And when he's older, I'll enrol him in the local primary school. He'll paint, cut felt, germinate beans against a wad of wet tissue in a jam jar. He'll learn his letters and his numbers, make friends, find his place in the world.

Yes. Perhaps we could stay here. Perhaps it will all be fine.

And then I remember who I am, and who he is. I remember someone is coming for us. And I know, without a shadow of a doubt, they will not let us get away, not if they can help it. My job now is to get us out of here, clean away.

My job is to keep X safe.

But then, wasn't it always?

4

Dolly

Much later, Westminster, during the Public Inquiry

Please state your name for the record.

Samantha Mc –

Speak up please. The panel must be able to hear your answers clearly.

Samantha McFarlane.

Thank you, Miss McFarlane. But most people call you 'Dolly', is that right?

Yeah, that's right. Everyone calls me Dolly.

*

I was Samantha up until the moment I was born. Or it might be more accurate to say I existed in a sort of existential limbo of indeterminate gender: *Samantha if it's a girl, David if it's a boy.* A kind of hermaphroditic Schrodinger's Cat, if you get me.

Science joke. Don't worry about it.

But I was never David, and I'm not Samantha either. Not really. I arrived eight weeks early, a featherweight three and a half pounds. Perhaps I was already rebelling against parental expectations. Anyway, you know the drill: incubator, oxygen, feeding tube, the works. And it was my Dad apparently, sleep-deprived and red-eyed with wonder that this tiny creature had made it into the world alive, who croaked out some sentimental rubbish about me being *like a little doll.* So Michelle, my nightmare of a bossy older sister (barely two at the time, but no doubt already bossy, already nightmarish) laughed out loud at Dad's comment, and called me Dolly.

Mum still managed to get Samantha onto the birth certificate. And she pulls it out occasionally, when she's got a point to prove. Like, in that text: I remember reading it on the Metro on the way into work at the Centre. I'd called them the night before – 'them' being my esteemed parents – to give them the news that their darling daughter had just been offered an important position on the most important medical research project in history. I guess I was expecting them to be pleased.

Ha. No chance. We'd argued about it. I'd slammed the phone down.

The following morning, there was the text message: *Please don't take it, Samantha. Don't do this to us.*

Yeah, cheers, Mum. Really helpful.

*

Perhaps you could start by telling us about your position on the IVG research project.

I'd been working at the Centre as an embryologist for a couple of years. But I was more interested in research, you know, I'd been figuring out how I was going to get my PhD. And I'd worked with Alex –

Dr Mansfield.

I'd worked with Dr Mansfield before. When she saw patients at the Centre. I knew about her work, obviously. Everyone did. And she knew I was keen to do something more –

Something more – ?

You know. Something more interesting.

*

Mum's objections to the job weren't ethical ones, and she'd never given two hoots what the neighbours thought. Like, that Christmas, when I came home from University for the holidays, nauseous with anxiety because I'd decided to *tell them*. And they were completely fine about it, weren't they? Dad gave me this humongous bear hug and whispered something into my ear, all hot and sherry-scented, about me being his *baby girl*. And Mum just raised her perfectly plucked eyebrows and said, 'Well, it's not exactly a surprise, is it? Your father and I have known you were gay since you were twelve.'

*

What were your responsibilities?

I was the lead from the embryology side. I was going to assist Alex – Dr Mansfield – assist her clinically, with patients in the trial. With egg harvesting, *in vitro* fertilisation, also some diagnostic work, if that was needed. And then, once we had a stable pregnancy, I'd be part of the research team.

Tell us about your research.

We'd be gathering a glut of data. Nutrition. Activity patterns. Sleep. Think about it, no one had done anything like this before. But it wasn't just research. It was part of the terms of the license, that we provide round-the-clock monitoring. So Alex needed a team.

I thought everything was automated.

It was. And the systems were mind-blowing. And we had all that hospital back-up just up the road. But the ethics committee specified that someone should be on duty twenty-four seven, just in case.

Just in case? If anything had gone wrong, what could you have done?

We could adjust the inputs, and all the environmental variables, at a touch of a button. But look, there are always risks, aren't there? There are risks in natural gestations, remember. I mean, in natural *pregnancies*. What I'm saying is we'd reduced the risks. We had all the bases covered, genetic and environmental. We kept saying, this is the safest pregnancy in history.

I suppose that sounds naive now.

*

Mum worried I'd get myself blown up. Or shot as I walked through the front door at the start of my shift. Taken down by a sniper from the roof terrace of the Geography building on the other side of the square. To be fair to her, those fears weren't completely unfounded. Alex had been candid enough to show me some of the letters.

But then Mum's always been overprotective. Neurotically so, some might say.

*

You never had any doubts?

What sort of doubts?

You must have been aware of all the public opposition.

There were people who didn't agree with what we were doing. But they were extremists mainly. Some of them sent threats to Dr Mansfield. Threatening to kill her, blow up the building, that sort of thing. But look, we've always had to contend with that in medical research, you can't just cave in to that sort of pressure. And you've got to understand, there was also a lot of public support, as well as all the wariness. With hindsight, it's easy to forget that. A lot of people were excited about what we were doing. It gave them – it gave a lot of people hope.

Did you ever have any doubts about Dr Mansfield?
Well, I –

*

There was this exhibition, which the Education Department ran, in the lobby of the Centre. They used to bring in school parties, science field trips, that sort of thing. There were these panels showing the history of fertility medicine, and two interactive touchscreen displays. One lunchtime, I was on my way out and I stopped to have a play on one of the touchscreens. It was a game for kids, a so-called genetic engineering simulation. You selected coloured "genes" in a jigsaw puzzle strand of DNA, swapped other bits in from your little box of tricks. Play the game to its conclusion, and the final screen would give you an image of the child you had "designed".

So, okay, it annoyed the *hell* out of me. I was all fired up to complain to the Education Department, but by the time I got back from my lunch, my irritation had died down, and after a while I forgot about it.

It gave so completely the wrong impression about what we were doing. It made everything look so clean, so precise: a quick snip here, a replacement there. As if the mapping of the genome was the end point rather than just the beginning. As if any of it was easy.

This wasn't just science, this was *medicine*. Our methods were super-clean and super-precise, but the outcomes were messy and inexact. Medicine can be messy. We weighed the odds, offered up guesses. Most of the time it was about making the best of a bad hand. Alex knew that, better than anyone. She wasn't just a scientist, she was a doctor too.

That's what I liked about her.

*

So, Miss McFarlane. Did you have any doubts about Dr Mansfield?

No. Not at the beginning. She was – I mean, she was just *brilliant*. I thought, if anyone could pull this off – it was her. And she was super conscientious. The most conscientious person I've ever met.

Not at the beginning, you say? You had doubts later on?

Later on. Yes. Yes, I suppose I did.

5

Alex

Now, Sussex

I'm sitting on a deep sofa in the living room. Through the patio doors I can see it's still raining. I'm upright, three cushions behind my back to prevent me from slumping, another underneath my left elbow. I am feeding X from my left breast.

He's getting better at this. He managed to suck my nipple right back against his soft palate this time, which makes it easier for him and minimises damage to me. A 'good latch' is what they call it. Something else I learned from Fiona.

Now X is chewing, slowly, steadily, opening and closing his jaws like a machine, like some small engine, running a pump. His eyes are closed. Not scrunched up closed, but smooth, relaxed. He is in a state of intense bliss. He's making small, rhythmic grunting noises, and the occasional ticking sound as he swallows what must surely be great gallons of milk.

I take the glass of water I've been holding in my right hand, and place it on the low table to the side of the sofa. I cup X's delicate cranium, stroke his hair. It is impossibly soft, and a buttery colour that will no doubt darken to brown in future years. Milk flows through me, and out of me, and I feel restful, emptied. We weren't like this ten minutes ago, when X cried and twisted in my arms and wouldn't latch on until we were both fretful and red-faced with hunger (his) and panic (mine). But already the memory of those moments is fading, emptying out of me with my milk. Also on the low table, next to the glass of water, is the TV remote. I have the picture on, but the sound turned off, waiting for the evening news. When it begins, I'm not surprised to see us mentioned in the headlines, and seconds later, we're up first.

We're famous. The whole country is looking for us.

I reach for the remote, hit the mute button to restore sound. The image on the screen is my workplace: the Centre for Reproductive Medicine in Newcastle upon Tyne. It's still light, I notice. An establishing shot then, filmed earlier today.

The scene cuts to a reporter, standing in the twilit square outside the building, the same square where the protesters used to stand, handing out leaflets. Today there are no protesters, though a small crowd has gathered. In the far right hand corner of the shot I see flowers laid on the steps of the Centre. A large blue teddy. A cardboard banner, the print indistinct. If it wasn't still raining, would these people be lighting candles?

The reporter is a woman in her twenties, wearing a heavy coat, holding an umbrella. I feel nothing as I hear her say: *Late last night, the child who has become known to us as Baby X was removed, illegally, from this research facility. Although it's too early to know exactly what has happened, police are searching for Dr Alex Mansfield, the leader of the research team, also missing. Tyne and Wear Police wish to stress that Dr Mansfield is not currently a suspect in any crime. Not at the present time. But they are anxious to locate her, and, of course, the baby.*

Strange that I feel nothing.

The scene cuts to a television studio. There's a middle-aged man in a grey suit, radiating scepticism, grumpiness, the hallmarks of authority. I recognise him, actually. He interviewed me a couple of years back, on this same news programme. Right now his name escapes me.

I remember the interview though, sitting very still under the hot lights, hoping my face wasn't flushed. The cameras spinning round to face us and a young man on the edge of the studio counting down. At the very last moment the grey-suit had leaned in close, nodded at my emerald green blouse and snarled, 'That colour'll bleed.'

Now you tell me. Thanks a million.

I'd barely caught his opening remarks, and then we were into a pre-taped segment, displayed in the studio on monitors. A reporter walking down a London street, speaking directly to the camera, trotting out familiar phrases, clichés really, about fertility medicine. Then a montage of images, more clichés: a gloved hand pipetting clear liquid into a Petri dish; fingers pressing pink lozenges from a pill pack; an ordinary looking couple at a kitchen table, the woman tearing open a manilla envelope, her man looking on, concerned.

I'd shuffled in my seat.

Then it had cut to the recently opened Centre for Reproductive Medicine, followed by another montage: members of the public were being asked their views by the reporter.

Excuse me, have you heard of IVG? People could rarely decode the acronym, even when they had strong opinions; the reporter had to help them out. *In vitro gestation. What do you think?*

A middle-aged man, apple cheeked and balding, in a brown leather jacket: *Well, we've had our kids, haven't we?* He laughed. *Wouldn't've missed it for the world!*

And now a young woman, work get-up, good quality

make-up, her shiny hair swinging. *I'm not really thinking about babies right now.*

Honestly. What nonsense all that media coverage had been.

And I remember the grey-suited interviewer giving me a hard time on air, sniping at me, accusing me of "playing God". You know, the usual shenanigans. And I remember his ostentatious distaste, the way he wrinkled his nose at me when he said, 'It isn't *natural*, is it?'

But as soon as the cameras were off, he had leaned in close again and muttered, 'They're just scared, you know.'

'Scared?'

'The proles. Don't pay any attention to them. We call it the *yuk-factor*. Same thing with organ transplants, when that started. But no one would turn one down now, would they?'

He's turning now, that same grey-suit, part-profile towards a big screen mounted to his left, a concerned frown on his jowly face. He's speaking directly to the reporter. *Dr Mansfield is a controversial figure, isn't she? What can you tell us about her?*

The reporter tells him all sorts of things about me. She tells him I was one of the original team involved in the development of *in vitro* gestation technology, or IVG as it has become known. She tells him I argued for this project to go ahead, that I have led it, and been the public face of IVG to the world. The impression she gives is of some driven, Frankenstein figure, proceeding in the face of public opinion. *Fools rush in where angels fear to tread.* I'll admit I've had detractors, but this seems disingenuous to me, and I am trying to work out a rejoinder in my head, a mental letter-to-the-editor, when a still photograph appears briefly on the screen. Black suit, emerald blouse.

Ah, that green blouse. The colour that would bleed on

camera. Still, I barely recognise myself. I'm so much younger, slimmer. So much more certain.

The frowning grey-suit interrupts to introduce an interview with one of my colleagues. I wonder briefly who agreed to talk. Then the scene cuts to Dolly in the lobby of the Centre, eyes red-rimmed. *I don't know how this could have happened*, Dolly says. *Alex – Dr. Mansfield. She would never let anything happen to – to the baby. She's committed to this project. To helping childless couples.* She looks like she might cry again, but then collects herself. *She's the most conscientious person I know.*

Poor Dolly.

Now another reporter is questioning Dolly, a man this time. *What do you say to rumours that Dr Mansfield has been unable to cope with the stress? Is it possible she's had a nervous breakdown?*

I see the doubt cross Dolly's face. She hesitates, then says, *It's been difficult. Everyone's been under pressure. Alex more than anyone.* She pauses again, glances guiltily at the camera, and for a second seems to catch my eye. Then she says, *I know Alex would always try to do the right thing. She'd move heaven and earth to keep that baby safe.* Her voice breaks as she says, *I just wish I knew where she was.*

Instinctively, my hand moves to X's head. I love the feel of his soft hair underneath my fingers. I run my hand down over his shoulder, squeeze gently, feel the give in him, and also the tension, the vitality of his warm, soft body against mine.

X finishes feeding, and falls back into a swoon, head tilted back, mouth open. He starts to emit small snoring noises. A dribble of milk is leaking from the corner of his mouth.

I glance back at the television, hoping that this is the

end. But no. Here is the reporter again, introducing another segment. The parents of Baby X have given a press conference, appealing for their infant son's safe return. Any second now, I will see Karen and Robert Frey's stricken faces on the screen in front of me.

Am I strong enough to bear this?

It turns out I am not. My hand moves to the remote, and the screen turns black.

6

Karen

Twelve months earlier, Newcastle-upon-Tyne

I wished I'd painted my toenails. It hadn't crossed my mind this morning when Rob and I were getting dressed in the half-dark, in time for the long drive up to Newcastle. Now I could see my toes, the varnish chipped, poking out at the end of the waffled green sheet they'd given me to cover myself.

Ridiculous, the things that went through your head. No one here was interested in my feet.

They'd unrolled a long piece of tissue paper and stretched it out over the plastic bed for me to lie on. My jeans, knickers and socks were folded in a pile on one of the two chairs next to the bed, my bag perched on top. Rob was sitting in the other chair. I propped myself up on my elbows to catch his eye, and he gave me a small *hang-in-there* smile.

He didn't need to come all this way, taking another day off work. He'd already done his bit: giving several sperm samples on previous visits, and Dr Mansfield had explained there was enough to fertilise another batch of my eggs *in vitro*. More than one batch, if necessary. So I told him: I'd be fine driving up and back on my own. If nothing else, we'd want to hang on to some annual leave for when the baby came, wouldn't we? But he'd insisted, like he always did. He said I might be in pain afterwards, or still woozy from the sedative. I hated to admit it, but he was probably right.

'Are you ready for us, Mrs Frey?' The voice came from the other side of the curtain. Dr Mansfield's assistant, the younger woman with short red hair who'd been at the other egg harvesting appointments.

'Yes, thanks. All ready.'

Dolly, her name was. Seemed like a nice girl, always polite and helpful. We'd had a little chat about Leicester, last time I was here. Dolly knew the city well, and parts of the county, although she'd never actually been to our town. Her housemate had been at university there, sometimes they went together to visit old friends. I made a mental note to ask if she'd been down our way recently, if the opportunity arose.

Now Dolly was pulling back the curtain. Dr Mansfield pulled up a chair and started to adjust the ultrasound monitor near to my sorry-looking feet. 'How are you this morning, Mrs Frey?' she asked.

'I'm fine, thanks.'

'You've taken some painkillers this morning, as I suggested?'

'I took them an hour ago.'

The doctor nodded. We were in safe hands with Dr Mansfield. I don't just mean she was clever. Which she was, of course, but she was more than that. She didn't just talk at us, she listened too.

'And how have you been on the follicle stimulation hormone this month?' she asked now.

'You'd better ask Rob,' I said, with a glance in his direction. 'He's the one putting up with my moods.' Rob rolled his eyes. 'Oh, it's all right really,' I said, trying to sound breezy. 'I'm just tired.'

We'd stopped in the motorway services for our breakfast. This time, I'd had an almond croissant. The first time we drove up for egg harvesting it was almost exciting,

34

like we were going on holiday or something. Several cycles later it was taking its toll. The hormone treatments, all the travelling, and then, each month, the news that it hadn't worked. We hadn't made a baby after all.

I didn't want to complain. Whinging wouldn't make anything easier. We were lucky we were on this programme, weren't we? I was just tired, that was all.

'You know,' Dr Mansfield said, adjusting the monitor. 'I went through a cycle myself a few years back. Just the one. But I've got some idea what you're going through.'

That was a surprise. Doctors were the people who did things to you, rather than people who had things done to them. Dr Mansfield, it turned out, was one of them, but also one of us. Was that why she was always so sympathetic? Had she suffered with infertility herself?

'I wasn't having IVF,' Dr Mansfield said, as if she'd guessed what I was thinking. 'I was a graduate student, and my professor asked me to take part in a clinical trial. A new egg retrieval technique.' Dolly had wheeled a trolley of instruments up to the end of the bed, and Dr Mansfield's attention slid to these. 'Well, it was new at the time.'

'You took the same drugs I've been taking?'

'Different drugs, similar effect.' She glanced at my feet. 'Can you bring your legs up now?'

I put my feet up on the metal plates, spread my legs wide. Dr Mansfield prepared the probe with lubricant. The first time we'd done this, she'd explained everything, first in advance, and again as we went along. But I was an old hand now. The probe would go right up inside me, and press against my ovaries so Dr Mansfield could get at my eggs.

'Ready?' she said now. I nodded. It didn't hurt, but it was a strange sensation, and not exactly a pleasant one, the feeling of being opened wide, the heavy thing inside me.

'And how did *you* get on with the hormones, doctor?' Asking questions was a good way to take my mind off what was happening down there.

Dr Mansfield kept her eyes on the monitor, making adjustments to the angle of the probe. Then she laughed. 'It was hell, to be honest. I burst into tears every day. Nuclear PMT.' She glanced away from the monitor to make eye contact with me. 'There are lots of eggs here, Mrs Frey. Well done.'

Rob squeezed my hand. 'That's great, isn't it, love? Lots of chances.'

Dr Mansfield held the probe in place while Dolly worked at the computer, counting and measuring the egg follicles. After a while Dolly said, 'Eight mature oocytes here. Seven on the other side.'

Everyone seemed pleased with me. Was I supposed to feel proud of myself? All I'd done was take the drugs and lie here with my feet up.

Dr Mansfield removed the probe. 'Did you recover quickly after last time?'

'You were in quite a lot of pain, weren't you?' Rob said. 'Once the drugs wore off.'

I bit my lip. 'I wasn't too bad,' I said. 'Some cramps.'

'And the bleeding?'

'A few days. Fine, really.'

Dr Mansfield was preparing the probe for the next part of the procedure, inserting the long needle which would draw out my eggs. 'Ready?' she asked.

I nodded, but my face must have given me away. 'Try to relax,' Dolly said, patting my arm as Dr Mansfield pressed the needle in through the ovary wall. 'Breathe through it.'

I thought about Dr Mansfield going through all this as a young student. I hoped the professor she'd mentioned hadn't pressured her into it. A young girl, too, and possibly far from home. 'If you don't mind me asking,' I said, 'but why did you do it?'

Dr Mansfield was concentrating hard now. Although I couldn't see the ultrasound monitor, I had an image in my head of what she was doing, from the video she'd shown us at the start. The needle was digging around inside my ovaries, picking open the egg follicles, then sucking out the eggs, one at a time. Even through the painkillers, I could feel it when she moved the needle. I did my best not to wince.

'I'm not sure,' Dr Mansfield said, frowning at the monitor. 'They paid me a bit. Not much, but that might have been a factor, I was perpetually short of money as a student. And I've always been interested in research.' She leaned forward, eyes narrowed. 'Knowing me, it would have been curiosity as much as anything.' She glanced away from the screen and up at me. 'And I had no idea how unpleasant it was going to be.'

She looked away and moved again to push the needle in, suck out another egg. I'm sure I felt the resistance as the egg popped out. But maybe that was my imagination.

Five little peas in a pea pod pressed. One grew, two grew and so grew all the rest.

Honestly, the things that went through my head.

Except, as Dr Mansfield had explained, a woman's ovaries usually produce one – occasionally two – mature eggs per cycle. And mine hadn't always done that very well. All the strong drugs they'd been giving me had pressed my body into producing twelve, thirteen, fifteen eggs, for several cycles in a row. No wonder I was feeling tired.

They grew and they grew and they would not stop. Until one day the pod went –

'I guess I don't really know why I did it,' Dr Mansfield continued thoughtfully. 'I'm glad I did though.' She sat back, moved the probe, went in again. 'We're half way there now, Mrs Frey. You're doing brilliantly.'

But I wasn't doing anything really, just lying here asking questions, thinking about what Dr Mansfield had just told me.

At our first meeting, she'd explained the risks involved in egg harvesting. For the most part, they were small, same as with any minor surgical procedure. And there were possible side effects from the hormones I'd been taking, and a few of these – the rarer ones – could be serious. She'd reassured us that the risks were low. I have to give her credit for being so clear about everything, and so honest. She'd even made a point of telling us that the long term risks of the hormone treatments weren't really known yet, because the procedure was still new. At the time it didn't mean much to me. All the side effects she listed were just words, words with numbers attached, percentages of patients effected. Pulmonary complications. Ovarian hyperstimulation syndrome. Even ovarian cancer. But cancer was just a word, wasn't it, when the chance of it happening to you was so small?

Then recently, I'd been feeling so tired. More than tired if I'm honest. Some days I felt quite weepy, low. I didn't want to go running with Claire. My colleagues at school had noticed, and the children too. Even Little Tyler at school, who struggles with empathy at the best of times, said to me, 'Mrs Frey, why are you so sad?'

'I hope I'm not being nosy,' I said now, 'but what did you do with your eggs?'

'I donated them to the Centre,' Dr Mansfield replied,

her head still dipped, concentrating on positioning the probe correctly, glancing up at the monitor now and then.

I glanced towards Dolly, confused for a moment, 'Do you all do that then?'

'No, not me.' Dolly looked at the floor, but the expression was clear on her face. *Not bloody likely*.

Of course not, how silly of me.

'There,' Dr Mansfield said, withdrawing the probe. 'All done.' She paused, and I sensed there was something else she wanted to say. This was it then, the point when she gave me the ultimatum. I felt my stomach drop. 'What we hope,' she began gently, 'is that these eggs will give you a viable blastocyst.'

'That's what we're all hoping,' Rob said, squeezing my hand. He was trying to stay strong for me, and I felt myself tense, waiting for what was coming next.

'But if that doesn't happen,' Dr Mansfield continued, 'maybe we need to take a break and work out the best way forward.'

'Take a break?' She was going to drop us from the programme. I'd been holding back the dark thoughts but now they crowded in – even when I wasn't *carrying* the baby in my own body, I'd still made a mess of things. I was useless, barely a woman. Pathetic. I'd let Rob down again.

'Perhaps we should consider involving a donor,' Dr Mansfield said. She smiled at Rob, and then at me. 'Look, we're all done here for today. But I think maybe we should talk about egg donation as a possibility.' She paused, letting the idea hang in the air. 'Anyway, let's see what this round throws up first. You never know, we might be lucky this time.'

7

Dolly

Much later, Westminster, during the Public Inquiry

So, the project didn't exactly get off to a flying start?

You'd expect it to be complicated. The Freys had a complicated medical history.

Then perhaps you could explain: why were they chosen as test subjects in the first place?

They were exactly the sort of people we wanted to help. People who'd run out of options.

But Mrs Frey might have fallen pregnant again naturally. And with treatment for her condition –

And given the additional morbidity we discovered later, she might have gone on to have another late miscarriage. Nobody wanted that.

What about the Freys? What did they want?

Dr Mansfield had those conversations with them; I can't tell you what was discussed. My understanding was that they didn't want to give up.

Is it possible that Dr Mansfield somehow coerced the Freys into participating when it wasn't in their best interests?

No, I don't believe that. She would never have done that.

Then let's pick up somewhere else. Tell us, Miss McFarlane, how did Mrs Frey's treatment begin?

We started by harvested eggs from her, and sperm from Mr Frey. We fertilized the eggs *in vitro*. We tried for several rounds, but no viable embryos were produced. Without a viable embryo, we couldn't proceed with IVG.

In vitro gestation.

That's right. In IVF, the egg is fertilised outside of the mother's body, but re-implanted into her uterus for gestation. IVG allowed us to gestate the baby outside of the mother.

In the artificial uterus.

That's right. We just needed a strong, healthy embryo.

So?

We'd already noticed it had taken Mrs Frey some time to conceive each of her earlier pregnancies. We wondered if there might be some additional cause of infertility. So Dr Mansfield ordered this procedure –

Pre-implantation genetic diagnosis?

You remove a cell from an embryo, dissolve the contents of the nucleus to release the chromosomes, stain them, and see what you've got.

And what did you find?

All the Frey embryos had chromosomal abnormalities. Blood tests on both the Freys enabled us to trace the faulty gene back to Mrs Frey.

Could you please explain the significance of this?

It raised the possibility that we might do best to try again with a donor egg. It wasn't the only option. Look, it's never black and white. You've got to weigh up the probabilities. Sooner or later, the Freys *might've* conceived a viable embryo. But how long would that take? Meanwhile, Dr Mansfield was keen not to put Mrs Frey's health under a lot of stress.

Put her health under stress?

The egg harvesting isn't without risk. Mrs Frey knew what she was doing. But still, with every round, the possibility of complications increased.

Perhaps you can explain something to me. If the egg wasn't Mrs Frey's egg and the embryo wasn't gestated in her body, then in what sense would she be the baby's mother?

Well, technically she wouldn't be. But that's not for me to say.

Did you voice an opinion at the time?

Well, I –

I don't need to remind you, Miss McFarlane, this is a Public Inquiry into the events that took place at the Centre for Reproductive Medicine last year. This inquiry has been called by Parliament and you have been called to give evidence, under oath.

I know, it's just.

So, I'll ask you another way. Did any of the team raise objections to the continuation of the Freys on the programme?

Look, we *could've* taken a decision to kick them off the trial, in favour of a couple who could conceive but not carry a baby. It would've made our job easier, that's for sure.

But you didn't?

Alex – Dr Mansfield – she didn't think that was right. If we abandoned every couple who turned out to have complex morbidity – I mean, that's what the Centre was there for, right?

*

Alex had been firm about it. She felt she'd made the Freys a promise; she wasn't about to let them down. Like I said, Alex always saw IVG as medicine, something to help couples with intractable fertility problems. If it turned out the Freys had a whole basket of intractable fertility problems, so much the better.

42

As test subjects, I mean. I don't mean so much the better for them.

I didn't quite see it that way, I might as well admit that now. It's not that I didn't care about the Freys. They were nice people, and they'd been through a lot. It's just, by that point I didn't see IVG as medicine. Or at least, not *just* as medicine.

I always thought Alex had invented something amazing, something universally, revolutionarily *amazing*, like – like the contraceptive pill, or the bicycle or, I don't know, the washing machine. Any idiot could see the invention of the washing machine would be life-changing for a whole lot of people. But it was like – and excuse me if I'm stretching the analogy here – it was like Alex held on to this belief that the only people who'd want a washing machine were people too physically disabled to get down to the river and wash their clothes by hand on a rock.

For such a clever woman she could be stupid sometimes. I mean, why would you choose to get sick, get fat, get piles – all that nonsense – if you didn't have to? Why go through labour – which everyone agrees is painful and terrifying – when there's really no reason? My sister Michelle was ill, and I mean, *really* ill, all the way through both her pregnancies. She vomited her guts up for the first six months. The second time she lost so much weight she ended up in hospital on a drip. Pretty much ended her career right there and then, all the time she had off sick. I mean, I ask you. Mum was having kittens with worry, you can imagine.

Sometimes Alex and I would have this conversation, in the lab, or occasionally in the pub. Alex argued that IVG would be too expensive for just anyone to do it, and so tied up in regulation it would only be available to people with the greatest medical need. But Alex didn't live in the real world. Some people have plenty of money, don't they? Others'll beg, borrow or steal if something's important enough. Look at private schools, look at plastic surgery. And as for regulation, well that's a joke, isn't it? We develop these reproductive technologies in the UK, then they get used in other parts of the world without the same restrictions, at a fraction of the cost. Eastern Europe, India for example. Even Spain.

I knew exactly how this was going to play out. First off, there'd be some high profile celebrity who'd have her baby this way. She'd get to keep her figure, keep making films, and pick up the baby at the end of the nine months without a single stretchmark to show for it. Perhaps she'd try to keep it secret at first, but it would leak out, and even though she'd deny it, the idea would be there.

Ten years down the road, everyone would be doing it.

Aimee laughed at me when she heard *that* little speech. 'You don't even care,' she said.

'No,' I said, 'I don't. I'm not about to get all nostalgic about pregnancy. Leave all that in the bloody dark ages.'

'But,' Aimee said, 'a few years down the line there'll be a backlash. Left-leaning, middle-class women, wanting to have their babies the old fashioned way. And by then, there won't be any maternity hospitals – or trained midwives – to help them through it.'

I frowned at her, trying to work out if she was joking. 'God,' I said finally. 'You're such a hippy.'

She smiled at me. That smile she did, the one with the dimples. Super cute. 'Some women enjoy being pregnant, right? Maybe I'd be one of them.'

'Urgh no. Bet *I* wouldn't. Bet I'd hate it.'

'You know what, though,' Aimee said, eyebrows raised, downing the remains of her beaker of wine. 'If this technology revolutionises reproduction, it changes the dynamics between men and women. Like completely. Forever.'

Another typical Aimee comment. She'd been taking this class in Gender Studies as part of her master's degree and she was always coming up with phrases like *structural power imbalance* and *intersectionality*. Most of the time I ignored it.

'What do you care about the dynamics between men and women?' I'd countered, reaching for her knee.

'I mean it frees women up,' she said. Deadly serious now. 'If they don't have to actually have the babies anymore. Maybe it changes everything.'

'I'll drink to that,' I said. And I did.

'And maybe it changes things for us, too,' Aimee said. Those dimples again. Man.

'How so?'

'Well, I know this isn't the way it works at the moment,' Aimee continued, looking away from me now, her voice suddenly tentative. 'But what if the next thing you discover is some way to take a woman's DNA, and put it into another woman's egg, and then gestate *that* embryo in one of your artificial whatsits.'

While we're at it, that was Aimee all over too. She might have known what *intersectionality* meant, but she didn't have the first idea about the parameters of human genetic medicine. 'It doesn't work like that,' I said, laughing. 'At least, not yet.'

'Why not?'

'Because you don't just stuff a load of Person A's DNA into Person B's egg and hey presto there's a baby.'

'You don't need to be like that about it. I was only saying.' She tucked a strand of hair behind her ear. 'I just thought it would be nice. That's all.'

*

So it was Dr Mansfield who suggested that you proceed with the Freys, even though their chances of conceiving a viable embryo looked slim. And in order to keep them in the programme, she put it to them that they should consider using donor eggs?

That's right. But you're making it sound much more – much more sinister – than it actually was. It was reasonable to suggest involving donor eggs at this point.

It was what any clinician would have done.

8

Alex

Now, Sussex

I carry X through into the kitchen. There's a bag of groceries on the table, things I grabbed at the petrol station on the way here. With my free hand, I eat an apple then a bar of chocolate. I'm still hungry, but can't think straight enough to make anything more substantial. There's food in the other bag, the one I brought from Fiona's. Pasta, I think. A glass jar of tomato sauce, some cheese. A couple of bananas. I should cook something. I need to look after myself if I'm going to keep feeding X. Let alone come up with a half decent plan.

It's starting to get dark in here now; I haven't put on the lights yet. All the same, from where I am standing at the kitchen counter I can see into the living room, a narrow slice of floor, sofa, and ceiling. And although I'm not really looking that way, out of the corner of my eye I catch movement. I turn my head sharply to see.

Is there a cat in here? Grannie didn't have a cat. All the doors and windows were shut up when I arrived. Anyway, the thing I saw was bigger than a cat. Person-sized.

Holding X close, I take a step towards the doorway. On the far side of the living room, I see a woman, her back towards me. She's young, with brown hair falling to her shoulders. And she's unnaturally still, as if she's examining a spot on the wall.

'Fiona?' I say quietly.

*

Fiona and I parted a few hours ago, in the early hours of this morning. I'd driven south via her house in St Albans, parked the car outside on the street, and then crept around the side, X in my arms, my big coat slung over my shoulders to shield us both from the rain.

I'd caught my sister round the side of the house in her dressing gown, lifting a black sack into the wheelie bin. I'd called out to her in a stage whisper, and she turned to see me, one hand flying to her sternum in shock. 'Jesus, Alex!' To give her due credit, I probably looked like a crazy person, wild-eyed and bedraggled, in odd clothes, my hair a mess. At least I was no longer covered in blood.

'I need your help,' I'd said. 'Baby clothes. Food. Cash if you've got any. I could do with a car seat.' I paused. 'And the keys to Grannie's house.'

Once she understood what was happening, Fiona's voice was low and calm. The voice she used with the kids when she was reaching the end of her rope, the one she got out on special occasions. Not dissimilar, funnily enough, to the voice people in authority use with mental patients holding weapons, or preparing to jump from bridges. 'Alex,' she said. 'You need to phone the police. He's a newborn baby. He needs to see a doctor.'

I nearly lost my patience then. 'I *am* a doctor, remember? And I'm his mother.' She'd looked at me strangely. 'Believe me, Fiona,' I'd said. 'I'm his *mother*. Besides, I've been caring for him since conception. I know better than anyone what he needs.'

*

Now, standing in Grannie's kitchen, I wonder: has my

sister followed me here? Something about the way she holds herself tells me this is not the Fiona I left early this morning. This is an echo, a memory of childhood summers together. A ghost, or else a hallucination.

Confused, I glance at X's sleeping face, and when I raise my eyes again, my sister is gone.

9

Karen

Nine months earlier, Market Harborough

My Head gave me the morning off work. I felt bad deserting Caroline, the Year 2 class teacher, and though there were other Teaching Assistants, it meant messing up the rotas, and moving my Nurture Group to Thursday. Little Tyler had never coped well with changes to his routine. He'd be sulky in class this morning, and clingy this afternoon.

But it was important to be at home when the call came.

I sat at the table in the kitchen, flicking through one of those free catalogues that comes through the door, nursing a cup of herbal tea. I hadn't touched caffeine for years, since my brother sent me a newspaper article on coffee and infertility. Not that any of that mattered now. I didn't have to get pregnant, or carry a baby. I didn't even have to produce eggs. I could drink all the coffee I wanted.

But I stuck to the herbal tea. Coffee would've made me jittery.

After the last batch of eggs failed, we'd gone back to the Centre to discuss our options. Dr Mansfield suggested we use donor eggs instead. I was so grateful she was keeping us on, I'd wanted to say yes immediately, but she asked us – she insisted – we take some time to think it over.

Rob struggled with the idea at first. 'As long as you're

sure it's what you really want,' he'd said. 'As long as you won't feel left out?'

It wouldn't make any difference, I was sure of that. We wanted a baby, and this was our best chance.

Dr Mansfield and the team used eggs that had been donated for medical research and stored in freezers at the Centre. This was unusual apparently, but she'd explained that the storage techniques were so good, the eggs would be perfectly healthy. We couldn't use foreign commercial donors, because of the strict terms of the license, and egg sharing, which IVF couples often used, was too risky in our case because the eggs would've come from women having fertility treatment. Older women. Or faulty women, women like me.

Instead, we'd have eggs from the experimental pool, donated by students, or young researchers. They were bright young women, healthy and strong, and the eggs would be healthy and strong too.

We didn't even have to travel up again after that. The team fertilized a batch of eggs with Rob's sperm, and after eight days we received a call from Dr Mansfield to say that one embryo – the strongest one – had been selected. They'd already carried out a chromosomal check, and the embryo was healthy. And male, she told us. They could tell that already, from when they'd checked the chromosomes, and we'd said we didn't mind knowing.

Now it was up to him, to implant himself into the warm woolly walls of the artificial uterus, to grab on and hold tight, so he could start growing properly. We'd been given the percentages. A lot of the test subjects had never managed it apparently, poor little mites. But if he implanted, the odds looked good.

Dr Mansfield had said she'd phone at ten. I glanced at the clock: five to. And that was when the phone rang.

'Is that Karen?' It wasn't Dr Mansfield's voice. Maybe she'd asked someone else to phone, but no, that wasn't like her. Anyway, everyone at the Centre called me Mrs Frey.

'Speaking.'

'Hi Karen, my name is Toni. How are you this morning?'

So this was one of *those* calls, a consumer survey which would only take up one minute of my time. An offer to reclaim money on my behalf. I'd have to wriggle free as politely as I could. 'It's not a good time,' I said. 'I'm expecting another call.'

'Are you?' Toni said, excited now. 'Are you waiting to hear from Dr Mansfield?'

How did she know about Dr Mansfield? A small shudder worked its way up my back. 'I'm sorry, but where did you say you were calling from?'

'I didn't,' said Toni brightly. 'But I'll tell you now: *True Life* magazine. I want to discuss something with you. A fantastic opportunity for yourself and your husband. Rob, isn't it?'

True Life magazine? One of those cheaply-printed mags where real people talked about discovering a husband's double life of sex addiction, or a teenager's struggle with anorexia. Not my cup of tea, to be honest.

'You know, Karen,' Toni said, 'the world is desperate to hear your story. *We're all absolutely gripped*. And we're on your side.'

I didn't know what to say. What did she mean anyway? I hadn't realised there were sides.

'And I'm sure you know as well as I do,' Toni continued, 'babies are expensive. And they get more expensive as they get older. Believe me, I know. My boys are at secondary school now.'

'Oh yes,' I said, at a loss. 'I'm sure that's right.'

'Look, this isn't going to be your only offer, but I really believe it's going to be your best. The most important thing is that we want you to tell your story from *your* point of view. You aren't going to get that sort of assurance from everyone, believe me. Talk to Rob about it. If you're with us and it's an exclusive, I mean, then all of those others will just have to leave you alone. Take it from me. It would be a sort of protection for you and your family. So you can just enjoy these next few months in peace.'

Protection. Peace. I could almost see the words hanging in the air. And their alternatives.

'And the money's got to come in handy, hasn't it? I know with my boys, it's always, *I need money for new trainers, Mum, I need money for clothes.* And kids these days, they don't want any old cheap rubbish, they want the real thing. Labels. Designer.'

'I'm sorry,' I said. 'I don't mean to interrupt. But we really don't need –'

'If you don't need it now, it could come in handy a few years down the line. A little bit to put into a college fund perhaps, those fees just keep going up, don't they? I know it seems a long way off, but it'll come round quick. Believe me, I know what I'm talking about.'

'Really sorry,' I said again. 'But I'm really going to have to get off the line. Just leave it with me and I'll talk to my husband later.'

I let her read out her number, and I dutifully wrote it down on the corner of my catalogue. I'm not sure why; I had no intention of calling her back. As I pressed the button to end the call, the phone rang again.

'Mrs Frey?' It was Dr Mansfield this time. Thank heavens.

'I'm here,' I managed.

'He's done it,' Dr Mansfield said. 'Implanted. He's cleared the first hurdle.'

I had an image of him in my mind, leaping over obstacles. My little athlete. The strongest one, wasn't that what she'd said? Not like my other poor babies, who'd never made it off the starting blocks. 'And he's okay?'

'Like we discussed,' Dr Mansfield said, 'it's very early days. But, so far –' I could sense the smile in her tone of voice. 'So far, he's – just *perfect*.'

10

Alex

Now, Sussex

I hear the sound of a car's engine. We're too far from the main road to pick up the sound of passing traffic, it must be making its way up the narrow track towards the house. I freeze, holding my breath.

Yes, definitely a car.

Soon I'll hear the crunch of tyres on gravel, the thunk of doors opening and closing. Forgetting my vision of Fiona, I act on instinct, pulling X close to me and hurrying up the stairs. It's only when I'm halfway up I remember I've left signs of occupation all round the house. A water glass on the small table in the living room, that apple core on the kitchen counter. I should go downstairs and clear those things away.

A car door slams. If I go downstairs now we'll be seen.

Come to think of it, did I lock the front door after I went outside for the car seat, or did I leave it on the latch?

On the landing I pause, hearing movement downstairs. Someone's in the house.

I listen, but no one calls up. For a moment I find myself hoping it's the police; the least appalling of several appalling options. But in my bones I know it can't be. They won't have found us this quickly.

I stare at X's face. Even in the darkness I can tell his eyes are open, he's watching me. Is he trying to work out what I'm going to do next? No, Alex, get a grip. He's a newborn baby. He can't have any inkling of the danger we're in. He isn't afraid. He is simply happy and trusting, because he is close to me, his mother, in the dark. He can smell me, hear my breathing, feel my beating heart.

The thought that I am comforting him calms me enough to consider our situation.

I inch along the landing, in the direction of Grannie's bedroom. Someone is moving around downstairs; I hear footsteps in the hall.

What do I do? Hide and wait to be discovered, or stand and fight? But how can I fight with a baby in my arms? I could put him down, but he might make a noise, might start to cry and give us away. Anyway, I can't put him down, not now. Whatever we're facing, we're in this together.

I reach the doorway of the bedroom. I have to turn this situation round. I have to be strong for X because he can't be strong for himself. Grannie's heavy dark wood wardrobe sits solid and ancient on the far side of the room, the first thing an attacker's eye would fall on, entering in the half-dark. The most obvious place to hide. I guess that the person coming will approach that wardrobe silently, with whatever weapon they are carrying. They will walk towards that closed wardrobe door and pull it open, hoping to find us inside. At this moment, knowing this, guessing it, ahead of our assailant, represents my sole advantage over someone who is stronger than me, better armed and less encumbered.

If I crouch behind the door, our attacker will stumble upon us before reaching the wardrobe. If I crouch behind the bed, I mightn't be completely hidden. There is that chest of drawers, though, which throws out that wide pool of deep shadow. Looking from the doorway, in the almost-dark, an intruder might not see us crouching there. I estimate just one stride between the chest of drawers and the wardrobe, and if a person had his back to us –

And that heavy bowl is only made of china – but if I swung it hard enough –

If he hits the light switch, he'll see us straightaway. It's only the way the shadows fall in the corner that would keep us hidden. But perhaps it's not quite dark enough yet for him to take the decision to switch on the light.

Another creak downstairs.

I don't have the luxury of a plan B. We're going to have to take our chances. I cross the room silently, and get myself into position.

11

Dolly

Much later, Westminster, during the Public Inquiry

But why did Dr Morvan contact you? Why not someone more senior in the organisation?

I'd met her before, you see. At a conference in Manchester, a couple of years earlier. She gave this presentation on stem cells and I went up to speak to her afterwards.

Stem cells?

It's the new frontier of medicine. We'll be able to do anything, regrow human organs, replace missing limbs.

That sounds like science fiction.

It's early days, sure.

I expect a lot of people here won't understand the connection to fertility medicine.

You can only get truly flexible stem cells from certain sources. Embryos, for example. And fertility medicine produces a surplus of embryos, through IVF.

A surplus?

That's right. Say, once a patient completes their family, and isn't going to have any further treatment. But still, some people are uncomfortable harvesting stem cells from embryos. And I suppose, if stem cell medicine becomes more widespread, the demand will increase. Which could – theoretically, I mean – create economic pressure to produce embryos simply to source more stem cells.

Spell it out for us, Miss McFarlane.

Because, and I should add, the jury's still out on this one, but some people consider an embryo to be a living human being. And then there are other people who don't believe an embryo is a person exactly, but they see that it has the potential to grow into one. Either way, some people don't like the idea of harvesting parts from a living being – even a potentially living being – to use in medicine.

Yes, I see.

It's not just that. Say you had a big global market in stem cells derived from embryos. That could create pressure to supply eggs and sperm for commercial stem cells production. And egg extraction entails some medical risks for the donor, small perhaps, but once you scale it up —

But I'm still not clear why Dr Morvan approached you.

Ah, well, yes. It was because of the foetal cord blood.

Explain –

There are stem cells in embryos, and there are also stem cells in the blood in a foetus's umbilical cord. Foetal cord blood is a waste product of IVG. No one could suggest it's alive, or has rights. No one's harmed – or even put at risk – by taking the cord blood from an artificial uterus and using it to create therapies.

Can't cord blood be harvested at ordinary *births?*

Yes, but it's more complicated. Harvesting foetal cord blood tends to lengthen labour, which arguably makes it riskier for the labouring woman. You could get into a situation where women are encouraged to labour in a certain way to supply the stem cell industry, rather than clinicians making their decisions purely in the interests of mother and baby. But of course, the IVG process is already automated, semi-industrialised, if you like. It's all so much cleaner and easier, it makes sense.

I see. So back to Dr Morvan.

After the lecture I introduced myself, and we ended up talking about IVG.

And then she contacted you?

Some months later. You see, Dr Morvan also heads up the European Cord Blood Bank. She was proposing a partnership between the Centre and the Bank to gather cord blood. Parental consent permitting, of course.

But you said this led to tensions between you and Dr Mansfield?

That's right.

Dr Mansfield didn't want to work with the European Cord Blood Bank?

No, she wanted to. She thought it was a great idea.

*

I'd felt smug that morning, walking past the protesters in the square. There were two groups, each clustered around their separate trestle tables, regarding each other with suspicion. On one side were the animal rights crowd, boys in ripped jeans, one girl with an impressive mane of multi-coloured dreadlocks. On the other side there was a local church group: middle-aged, cardigan-wearing, collected round some chirpy-looking young man in a dog-collar arranging pamphlets in neat little piles.

When I got to the lab I presented Dr Morvan's proposal to the team. Everyone was gathered: Alex, obviously, and Laura, our post-graduate student, along with super-sensible, recently-married, baby-on-the-way Matt. And James Connelly. The same age as Matt, James still looked like a student, in his grungy t-shirt and combats, tatty designer trainers. I saw through his whole alternative get-up though: James was on a graduate training programme with Verlaine and seconded to the Centre. He was destined for management, you know the deal: career trajectory, a proper salary. Jammy sod.

Daniel Hall was there too. He often spent time in the lab with us, when he wasn't tied up in meetings with management at the Centre, or back at Verlaine HQ. He was always the first to get a round in after work; he understood we junior researchers were perpetually short of cash. And he did his best to make things easier for us. Like, a few weeks earlier, we'd been complaining about the lack of facilities in the dorm, the little room adjacent to the lab we used for sleepover shifts. There were some lockers in there, and a side table with a kettle, and the bed was comfortable enough, but otherwise it was pretty basic. Anyway, Daniel had heard us complaining, and the following week he'd turned up with a smart new TV and a DVD player, courtesy of Verlaine.

I'd kicked off the meeting, explaining that Dr Morvan had contacted me about the IVG project cooperating with the European Cord Blood Bank.

'So, let's be clear about it,' Alex said. 'Storing this blood won't directly benefit the Frey's baby?'

'Probably not,' I explained. 'If *this* child becomes ill one day, stem cell therapies from his own cord blood won't help him.'

'Because those stem cells would carry the faulty genes that caused him to get sick in the first place?'

I nodded. 'His cord blood might help a future sibling, but that's not Dr Morvan's plan. This is about developing a public bank of stem cell resources.'

'So in the future,' Daniel said, 'there'll be stem cell resources available for everyone.'

Matt was busy thinking through the clinical implications. 'We couldn't risk restricting foetal blood supply during delivery,' he said. 'But we could allow Dr Morvan's team to collect from the placental side of the clamp, immediately after the cord's been cut.'

'I'll think about it,' Alex said.

She agreed to make contact with Dr Morvan, so the two institutions could talk. She'd discuss it with the Freys too. It was a legal grey area – I mean, the blood wasn't part of Mrs Frey's body, and it wasn't part of the baby's body either, so I'm not sure they'd've had a leg to stand on – so to speak – if they'd decided not to go ahead with the blood transfer. But Alex wouldn't have proceeded if the Freys weren't happy.

I stared up at him – X – on the big screen in the lab. I remember thinking, what an amazing creature. All that potential, you know?

You've probably seen an illustration of an embryo in a biology textbook, and that's what you're thinking he looked like. Well, scratch that from your mind. For a start we were peering at him through all this gunk and goo floating in the fluid, and even on the big screen you had to view him through this thin skin, a kind of bubble. That was the amnion. The bubble was gathered at the base, and anchored against the wall of the AU by this plant-like mass of red tendrils, like something out of a horror movie.

In the beginning you had to zoom in close to catch him, just this black clot, with red tendrils attached. Pretty icky, really. And a little later on, when he started to emerge out of the mass of stuff you still couldn't tell what he was, with his grotesque curved spine and oversized head.

His body was so pale it was almost blue. And semi-transparent too, so when he moved in front of the light you could see all the bright scarlet threads of his veins and blood vessels. At the beginning, he didn't really have arms and legs, just these little stubby webbed buds. And he didn't look solid. It was like his bones were just floating around in all that translucent flesh. The only solid things were his eyes, which were like giant black beads, no white or iris, all pupil.

Nobody ever said it, but everyone knew what everyone else was thinking: *We all started out like that.*

12

Alex

Now, Sussex

I'm crouching in the dark, holding X close, feeling his heartbeat, a rapid flutter against my belly. Someone's coming up the stairs. And now, a heavy tread on the landing. They're heading straight for this room, my grandmother's room, where we are hiding, waiting to be discovered.

I keep hoping the intruder will cry out, assure us they are friend not foe. I want to hear, 'Alex, don't worry, it's only me, it's Dolly.' Or 'It's Fiona. I've changed my mind. I'm here to help.'

But there's no greeting, no warning. Anyway, that was a man's tread on the stairs. A big man. Whoever is coming is trying to creep up on us, and I'm not naive enough to misunderstand his intention. I too could cry out, of course. I could call, 'Who's there?'

Invite communication. Alert him to our hiding place.

Not bloody likely.

The silhouette of a man appears in the doorway. It's too dark for me to make out his features. Which is good: that means it's too dark for him to see us crouching here.

The silhouette of a man. As if there was any ambiguity about his identity. I'd recognise that shape anywhere. Those broad shoulders, the shaggy haircut, the sloping bulk of him.

*

I remember the day I first set eyes on him. There was grey slush on the steps of the Centre, refrozen in the night; I was glad of my good boots. He was standing outside the building, close to the revolving glass doors. Staff and patients smoked out there, despite all the signs telling them not to. But he wasn't smoking. He had both his hands stuffed deep into the pockets of a heavy overcoat, and was shuffling his feet against the cold. As I climbed the steps I got the sense he was waiting for me.

A patient? Not one of mine. A member of staff? I didn't recognise him.

Or – oh hell – not another journalist.

'Ted Hayward,' he said, holding out his hand.

He was an attractive man, in a big, handsome way; broad-faced with strong, even features. A little younger than me, or perhaps that was just the impression created by his casual clothes and demeanour, the way he moved his feet, hanging around outside like a teenager playing hooky. Dark hair with a slight curl to it, almost hidden under a dark blue beanie. Something awkward about him too, something sad, as if he wasn't quite sure what he was doing. Though his smile reached his eyes, there was a hesitancy to it. And that roundness of his shoulders, as if he wanted to crawl back inside himself.

Or maybe it was just the cold.

I took the offered glove, and shook it. 'Alex Mansfield.'

He smirked. 'I know.'

Of course he knew who I was. Since the television appearances, everyone did. To my disadvantage, I sometimes felt. I glanced towards the revolving doors. 'Are you coming inside?'

As we crossed the lobby towards the lift, he told me

he'd recently started working for the National Gamete Service, which was housed in our building. In the context of declining fertility, the National Gamete Service had been tasked with promoting egg and sperm donation, and managing the unenviable job of keeping track of whose donated eggs and sperm had successfully been used in the creation of which babies.

When I got out of the lift on the third floor, he smiled at me; again there was that same sad, smile. Nothing to the encounter really, but it stayed with me. And after that I saw him around. I couldn't help noticing the way he looked at me when we shared a space, the way his eyes sought me out across the lobby or the square. It was disconcerting, unsettling I suppose, but I liked it. Now and then I caught myself looking out for him.

All the same, I remember wondering what he was after. Was he angling for a job, hoping for some help with his career? Or was it something else? You'll laugh at me, I suppose, at my naiveté. But I've never been very good at that easygoing back-and-forth of early attraction. I barely know what it is when I feel it, and I'm not good at spotting it in others. Fiona says I'm too high strung to be good at flirting, too spiky. So even when I bumped into Ted on another chilly morning, and he stopped to talk to me, I wasn't sure how to read the cues.

'I've been meaning to catch you,' he said, his eyes meeting mine before sliding away. 'I wanted to ask if you'd like to meet me for a drink. After work, one evening.'

We met in a bar on Newcastle's Quayside, and shared a bottle of wine. We started off talking about work, naturally enough, I suppose, but even then it struck me how many questions he asked. Enough that alarm bells marked 'undercover journalist' were going off in my head. I remember my twang of disappointment then, along with some regret that I'd bothered to dig out – and iron – my good black dress.

I'd answered his questions, confident I could deflect any likely to compromise patient confidentiality or commercial secrecy. And he *was* interested in Verlaine, our commercial sponsor and partner, I remember that too. He asked a lot about the relationship between the Centre and the international pharmaceuticals company. Who benefited, and how. I remember wondering, is that it? Is that what he's after?

After it got dark we went for a walk along the river, under the lights of the Baltic Centre for Contemporary Art and the invertebrate curves of the Sage on the other side of the water. We'd moved on somehow, from work-talk, into more personal territory. I was telling him something about my sister, I think, when he stopped and turned to face me, and I thought, ah, now. This is when I get to find out what's going on.

But instead of asking any more questions, he put his big hand to my cheek.

Okay. So he wasn't looking for career advice, or a scoop. This wasn't an interview, or some low level industrial espionage. This was, in fact, a *date*. And although I was surprised, I was pleased as well, pleased by his hand on my cheek, by the way he was looking at me. More pleased than I like to admit now, considering what happened later.

Between the constant demands of the project, and the press, and the ethics committee, I didn't have a lot of time to spare for a personal life. But we met up again, a few times for drinks, and then dinner, and gradually, over the months that followed, we started to get close. At least, I'd thought we did. At one point, I even started to think that maybe – just maybe – I was falling for him.

*

And now here he is, standing in the doorway, staring into the darkness of the room. Looking for me. Looking for X.

So yes, I feel pretty stupid now.

13

Karen

Nine months earlier, Market Harborough

Claire and I were running. Back at the house, I'd told Claire our news, and she kept saying how great it was. On the one hand we were pregnant, Rob and I, and this time it was going to work. On the other hand, I could run marathons if I wanted to, right up until the end. I could jump out of an aeroplane strapped to a freefall instructor, I could do a deep sea dive. I could eat what I wanted, drink what I wanted, go where I wanted.

'I know you didn't choose to do it this way,' Claire said, as we jogged on the spot at the traffic lights. 'But you might as well make the most of it.'

So, here I was, making the most of it, picking up speed as we headed for the gates and into the park. I wanted to run fast today, work up a sweat, shake off this strange jittery feeling.

'Whoa,' Claire said when we stopped by the bandstand, bending over her knees as she caught her breath. 'Give me a minute, eh?'

Where had this feeling come from? Why this sense that I wanted to bolt? The other day at school, an "incident" with Little Tyler had rattled me. He'd bitten one of the Reception girls on the arm, bitten her hard – I'd seen the neat red row of teeth marks. And Little Tyler wasn't even so little anymore, he was in Year 2 now and ought to know better.

But that didn't explain the way I was feeling today. Little Tyler wasn't my problem, was he?

Admittedly, I worried about him. He might not have been a particularly likeable kid but I'd lost count of the times I'd wanted to scoop him up and bring him home, be a good mum to him. Because being a good mum wasn't all about biology, was it? It wasn't about giving birth, or producing eggs, or even being genetically related to your child. It was about sitting up all night holding them when they had a fever, and hearing them talk through the difficult day they'd just had at school. It was about being the one person in the whole world who'd always be on their side.

Like, before we started our treatment at the Centre, all those months ago, Dr Mansfield sent us to see a counsellor, and then later on, when we were thinking about using donor eggs, we'd been advised to go back again. I knew why Dr Mansfield had insisted. They wanted to make sure we'd be able to love our baby if he was grown in an artificial uterus, and then, if I'd be able to love him if he wasn't related to me.

It reminded me of this training course school sent me on a few years back – when I was working towards becoming a Higher Level Teaching Assistant, and specialising in working with kids with emotional difficulties. I might not've been very academic at school, but I'd understood all that sort of thing easily enough. They used big words like 'attachment', but what they were really talking about was love. Kids needed enough of the right kind of love when they were tiny. Without it, they struggled. The way Little Tyler struggled.

The first time we met with the counsellor at the Centre, I kept thinking, *of course I would love him*, of course I would. Anyone who knows me must know that.

And afterwards, I'd asked Dr Mansfield, 'Did we pass then?'

'Pass?' Dr Mansfield looked surprised, and then she smiled. 'Dr McCarthy didn't have any concerns about your ability to bond with a baby gestated *in vitro*, if that's what you mean. She said – and I quote, although I think she was being tongue-in-cheek – "Karen would love an ugly baby left on her doorstep in a snowstorm."'

That counsellor saw right through me, didn't she? And what about Rob? Maybe it was easier for him, because he and the baby would be genetically related. And anyway, wasn't it always this way for men, one step removed?

Perhaps that's why I'd been feeling this distance between us. There wasn't any problem exactly, I mean, we weren't fighting or bickering. But sometimes I felt like Rob didn't quite get what it was like for me. I wanted him to understand all the swirling thoughts and questions going round in my head, but I didn't know where to begin. I just wanted him to understand, without the need to explain. Was that so much to ask?

'So, what's up with you?' Claire asked, when we slowed to a walk.

'Sorry,' I said. 'It's nothing, really.'

'You seem thoughtful. Quiet.' Claire upended her water bottle, took a long drink.

In the end it didn't matter that I didn't *feel* pregnant, running round the park. None of that mattered. All that mattered was that I'd love the baby. And I knew I'd be able to do that.

But then, the other day, Carole, who's one of the other teaching assistants at work, said something that got right under my skin. She hadn't meant to upset me, it's just that sometimes she lets her mouth run where it shouldn't. We were in the staffroom at break time. I'd just made myself a cup of peppermint tea, and Carole was drinking her coffee and flicking through a newspaper. There was an article about kids in care, the shortage of foster places, lack of resources. The usual.

Carole read out some of the more shocking statistics, and we all ummed and ahhed in sympathy. Then Carole said, 'Didn't you ever consider adopting one of those poor kiddies, Karen?' She just came straight out with it, and I didn't know what to say.

I understand people have questions about what we're doing. It's just, people don't ask those sorts of questions to healthy couples, do they? Couples who manage to have babies the normal way.

But I thought about it afterwards. Should we have adopted? Would that've been the right thing to do?

'I've just got a lot going on in my head,' I told Claire. 'Sorry I'm not very good company.'

'Oh, don't worry about t*hat*,' Claire said. 'I'm just concerned about you. Do you want to talk about it?'

I took a deep breath. I wouldn't even know where to start.

She looked me in the eye. 'It's going to be okay, Karen,' she said. 'You know that don't you?'

My voice was shaky as I said, 'How do I know we're doing the right thing?'

'You are *absolutely* doing the right thing.'

'But how do I know – how do you know I'm going to be able to do it?'

'Do what?'

'I don't know. Be a good parent. Love my child enough. Love him right.'

She put her hand on my arm. 'Karen. You're going to be a great mum. I know it. You know it.'

I looked down at the path, the backs of my eyes stinging.

'Look,' Claire said. 'Your situation isn't exactly normal, okay? But doubts and wobbles are normal. We all have doubts and wobbles.'

I looked up at her. 'I feel so unsure of myself.'

Claire puffed out a long breath and draped an arm around my shoulder. 'Welcome to the club, honey,' she said.

14

Alex

Now, Sussex

The figure stares into the room, but doesn't reach for the light switch. He notices the wardrobe and takes a step in our direction, then another. I'm almost hysterical with relief that he's going to do exactly as I predicted. It gives me, it turns out, an unrealistic sense of my own power.

As he leans towards the wardrobe door, I straighten up and take a step forward. With my left arm still holding X to my body, I grab my grandmother's bowl with my right hand and lob it with all my might at the back of Ted's dark head. Except, before the thing hits him, he turns. The bowl smacks him in the shoulder, and rather than smashing in a satisfying manner, it bounces off his solid body and falls ineffectually to the floor.

He grunts. 'What the –?'

I clutch X tighter to me and make a dash for it, towards the door of the bedroom, then spring along the landing and down the stairs. As I step into the kitchen I hear Ted calling out from upstairs. Yes, now he calls out. 'Alex. Alex, it's only me.'

What sort of an idiot does he take me for? I look around the kitchen, my eyes running over each object to see what I might use as a weapon. I flinch away from the wooden knife-block.

'Alex. It's me, Ted.'

It's funny, in a way. He believes I only threw the bowl

at his head because I'd mistaken him for someone else. I resolve to use this to my advantage. Keeping my voice even, I call out, 'I'm in the kitchen.'

I hear his steps on the landing. 'You're not going to attack me again, are you?'

Hanging from a hook on the wall there's a heavy-bottomed frying pan, the kind with the terracotta-coloured ceramic finish. Unhooking it with my right hand is enough to convince me I'll need two hands to wield it.

'I'm really sorry about this, sweetheart,' I whisper, placing X down on the bare tiles. I don't like to leave him there, so vulnerable. I don't like letting go of him at all, but I don't see that I have much choice. There's nowhere else to put him down in here and I'm not about to risk putting him in another room.

The kitchen opens onto the hallway, and I hear Ted's steps coming down the stairs. I step into the only space in the kitchen I won't be seen as he descends, and raise my arms, holding the heavy-bottomed pan aloft.

For the first couple of seconds after I put him down, X is quiet but alert, rolling his newborn eyes and stirring the air above his face with sorcerer's hands. Then his face cracks into a grimace and he issues a plaintive cough. This is the first time I've heard such a sound from him, but to my surprise, I understand it. I speak X, apparently; I'm as fluent as a native. The noise means, *Where did you go?* It takes some self-restraint not to pick him up, or even answer.

Concentrate, Alex.

I force all my attention into listening for the moment when Ted steps from the hallway into the kitchen. By the time he does, the muscles in my upper arms are already starting to burn, but by then it's too late for Ted. I swing the frying pan with all my strength at the height where I am expecting his head to appear.

Heavy pan connects with human face. Man grunts and crumples to his knees on the tiles. For good measure I hit him one more time.

I don't know who I'm more furious with: him, or myself for being taken in.

No, scratch that. I do know. I'm much more furious with him.

*

It was Daniel who first warned me Ted wasn't the person I thought he was. Ted and I had been dating for a few months by then, taking it slow. X was growing nicely, and although there'd been a lot to cope with, the project was going well. Another four months and we'd birth him and hand him over to his parents.

Daniel Hall had been assigned to our project from Verlaine, our commercial partner. Along with Dolly, he'd turned out to be one of my closest allies at the Centre. One evening he'd asked me to meet him in the pub at the end of my shift. This wasn't unusual, we often got together to talk through the latest developments, scientific or otherwise, and I relied on him to cheer me up when the latest media nonsense about us – about me usually – was driving me nuts. But this time he was the one who seemed worried.

'Come on then,' I'd said, placing his pint on the table in front of him. 'Out with it.'

He ran a freckled hand through his pale hair. 'That man I saw you with. Ted Hayward. Are you and him – I mean, are you seeing each other?'

I must have frowned then, because Daniel looked uncomfortable. 'I'm sorry, Alex. I know it's none of my business. I'm just looking out for you.' He took a gulp of his lager. 'I know him. I mean, I don't know him, not really. But I recognised him.'

That seemed unlikely. Ted had only moved to the area recently, and for that matter, Daniel's last project had been at Verlaine's San Diego headquarters. But I hung back to let him continue.

'There was a scandal,' Daniel said. 'A few years back, at Verlaine. A researcher lost his job. A serious case of malpractice. I don't know much about it, except that a research subject was hurt, and a drug trial had to be stopped.'

Maybe I was already putting up defences. I just couldn't see what any of this had to do with Ted.

'It was him, Alex,' Daniel said. 'I'm sure of it. Ted Hayward was the researcher.'

I remember the feeling of relief spreading through me then, and I paused to take a sip of my drink. 'You must've made a mistake,' I told Daniel. 'Ted's never worked for Verlaine. He's never even worked in research.' We'd had a dozen conversations about Verlaine by then. If Ted had ever worked for them, it would have been odd not to mention it. More than odd. Dishonest.

Daniel put his hand in his pocket, and drew out a piece of paper. 'I wasn't sure at first,' he admitted. 'So I went off and made some enquiries. Got hold of his personnel file.'

I smoothed out the paper. It was Ted all right. Younger, more smartly dressed, but definitely Ted. 'There's got to be another explanation,' I said weakly, although I couldn't think one. Why would Ted have lied to me?

'I've been over and over it,' Daniel said. 'Trying to work out if I was right to tell you. I know a man's past is his own business, up to a point. But –'

'But what?'

'He hasn't worked anywhere near research for years. Then, this high profile Verlaine project runs in partnership with the Centre, and all of a sudden he turns up here?'

'He works for the National Gamete Service. It's just a coincidence that their offices are based in this building.'

Daniel looked at me. 'Has he been asking you a lot of questions? Maybe being here, and getting to know you… it gives him proximity to the project.'

'But why would he want – ?'

'It's an explanation for the covert activity Security has discovered in the system. We already know someone's trying to steal from Verlaine. So far we assumed it was straightforward industrial espionage. But what if it's someone with a grudge?'

There had to be another explanation. Sure it was strange Ted hadn't told me about working for Verlaine. Worse than strange, tantamount to a lie. But what if there was a more innocent explanation? What if Ted did have something difficult in his past and was waiting for the right time to tell me?

'I know it's hard for you to hear this,' Daniel said. 'I'm only telling you as a friend.'

I needed more information, ideally from an independent source. 'Where did this happen?'

'Our Bristol research centre. About six years ago.'

That's when I thought of Miles Berger, a friend and former colleague of my father's. Hadn't he worked at that centre some time ago? Miles would be at my father's birthday party, a week from now. I'd talk to him.

15

Dolly

Much later, Westminster, during the Public Inquiry

So relationships with your colleagues were good?
Yes, we all got on okay. But I don't really understand –
And Dr Mansfield? Was she a good manager?
She was great. Look. Why are you –?
What about disagreements? Were there any of those?
Sure. We disagreed about stuff. Of course we did, there's nothing wrong with that. We discussed things. As a team.

*

Like, for example, how we should refer to the foetus. I used to wibble on to him when I was going about my day-to-days. Like, I'd be sitting at my computer terminal, I'd hit the button on the panel to discharge nutrients into the system, and I'd say, 'There you go, baby. Yummy breakfast coming right up.'

I saw Alex's shoulders stiffen. 'Listen to yourself, Dolly,' she muttered.

At that point I was having this particular flavour of argument – or a variation of it – at home too. Aimee, deep into her module on Gender Studies, had pulled me up on calling him 'the baby'.

'That's what he is,' I'd countered. 'He's a baby.'

'He's not a baby, he's a *foetus*.' Then she caught

herself. '*It*, I mean,' she corrected. '*It's* a foetus. Right?'

'Actually,' I'd said, feeling smug, 'until ten weeks, he's not a foetus, he's an embryo.'

And anyway, whatever. I can't say I was exactly *au fait* with the politics, I never cared very much about that. As far as I could tell our boy was definitely a 'he'. He had a Y chromosome: I'd seen it with my own eyes through a microscope. And even if he wasn't a baby yet, he was sure as hell going to be one soon.

Alex's objection to baby-talk was different. 'It's about maintaining professional boundaries,' she said.

Laura piped up, 'The newspapers have started calling him *Baby X*.'

'For God's sake,' Alex said darkly. 'Don't pay any attention to what the newspapers say.' She was still sore over the Dr Frankenstein thing.

'They're doing it because we wouldn't tell them the names of his parents,' I said. 'They invented a name which draws attention to his supposed anonymity.' Everyone was frowning at me, so I added, 'It's a joke.'

'Not much of a joke,' said Matt.

'Not a laugh-out-loud kind of a joke. More a sarcastic comment.'

'That sucks,' James said.

'I don't understand,' said Laura. 'The Freys' identities are known now. But the papers are still calling him *Baby X*. Why don't they switch to *Baby Frey*?'

'*Hash-tag* Baby X,' I said. Aimee was following it all on Twitter. She noticed these things.

'I don't even know what that means,' Alex said. 'And I'm fairly certain I don't want to find out.'

'It's the way people tag their tweets,' Matt explained, sounding a bit like he was talking to his elderly grandmother, 'so other people can follow the story.'

'Like I said.' Alex put her fingers in her ears to emphasise her point. '*La la la.*'

'But seriously,' I said. 'What *are* we supposed to call him?'

'The embryo,' Alex said firmly. 'And later on, we'll refer to him as the foetus.' She turned back to her computer. 'Right, everybody. Back to work.'

Except, Alex's solution didn't really solve our problem. The woman was smart all right, but sometimes she missed the obvious stuff. Like, what were we going to do when we had a bank of thirty babies gestating here at the Centre? Would they be known by numbers? By family surname?

Somebody check the status of the Williams Foetus. Which foetus is that, boss? *Foetus 27.*

It was quiet in the lab again. The pipes went *shush-shush-shush*, and a few seconds later, the soft tap-tap of fingers on keyboards started up. On the big screen the embryo twitched, flinging out his stumpy limb buds.

'There, there, baby,' I whispered.

*

We got into worse disagreements, as time went on. Like that morning I marched straight into Alex's office, all fired up. 'I just got a call from Dr. Morvan. The Cord Blood Bank, remember?'

'Well, good morning, Dolly. Why don't you take a seat?'

'She says you've refused to cooperate.'

Alex sighed, sitting back in her chair. 'I'd like to help, but –'

'The Freys refused consent? Why didn't you explain?'

'I didn't talk to the Freys. It never got that far.'

'Then what the hell is going on?'

She pressed her lips together, watching me fume. Then she said, 'I can't tell you. I'm sorry, Dolly.'

What possible reason could there be for Alex not to explain? Unless. 'Has this got something to do with Verlaine?'

The look on her face told me I'd guessed correctly. 'There's a non-disclosure agreement in the contract. I shouldn't even be telling you this much.'

'So go to Daniel.'

'Daniel can't fix this.'

I didn't believe that. He'd do anything to keep Alex sweet, that guy. I mean, he was so helpful, it was ridiculous. Sometimes I wondered if he had a bit of a crush on her, you know? Like the stuff he'd got us for the dorm, he'd said it was for the research team, but I reckoned it was Alex he was trying to impress. We all knew there were other things, things that mysteriously got sorted. Extra lab equipment she'd been struggling to get the Director to sign off on. If anyone could fix this, my money was on Daniel. Why wouldn't Alex try?

And for that matter, why would Verlaine stop us talking to Dr Morvan? That's when it came to me. 'They're developing their own stem cell resources.'

'Please, Dolly, just leave it – '

'And they want to use the IVG programme to feed their commercial cord blood banks.'

Alex stared at me, lips pressed tight. She didn't have to explain. If the resources generated from IVG were owned by a private company, the bright new future of stem cell medicine would only be available to people who could pay Verlaine for treatment.

I turned on her. 'I can't believe you let this happen.'

She laughed. She actually laughed. Like, you know, like she wasn't taking it seriously. 'Me? I didn't negotiate the Centre's contract with Verlaine. You don't think they'd let me get involved with that side of things, do you?'

'Why aren't you doing more to stop this? You're a public figure now. Go to the papers, kick up a stink.'

'I can't risk our relationship with Verlaine. We're in this now, we've got to deliver a healthy baby to the Freys.'

I stormed out. Where was her integrity?

Back in the lab the rest of the team were working quietly. The artificial uterus sat there on the bench, the grey and yellow logo in raised plastic, *Verlaine International*. When you came to think about it, that logo was on everything. All the stationary: our biros and sticky note pads. Our white lab coats, those good quality chairs even. The new lab equipment that mysteriously turned up two days after Alex and Daniel went to the pub together. Matt and James liked to joke that the little fella would come out with a Verlaine logo stamped across his tiny red arse.

I sat on my ergonomic Verlaine chair and ran my thumb over the raised plastic logo on the corner of my Verlaine mouse mat.

Suddenly, that joke didn't seem so funny anymore.

16

Alex

Now, Sussex

Ted is lying on his belly on the kitchen floor, legs splayed. He isn't moving, but there is a groaning sound coming from deep within his chest.

I'm glad he's not dead. Don't get me wrong, after what this man did to my child I hate him as only a mother can. There's a part of me, the animal part, that could finish him off with my bare hands. But there is another part of me that's still human, and a doctor at that. I'll do what I must to protect X, but I don't want murder on my conscience.

I stare at Ted, wondering what to do now. Meanwhile, X's plaintive cough has turned into a low whine. It means, *Pick me up.*

'Just here, baby boy,' I murmur. 'Won't be a second.'

I need to secure Ted's hands behind his back. I start searching the kitchen, hoping vainly for inspiration. If only I'd planned this better. In one of the kitchen drawers I find my grandmother's gardening gloves, some heavy duty scissors and a roll of twine. I cut a length and set about tying Ted's huge hands behind his back. Even his arms are heavy; how I'm going to move him, I don't know. Several hefts and grunts later, I manage to lift him onto his side, and then get enough of my own weight underneath his ribcage to roll him onto his back.

Ted's eyes flicker, but don't open. He's still groaning. On the side of his forehead, just above his right eye, a lump is swelling rapidly. I hunker down, knees bent behind Ted's head, my hands hooked into his armpits. He makes a sound that might be an attempt at speech, but I ignore it, dig my heels in, and drag.

It's lucky these tiles are so smooth. I wouldn't be able to shift him on carpet. I manage to heave his bulk across the kitchen floor, through the open door and into the room we always called the back kitchen, a sort of extended, walk-in pantry that my father nagged Grannie about converting into a utility room, though she ignored him.

I've only moved Ted a few feet. Back in the main kitchen, X has started to howl. I drag Ted as far as the boiler. Boxing in the exposed pipes was another job Grannie never quite got round to, and boy am I glad of it now. I haul Ted so his back is against the wall and start tying his wrists to the pipes. He winces, and I recognise the impulse in him to raise a hand to his swollen face, trace the contours of the bump with his fingers. But he can't do this, because his hands are tied behind his back.

'Consider yourself lucky,' I say. 'If I'd have swung any lower I'd have broken your nose.'

He blinks, watching me. 'Jesus, Alex. These pipes are hot. You'll burn my fucking wrists.'

I am not a monster. I go back into the kitchen, grab a tea towel. X's howling has become an alarm, a siren. *Wah-aah wah-aah wah-aah*. 'Just here, my love. Won't be long.' The sound runs through me and into me, jangling my nerves and raising my blood pressure. As I head back into the back kitchen and see Ted again, I feel an impulse to punch him, or shout at him, anything to release the tension of X's crying.

Accessing all my reserves of self-control, I kneel at Ted's side, fold the tea towel into a pad and press it between the pipes and his wrists. Then I tie him as tightly and thoroughly as I can, with another length of gardening twine. All the time I'm thinking, was that a mistake, the tea towel? Will that allow him to escape?

It occurs to me that he will escape, eventually. All I'm doing is buying myself some time. Anyway, the police will be here soon.

'You're a bloody maniac,' Ted mutters. 'Why are you doing this?'

The twine won't do what my fingers want it to, won't stay nice and tight. I don't know anything about tying effective knots. Not for the first time in the last twenty-four hours, I am discovering yet another life skill I have failed to acquire, even at the ripe old age of thirty-nine. Exactly what I've been doing with my life is a mystery to me.

X's cries have moved on now. He is no longer emitting that same siren wail, but making a tremulous, broken sound, like a lamb, or rather, the electronic approximation of a lamb, a hidden mechanism in the belly of a child's cuddly toy. It sounds like *laaa-ha-ha-ha, laaa-ha-ha-ha*, and is punctuated by shaky, hiccupping breaths, as if he's almost exhausted his store of hope that I'm coming back.

'I should've realised you were a bloody mad woman from the beginning.'

I scream at him, 'Shut up!' and then say more quietly, 'Or I'll have to gag you too.' He flinches and shuts up.

The twine is secure enough for now. It'll have to be, I'll have another go at it later. I go back into the kitchen and pick X up off the floor. He stops making the 'la' sound, but his breath is ragged with crying. I hold him tight to my chest, and he closes his eyes.

'There, there, baby. Relax, now. Mummy's here.'

'Mummy?' Ted says. 'Is that what this is then? You're even madder than I thought.'

I will not yell at him with X in my arms. I don't want my baby to hear my voice raised in anger. Instead I whisper, 'Shut. The. Fuck. Up.' My arms and legs are still shaking from the effort of dragging Ted across the floor.

But it isn't only that. I feel rough, actually. Really terrible. I wonder if I'm running a temperature.

*

Not long after my drink with Daniel, I got my chance to quiz Miles Berger. I'd been keeping my distance from Ted, which was easy enough, given how busy I was; we often struggled to spend any time together from one week to the next. Then, that weekend, I got the train down for my father's birthday party, and arrived late, to Fiona's frustration. I hugged and kissed my family and then went straight off in search of Miles.

'I don't suppose we could have a quiet word?' I asked when I found him.

'Alex, dear girl. How lovely to see you.'

Miles was becoming raggedy in late middle age, his blue bowtie slightly crooked, his eyebrow hair in need of a trim. I linked my arm through his. 'Let's get a drink. Shall we?'

Excusing himself from his conversation, Miles let me guide him to the bar. 'Very cloak and dagger, I must say. Something about your father, is it? Nothing wrong with the old devil, I hope?'

'No, nothing like that.' Miles was a surgeon, like Dad. Dad had supported him early on in his career, and never tired of telling everyone how proud he was of the way his protégé had turned out. His dear boy, the son he'd never had, yada yada yada. But yeah, all water under the bridge. I was over it. Really. 'There's something I need to ask you, Miles. A professional matter.'

'Go on.'

'Am I right in thinking you spent some time working at the Verlaine Biotech lab in Bristol?'

'Yes, that's right.'

'I need to find out about something that happened there, about six years ago.' I nodded at the barman, who came over and took our order. 'A scandal,' I said, 'involving a clinical trial. And a researcher, Ted Hayward.'

He frowned. 'I'm not sure. We're going back a while.' He raised the glass the barman handed him, nodding to me. 'Cheers, by the way.'

'Cheers.' I took a sip of my wine. 'I brought a photograph, in case that helps.' I handed him the print-out Daniel had given me.

Miles took it, smoothing out the paper. 'I do remember him. Yes, Ted Hayward, that was it. Gosh, Alex, what's this about? Has he applied for a job with you or something?'

'Something like that.' I kept my voice steady, despite the image that flashed through my mind: Ted's face close to mine on my pillow, his arms around me.

'I suppose people ought to be given a second chance.' The corners of Miles's mouth turned down doubtfully.

'I'm sensing a "but".'

'Absolutely. If it was my project. Or let me rephrase that. If it was my career-making, once-in-a-lifetime, history-changing project, I wouldn't touch a character like that with a ten-foot pole.'

I took a big mouthful of wine, swallowed it back hard. 'Why's that?'

'Well, I'm not sure of the details. But in the investigation that followed this fellow, Hayward, was accused of gross negligence. And there were rumours of worse.'

'Worse?'

'That he'd messed with a sample to sabotage the programme. Fellow could've gone to prison. Not sure why he was never prosecuted, sounded like a very suspect character to me. And of course, in your field, you're working with vulnerable people, aren't you? The patients, not to mention the – er – foetuses.'

I managed a nod, my guts churning. So it was true.

'You know,' Miles said. 'There are some people, some very dangerous people, I might add, who don't see research subjects as fully human. They manage this sort of mental sleight of hand, believing the good that comes out of research is more important than the rights of individual patients.'

'Seriously, Miles, you'd put this man into that category?'

'What do I know? I wasn't directly involved. I never had an opinion on him, at least until it all came out. But no, I wouldn't risk working with him. Even in a very lowly capacity, with someone standing over his shoulder. You just don't know what someone like that is capable of.' He paused frowning, and then he said, 'It was Dekker, wasn't it?'

'Excuse me?' For a moment it was like the floor was moving beneath my feet. I reached out to the bar to steady myself.

'This chap, Hayward. The scandal involving the research subject. It was Dekker's research I believe.'

It couldn't possibly be. 'Are you sure?'

'Yes, now I come to think about it.'

'Dekker. You mean, *the* Dekker?'

'Yes. Only, that's odd, isn't it?'

Odd didn't begin to describe it. Dekker had been developing synthetic immune products. His theory had been that these could be used to retrain the rogue immune systems of people with auto-immune disorders, terrible diseases such as rheumatoid arthritis and multiple sclerosis. It could've been the biggest discovery in medicine since antibiotics. Could have been, that is, if it hadn't been a total failure.

And Ted had been involved in *this* research?

'But didn't you end up using Ig240 in *in vitro* gestation?' Miles asked.

'Yes. Yes, we did.'

Dekker's synthetic immune products hadn't provided a breakthrough cure for autoimmune disorders, but they had made IVG possible. We now used one particular immune-product Dekker developed – Ig240 – to substitute the work of the mother's immune system *in utero*, protecting the foetus from infection and training the foetus's developing immune system to manufacture its own antibodies. Dekker's therapeutic cul-de-sac had been fertility medicine's gain.

'And now this chap wants a job with you,' Miles continued. 'Maybe that's just a coincidence. Still.'

A coincidence. I downed the rest of my wine, my pulse racing. 'Thanks, Miles. You've been very helpful.'

'I must say, dear girl, you're looking very pale. Feeling all right?'

I shook my head, smiling. 'I'm fine. Really. You've given me a lot to think about.'

There it was. Ted had been lying to me this whole time. Was there still a part of me clinging to how I'd felt about him? I couldn't get it to add up. Daniel had accused Ted of medical negligence, but what Miles was telling me was worse. Not just a mistake, but something callous, calculating. And the connection with Dekker was stranger still. What was Ted playing at?

But all this was hearsay, wasn't it? Miles and Daniel

could both have got their facts wrong. Perhaps there was another side to the story. I had to give Ted the opportunity to tell me the truth. I spotted Fiona, talking to one of our mother's friends from the golf club. I kissed Miles's cheek, thanked him again, and then made my way over to my sister.

'I'm really sorry about this, Fiona, but I'm going to have to go.'

'Go?' Fiona looked crestfallen. 'You only got here a moment ago.'

'I'm sorry. Something's come up. I have to get back. Could someone call me a taxi to the station?'

'Come on then,' Fiona said, shaking her head. 'I'll drive you.'

17

Karen

Six months earlier, Newcastle-upon-Tyne

'Oi, Karen! Over 'ere!'

I kept my head down and held on tight to Rob's hand. The stuttering cameras sounded like gunfire.

'Come on, Karen, give us a smile!'

Dr Mansfield suggested we come to the back door of the Centre, so she could sneak us inside without any trouble. But the photographers were one step ahead of us. As usual.

It all started a couple of weeks ago. I'd been doing the weekly food shop on a Saturday morning, when a man came up to me in the supermarket and took my photograph. He'd jumped in front of me, clicked his camera and dashed off. The following Monday, in the staffroom, Carole had brought in a copy of a national newspaper to show everyone. On the front page there was a picture of me, pushing my trolley down the household cleaning products aisle, wearing a pair of weekend jeans and a sweatshirt. On my feet were my old running shoes, the ones where the soles are so worn I don't run in them anymore. No make-up, naturally. I could have died of embarrassment.

The headline said: BABY X MUM WORRIED BY LATEST HEALTH SCARE.

For a few moments, I couldn't get to grips with the meaning the headline. I just stared at my face in the photo. That was probably my normal supermarket-shopping expression, a bit bored, a bit distracted. I thought, *I wasn't worried, that's a lie.*

And then I thought, *latest health scare?*

The other teaching staff were awkward around me. They didn't mean to be unkind, but no one knew where to put themselves. I was on playground duty at lunchtime, so the first chance I had to phone Dr Mansfield was in the middle of the afternoon. All day I'd been thinking, he can't be sick, he can't be. I kept remembering what Dr Mansfield had told me when he implanted. He was the strongest one, wasn't he? He was perfect. Good eggs from a healthy young woman, and then they'd picked the strongest embryo of the bunch. I was the lame duck, not him.

I got through to Dr Mansfield straightaway, thank goodness. She was quick to reassure me. There was no health scare. Everything was fine with the baby, the team had absolutely no concerns, none at all. The newspapers just made these things up, she said. She didn't know why they did it, but that's what they did. She hoped I trusted her enough to know that if there were any concerns about the baby's health, anything at all, Rob and I would be the first to know.

After work, Claire came round for a cup of tea. Turns out she'd seen the paper in the newsagent's that morning.

'There's no health scare,' I told her. 'That's not even my worried face.'

'Show me your worried face,' Claire said.

'I'm wearing it now.'

As first I'd just been relieved there was nothing wrong with the baby. Then I started thinking, why did they do it? Why did they write that headline? Did someone really think there was a health scare? Or had the photographer just taken a photo of me, and someone else had made up a headline as an excuse to print it? They didn't do that, did they? Not nowadays.

Claire had been more cynical about it. 'Wouldn't put it past them,' she said. 'The only news story here is a woman's been bothered by a photographer.'

'Not exactly newsworthy,' I said.

'Bet we can think up a better headline,' said Claire, 'How about: Baby X Mum Harassed by Pap in Frozen Food Aisle?'

I laughed. Yes, that was more like it. Claire always knew how to make me feel better.

But still, the niggling worry. Dr Mansfield said something else too: that, in her opinion, this was sympathetic coverage. There was no criticism of Rob and me. She was really sorry it had happened, she said, but frankly, it could have been worse. To the newspapers we were ordinary people who couldn't have a baby, and now we somehow stood for all those other ordinary people out there struggling to conceive. IVG had given us the chance of a happy ending. It was the sort of story people liked.

I understood what she was getting at, she didn't have to spell it out. The media coverage of her was very different, not sympathetic *at all*. I'm not sure why exactly, but they almost never used her name without throwing in some adjective that made her sound crazy, or like – like the other doctors mistrusted her, or something, when we knew she was very well-respected. *Controversial*, they called her. They said she was a maverick. And then there was the fact that she didn't have children of her own. That always got mentioned.

I did feel sorry for Dr Mansfield. She had a lot on her plate and as far as I could see she was doing her best. Still, I'd got off the phone feeling shaken, and somehow disappointed, as if she hadn't really understood. This nonsense from the newspaper – surprising me into an unflattering photograph while I did the weekly food shop and then printing that photograph in a national newspaper so that people – nice people, but still – could embarrass me with it at work, all this, and making up a story that my baby was ill – this was what they did when they were *on your side*? I couldn't work out how I was supposed to feel when she said it could've been worse. Was I supposed to feel grateful?

And it was confusing too. I understood why people were interested in IVG. The technology was new and strange, and held out hope for such a lot of people. I would have been interested, myself. I just couldn't work out why everyone was so interested in *me*. In me especially, they didn't seem half as interested in Rob. No one printed photos of him. No one was calling out his name now, on the steps of the Centre.

I was just an ordinary person, not a celebrity, or a public figure. But then, when you came to think about it, weren't there other ordinary people who ended up in the papers? People who were ordinary until something extraordinary happened to them. A natural disaster. A missing or murdered child.

I suppose it made me nervous. If they'd wanted to, what was to stop the same people who'd followed me to the supermarket from going through my bins? Or hassling my family, or neighbours for information? And if they wanted to, could really twist whatever they found to suit the story they wanted to tell?

And what about when our child was born? Would they follow him around too? If I'd already annoyed them by not co-operating, would they be more likely to say nasty things about him?

There was this other word that got used, you see, a word that I hated more than any other. It had already made me turn off the radio news, stop reading the papers. It was a horrible word, mean and nasty. A word that made my blood run cold.

Frankenstein.

So far, they'd only used it about Dr Mansfield. Because I knew from the old films, Frankenstein was really the doctor, wasn't he? Not the doctor's creation.

Not the –

At the back door of the Centre, surrounded by photographers, I had a decision to make. I'd be giving them what they wanted if I looked up now and smiled. They could write their story about our struggle for a baby of our own, our hope for a happy ending. They could pad it out with other details from a Centre press release: information on his weight and length, a quote from Dr Mansfield saying everyone was doing well.

Without the smiling photo, they might print one of me looking anxious. Or worse, angry.

Despite assurances from controversial fertility doctor, Alex Mansfield, that Baby X is growing normally, mum-to-be Karen Frey looked anxious as she arrived for her appointment at the Centre for Reproductive Medicine this morning.

I couldn't risk it. I took a deep breath and stood up straight, turning to face the photographers with a smile. They went wild, shouting, 'Karen, Karen,' and calling out questions.

'How are you feeling, Karen?'

'Karen, are you nervous?'

Enough. I was exhausted already. I held onto the smile for the time it took Dr Mansfield to open the back door, and bundle us into the building.

18

Alex

Now, Sussex

I'm still holding X as I dig inside Ted's jeans pocket, retrieve his mobile in its leather case, and flip it open one-handed. The phone should contain the information I need. You see, I've worked out Ted must've had an accomplice. There's too much he couldn't have done on his own. And although it hurts me to think about it, the most obvious explanation is that someone on the inside has been helping him.

*

It was six months ago now, when Jim, our head of security, first called me down to his office. 'Sometimes these hackers are just kids,' he'd explained. 'They just want to try their hand, see what they can break into, whether it's a high street bank or the Pentagon. But we've been monitoring this guy's activity on the system, and the most likely explanation is industrial espionage. He'll be in the pay of one of Verlaine's competitors. When there's this much money at stake, Alex, nothing shocks me.'

'But it's already too late to copy the work. There are patents –'

'Yes, but, if they take the data before publication, it gives them the head start on creating their own version of the technology. And anyway, patents don't cover every corner of the planet, this guy could be working for the Chinese. But listen to me, Alex. We think this is just data theft, but we have to be on the lookout for a more serious sort of attack.'

'More serious?'

'I don't have to remind you about the hate mail we've received. What if these same people could hack into our systems and do some real damage? Think about it. You've got all the control systems for the artificial uterus lab accessible remotely. Someone could disrupt the foetus's food supply or worse, his oxygen, or trigger the birthing protocol.'

Jim smiled kindly when he saw the panicked look on my face. 'So I've taken the liberty of introducing a little extra security. Think of it like a trip wire. If he tries to enter the AU system we'll know about it.'

I felt the knot of anxiety tighten in my guts. 'What if he tries to hurt the foetus?'

'Right now he's just digging around in the files. He's probably copying data, sending it offsite. If we close him down too early, he'll know we're on to him. This way there's a chance we can work out what he's up to, catch him in the act. Don't worry, Alex, the second he trips the wire, we close him down. He won't get access to the foetus. No way.'

And that was how they caught him, four months later.

I was on the train back from my Dad's birthday party, fresh from my conversation with Miles, when I took the call from Jim. Ted tripped the wire security had set, and the police traced the intrusion to his IP address. They'd arrested him that very afternoon.

I remember the pity in Jim's voice. By then everyone knew Ted and I had been dating. Everyone knew I'd been played. 'Don't worry, Alex,' Jim had said. 'You don't need to be scared about that bastard ever coming back.'

I stared at my face in the window of the train carriage. 'I'm not scared,' I said. 'Just angry. If I ever see him again I'll kill him, the treacherous shit.'

*

Now I slip Ted's phone into my own pocket, and glare at my betrayer, tied up against the pipes. X has calmed down and is sleeping in my arms. Every now and then he takes one of those little shaky, raggedy breaths, but for the most part he's still, his breathing even. I decide to risk putting him down to rest on the sofa while I check outside.

I go out onto the gravel, where Ted's car is parked in the front of the house. It's empty, which is a relief. I'd started to half expect someone else to jump out at me. The rain has slowed to a drizzle. Heavy cloud cover, a low-slung, wet-black sky. I go back into the house and check on X, then I drag one of the ladder-back chairs into the back kitchen, placing it in front of Ted.

Ted has his eyes closed, the welling egg on his eyebrow looks as if it might burst. For a second I almost pity him, this frail human, who has the face, and the body, of a man I had started to love. The man who played me to get access to X. My anger returns, hard and hot in the back of my throat.

Those knots won't hold forever. Besides, X and I will have to be away from here soon. Still, Ted has the answers I need. This is my opportunity to find out what he did, and why. I may never get another chance.

I sit down on the ladder-backed chair. 'How did you know where to find me?'

His eyes open, then close again. 'I worked out this is

where you'd come. We'd spoken about you spending time here, hadn't we?'

'But the address?'

'It wasn't difficult to find. You'd told me the name of the village. It isn't exactly a big place. I asked after your grandmother in the local pub. I told them I was a friend of your family, coming down to look at the place, thinking of buying it. I told them I was lost, and they gave me the address.'

Snooping, sneaking bastard. 'Who were you working with?' He doesn't answer. 'Come on,' I say. 'You couldn't be in all those places at once. And anyway, after you were arrested –'

He looks down at the floor, shakes his head.

'Don't give me that. I know about Dekker.'

His eyes flicker again, and recognition crosses his face. He closes it down quickly, but it's enough. I've got him. 'There was someone in my lab team, wasn't there? Who was it? Laura, James, Matt?' As I utter each name I watch his face, waiting for him to give something away. Nothing. The worst I leave for last. 'Was it Dolly?'

He shifts his weight against the boiler pipes, looks up at me. 'You've got this all wrong.'

'Don't give me that. We found your fingerprints all over the system.' For a moment, I feel myself reel and I'm glad I'm sitting down. My fever must be getting worse.

'Fingerprints?' he says.

'The dummy email account. You were retrieving data from the system, and sending it off site.'

He looks down at the floor. 'Ah, that.'

He's admitted it then. I hear X chirrup from the living room, and rise from my chair.

'I need some water.' Ted says. 'My head hurts.'

No kidding. I need some water and paracetamol

myself, maybe a thermometer to check my temperature. I'm going to need to be sharp to question Ted.

But first I need to see what X needs. Like I said, I'm a mother now, and that changes a person's priorities. Ted will just have to wait.

19

Dolly

Much later, Westminster, during the Public Inquiry

You faced opposition though, didn't you? What can you tell us about that?

Where should I start? You know about the bomb scares already, right?

*

I remember the alarm, clanging, insistent, everyone streaming out of their labs and offices like lemmings and making their way down the main staircase to the lobby. I remember a flow of nurses and technicians in blue and green scrubs and brightly coloured rubber clogs, doctors in white coats, patients with blank faces, carrying their coats and bags over their arms.

Outside in the courtyard it was a perfect spring day, bright and cold. Groups of passing students craned their necks to see what was happening *this time*, used to noise and drama after all the months of angry demonstrations.

I stood close to Alex in the sunshine. Her bony hands were locked together, her knuckles pale.

Look, I wasn't scared. No really, it was all bullshit. We'd been here before. There was no bomb, and let's face it, I'd been right about that, time and time again. We'd stand out here for the next hour while the police and the fire brigade checked the building, and then we'd all head back in.

Mostly I was thinking about what Mum would say when she phoned later, rehearsing the arguments in my head. It was a hoax. They're just trying to scare us. All we have to do is stand firm.

I thought back to our last conversation, before I put the phone down on her. The one where she said, 'What do I have to do to convince you to leave that place?' her voice shaking with emotion.

'Don't worry,' I told Alex now in the sunlit square. 'It's nothing. Everybody's out.'

When she turned to me her face said it all. And yeah, okay, I regretted that last comment.

So I said firmly, calmly, 'It's all right, Alex. There's no bomb. Safest pregnancy in history, remember.'

Honestly, it was like I was looking after her. And to think I used to look up to her.

*

How did your family feel about you working there, Miss McFarlane?

Not great, to be honest. My parents were worried about me. My mum totally freaked after the last bomb scare.

Would you hold up that plastic wallet, please?

This one?

Do you know what that is?

I do. It's a quote from the Bible.

Have you seen it before?

I have.

When have you seen it?

Someone was handing them out in the square.

Would you please read what's written on the piece of paper, Miss McFarlane?

I can. It says, 'And he said to the woman, 'I will increase your trouble in pregnancy and your pain in giving birth. In spite of this, you will still have desire for your husband and will be subject to him.' Charming, eh?

*

At first I almost didn't notice the package. I already had my coat on, my record bag slung across my chest, rubberised buds of earphones nestled in my ears. But there it was on the mat: a white jiffy bag, the address written in block capitals. My name, no stamp.

I walked back into the kitchen frowning. Aimee had the radio tuned to Six Music and was attempting to sing along to a song she liked, at the same time as shovelling sugary cereal into her mouth. 'That shit's bad for you,' I said. 'Addictive. Messes with your brain chemistry. Not to mention what it does to your teeth.'

Aimee glanced at me, then at the package, then back at me. 'What's that?'

I stared at the package, turning it over in my hands. 'Erm... letter bomb?' I held the blank expression for a moment before letting my face break into a goofy grin. I thought she'd laugh. You know, whack me maybe, but definitely laugh.

'Don't open it,' she said, those pale blue eyes wide and totally serious. 'Put it down over there.'

'I was joking,' I said. 'Oh, come *on*.'

The package was large enough to hold an A5 notebook, although it was almost empty, just a small bump inside, under my thumb. I didn't recognise the handwriting. The rear side of the envelope was stapled, the staples showing as raised bumps beneath a strip of shiny brown packing tape. I traced the bulge between the layers of brown paper and bubble-wrap: soft. Something small, wrapped in something soft.

I slid my fingernail under the loose corner of the packing tape and peeled it back.

'Seriously, Dee,' Aimee said. 'I don't think you should open it.'

'It's not a letter bomb,' I said. 'You couldn't make an explosive devise this small.' Like I knew anything about letter bombs. But really, there was no part of my brain capable of believing this package would explode in my hands. And I wanted to know what was inside.

I'd already started to formulate a hypothesis. Someone had sent me a memory stick and wrapped it in bubble-wrap, before putting it into the padded envelope. Someone was passing me information, but why? It was creepy, but exciting too. Maybe it was connected with this case of industrial espionage, like Jim from Security explained, at the briefing. We all had to be vigilant, apparently.

'I don't hear ticking,' I said, giving the package a little shake, kind of enjoying the look of horror on Aimee's face. I pulled open the seal, feeling the satisfying release as the staples gave in.

Inside: something wrapped in tissue paper. I upended the package onto the kitchen table. The thing landed with a flump, right next to Aimee's cereal bowl.

'Oh my God, what is it?' she whispered.

I lifted the thing into my palm, peeled back the layers one at a time with the very tips of my fingers.

The corpse of a baby mouse. Eyes closed. Perhaps they'd never opened.

It was tiny, pink, completely hairless. And it reminded me of something, the way it lay curled on its layers of tissue: a book I'd seen once, about life before birth. An expensive book on good quality paper, full of glossy images, claiming to show a true inside view of a pregnancy, brought to you by the miracle of modern photography, you know the sort of thing. But there'd been a controversy: most of the images were set-ups, lifeless embryos and foetuses, many the result of terminations, lit and coloured to appear living, using photographic tricks.

'Jesus,' Aimee breathed, 'that's just so fucking weird.' I could feel her looking at me, but I couldn't stop looking at the mouse. 'What does it mean?'

'I don't know.'

'Has this got something to do with your work? Is it a message? Is someone threatening you now?'

Of course it was about work. Don't be a doughnut, Aimee. 'Look inside the jiffy bag, would you? Check there's no note.'

'Nothing.'

I rewrapped the dead baby mouse in the tissue paper, and slid it back inside the envelope. Then I opened the flap of my record bag, placed the envelope inside.

'Aren't you going to phone the police?' Aimee said. 'Whoever sent that's got our home address.'

'I'm going to work. Alex'll know what to do.'

My confidence was about ninety-seven percent bravado. Would Alex know what to do? She'd been so weird and stressy recently, and so uncommunicative. I didn't know what was going on with her. Not that I was feeling particularly warm or friendly myself, I was still pretty upset with her that she wouldn't stand up to Verlaine about X's cord blood.

I hadn't touched the mouse, only the tissue, but on second thoughts, I washed my hands anyway. Then I leaned down to kiss the top of Aimee's head. 'Don't worry, I'm sure it's nothing.' See how cool I was? Like the hero of a spy thriller. Maybe Alex was falling apart with the pressure, but I was doing fine. Yes, sirree. Absolutely fine.

I spotted Daniel Hall on my way into the Centre. There he was, neat in his suit, ginger hair close cropped, purposefully crossing the lobby. I told him what had happened. He was fantastic about it. No, really, took it seriously, but was super-calm too. Like a proper leader, you know? And then we went to see Jim, the head of security, together. Jim took the mouse from me, told me he'd notify the police, and we talked about precautions I could take to keep myself safe. Jim also said he'd discuss the whole thing with Alex, once he'd involved the police and had a better idea of what was going on.

Afterwards I said to Daniel, 'Thanks for your help. I wasn't sure how Alex would take it. You know what she's been like lately.'

Daniel said, 'Alex is a brilliant scientist, a brilliant doctor. But like a lot of brilliant people she can be a bit –'

I noticed the unfinished sentence, but although I had adjectives aplenty to supply, I didn't offer any.

'She needs someone like you looking out for her,' Daniel said.

I breathed out hard through my nose. It was difficult to express what I wanted to say, which was yes, I was happy to look out for Alex, but this was turning out to be difficult for everyone, and she was our boss, right? Wasn't she supposed to be looking out for us?

'Give her a break, Dolly,' Daniel said. It was like he'd read my mind.

'All right,' I said, sullen as a teenager.

20

Alex

Now, Sussex

X woke up in a terrible state after all that crying earlier. Milk was the only thing that would placate him, and even that took a while to organise, as he moaned and fretted, turning his head angrily from side to side, refusing to latch on. I suppose, being left to cry on the kitchen floor while his mother decks a stranger with a frying pan is no more peculiar than anything else he's been through in his twenty-four hours of post-birth existence, all of which has been – let's face it – dramatic. But I wonder if he's picking up on my anxiety, on the air of danger and violence surrounding us. Perennially, I worry about the level of stress he's under, the amount of cortisol racing through his bloodstream.

Yes, I worry about it; so sue me. Old habits die hard.

*

It was about halfway through the pregnancy when we discovered markers seeming to indicate X's cortisol levels were high. Well, higher than anticipated, anyway. This wasn't too serious in itself – plenty of babies were subject to higher cortisol levels than X, and suffered no ill effects. But although X's cortisol never exceeded unsafe levels, we couldn't work out why it was so high. And this was a concern.

In a normal pregnancy, cortisol fluctuations could be explained by maternal stress, or toxins entering the foetal environment, tobacco smoke, for example. But X wasn't subject to any of these stresses, so why the extra cortisol?

I remember talking it through with Fiona over the phone. 'What if there's something I haven't controlled for?'

There were already internet rumours, and rumblings were starting up in the mainstream media too. Baby X would be born with some defect. It wasn't natural, was it, growing a baby in a box? Something had to go wrong, that's what people were saying.

Not that I believed any of that nonsense, but to be frank the climate was making me jumpy. Not least because I knew we had to keep quiet about X's cortisol levels, even to the Freys. If this got out, the papers would have a field day.

'We've replicated everything a biological mother would provide,' I told Fiona. 'Oxygen, nutrients, warmth, blood supply, even immune support. But what if the mother plays some unknown role in regulating foetal stress?'

'What about feeling held?' Fiona had said. I knew the project made her uncomfortable, though she struggled to express why she felt that way. Is that why I went to her to thrash out my doubts, as if she somehow represented the sceptical public and I needed to practice defending myself? No, it was more than that. This was an argument we'd been having between ourselves for years, one we kept returning to.

'He is held,' I'd countered. 'He's held by the walls of the AU. And the amnion bubble expands to accommodate him.'

'What about movement? He isn't rocked by a mother's walking.'

'That's true. It's a different environment. It smells different, it sounds different; the light levels are different. But I can't see how those things would trigger a stress response like that.'

'Okay,' Fiona said. 'But what if he needs – ' She might not have known how to finish the sentence, but the question came through loud and clear: *What if he needs a mother?*

And I couldn't help the answer that sprang into my mind: *He's got me.*

*

Now I'm sitting at Grannie's kitchen table, eating a thrown-together sandwich with my left hand. My right hand is busy holding X in a comfortable position at my left breast. I've finally put the lights on in the kitchen. It's properly dark now and the rain's still falling outside.

The list of things I haven't yet achieved outstrips the minor triumphs of having made myself a sandwich and switched on the kitchen lights. Honestly, I just don't know where the time goes. I haven't washed X or changed him into the pyjamas I feel he should now be wearing. I haven't had a second to work through the contacts and text messages on Ted's phone to find out who he's in communication with. I haven't looked at a map, or done anything that could be seen to contribute towards making a plan. I haven't gone hunting round the house for something better to tie Ted's wrists and ankles with so I can sleep easier tonight. Naturally enough, I haven't slept. Nor have I managed to make my way upstairs to hunt out Grannie's old mercury thermometer.

I'm assuming she must have had one. It's probably in the bathroom cabinet, or else in one of the drawers of the dresser in the bedroom. It's been forty minutes since I swallowed 400 mg of paracetamol, but I still feel weak, dull-headed and shivery. I know fever symptoms, even when feeling my forehead with my own hand reveals nothing bar a slight dampness on my skin. Trust me, I'm a doctor. And this is no time to be coming down with the flu.

You see, there's a man tied with not-quite-strong-enough gardening twine to the exposed boiler pipes in the back kitchen. Last time I looked in on him, I was pretty sure he was sleeping. But I locked the door all the same, and double-checked the back door was dead-bolted too. I'm still convinced that left to his own devices, Ted will escape sooner or later. The only question is, before the police arrive, or after?

And while we're at it with the unusual and problematic, there's another thing: Fiona is sitting at this table with X and me. Except it isn't Fiona, not really. She's younger-looking, slighter, her hair hangs loose down her back, longer than she's worn it for years. Part of me, the sane, rational part of me, knows Fiona isn't really here. I don't think there's anything to be gained by asking her if she is a figment of my imagination, or wasting time trying to work out how she got here. Instead I remember the disagreements Fiona and I had about the IVG programme. There's a clue in this, I think.

Fiona is here for a reason, even if she's only in my head.

But my head is banging like a pneumatic drill and I feel like hell. So, after a few minutes of watching each other, I venture lightly, 'Well then, sis, did you see any of this coming?'

She has the good grace to laugh. 'No, my darling. I can honestly say I did not.'

'You aren't here to say I told you so.'

Her eyes are bright. 'I think you have a fever,' she says tenderly.

'I think so too.'

'You should be tucked up in bed.'

'I've been meaning to get upstairs. To look for a thermometer.' I glance down at X, still chomping heartily. 'But I'm finding it surprisingly difficult to get anything done.'

Through the wall that divides the main kitchen from the back kitchen, I hear Ted call out, 'Alex, who's there?' For a second, I wonder if Fiona can hear him, and worry what she might think of me having a man tied up in the next room. Then I scold myself for this highly irrational thought. Fiona's not here; it doesn't matter what she thinks about Ted.

Ted calls out again. 'Are you talking to someone?'

Fiona and I both ignore him.

'So, Alex.' Fiona tilts her head, smiles at me.

I raise my eyebrows. 'Go on.'

'What are you going to do now?'

I press my lips together. X is becoming fretful again; I think the milk on this side is finished, and my boy is not yet sated. 'Hang on a second,' I tell my sister, while I edge back my chair to give him some space, and then swing him round to attach him to the other breast.

Fiddling with my bra, I notice my right breast is hot and sore. It's only when I pull up my shirt to move X into position that I notice the mark.

It's about the size of a twenty pence piece, and furious, fiery red, and it appears to float just below the surface of my skin. The breast itself is as swollen and hard as a bowling ball. I know it's full of milk, but I don't think the other was like this, even before X drained it dry. Tentatively, I place a fingertip over the mark. The flesh is burning hot. I apply gentle pressure, and tendrils of pain shoot through me, down through the breast tissue into my chest, and out along my arms, as if broken glass were passing through my veins. For a second I find myself reeling, as if I might slip from the chair, collapse onto the floor. I know what this means, there's no getting away from it.

Mastitis.

Fiona's eyes are kind, but practical. 'Poor darling,' she says craning her neck to look. 'That looks bad. You might need antibiotics.'

Now I know for certain this is not the real Fiona. Fiona would have offered me some homeopathic remedy, some minutely diluted sugar pill, to take away the raging infection. She was never one for what she called "Western medicine". I remember her perched on her silver birthing ball, belly distended, cradling a mug of nettle tea and lecturing me on the evils of pain relief in labour.

'No one's going to give you an epidural unless you ask for one,' I'd told her.

'Women have been doing this for millennia, you know,' Fiona had breezed.

And dying of it, I'd wanted to say. But that was too harsh, what with Fiona so heavy with her first pregnancy, and such a long way from any easy way out, her hips splayed and her feet flat from the effect of the relaxin on her ligaments.

'Antibiotics,' I echo now, sitting at Grannie's kitchen table with this ghostly vision of my sister. 'Don't suppose you've got any?'

Unsurprisingly, given she's a hallucination, Fiona shakes her head.

21

Karen

Six months earlier, Newcastle-upon-Tyne

I held onto Rob's hand and we stood behind Dr Mansfield as the lift took us up to the third floor. Dr Mansfield's back was straight as an ironing board in her white lab coat; if anything she seemed more nervous than us. I couldn't make sense of it. What did she have to be nervous about? She'd told us everything was all right, hadn't she? She'd promised.

I wanted to have a minute on my own with Rob, to touch base, breathe, calm down. There was so much I wanted to say to him, and recently never the right moment to say it. But the lift doors were already sliding open and here we were, stepping out into the corridor. We didn't pass anyone as we followed Dr Mansfield's white back along the lino floor, past rows of doors. When I glanced up I noticed the red eye of the CCTV camera staring down at us.

At last, Dr Mansfield paused in front of a particular door, tapping a key code into the security lock. A light flashed green, and she turned to face us.

'Try to forget all your preconceptions,' she said quietly.

A blank slate then, a whole new experience. Okay. Good. I was happy to put all those previous ultrasound scans behind us. This time things were going to be different. I glanced at Rob. His eyes were wide, his lips pressed together. If only I knew what he was thinking. I felt his hand move against the middle of my back, his fingers spreading.

I'm here, Karen. We're in this together. It's going to be fine.

Grateful for his touch, I straightened my back, took a deep breath and stepped through the door. Perhaps this experience was different for each of us, but we were in this together. It was going to be fine.

I just had to keep telling myself that.

Inside the lab, two young people in white coats were working at computers, a man with short curly hair and a beard, and a woman with a long dark plait falling down her back. They both seemed very young to me, but Dr Mansfield knew what she was doing. She introduced the two young people to us although within seconds I'd forgotten their names. It wasn't like me, I'm normally so good with names. I found myself wishing that nice girl Dolly was here with us. It might have helped to have another familiar face around. I could have asked her about her flatmate, recent visits to Leicester.

But there was no sign of Dolly. So I looked around the lab, trying to work out where the baby was. White walls, white floor tiles, white benches. White everywhere.

Dr Mansfield had brought us into this room once before, months ago now, when we first came to the Centre. She'd shown us all the computers and the equipment, and that white box, raised up on one of the benches. I remembered it now: that was the artificial uterus. But somehow I couldn't put the two things together: our previous visit, and being here today.

Could our baby be in that white box? It had seemed possible before, but not now.

And why was Dr Mansfield acting so strangely? She was talking too fast, her shoulders tense, her hands moving. The baby was fine, wasn't he? She'd been telling us that, over and over. He was the strong one, the best of all of them. She'd promised us. I had to hold on to that.

There was a giant black screen mounted onto one wall, like a huge TV, and now it buzzed into life. We all turned to face it, and that was when everything started happening too quickly, when I started to feel the ground slip and slide under my feet. Like part of me was here in the lab, and part of me had been left out there, on the doorstep with the photographers pointing cameras at me and telling me to smile.

I had to be firm with myself. Stop being so silly, Karen. None of that mattered now. I was here to see my baby for the first time.

My baby.

I stared at the screen. Everything was so strange, and so – oh! So red! My mind went blank. I needed something to hold on to, some experience or image to make it stick, to make it mean what it was supposed to mean. But nothing seem to connect, there was nothing here that meant my baby.

This was more like looking through a window of a spaceship, out onto the surface of another planet. Yes that was it, another planet. A planet of thick red gas, layers of swirling stuff.

Dr Mansfield must have been controlling the camera, or one of the young people was controlling it, because now they were moving through the image, panning and zooming, until there, floating, was the baby.

Yes, that was him. It had to be.

I'd been expecting pale pink skin, the colour of a baby's skin. But instead he glowed bright red, the way your hand glows when you shine a torch through your flesh in the dark. He was lovely, no doubt about it. You'd have had a heart of stone to look at him and not know he was lovely.

But –

I wanted to say something. But what on earth could I say? What would Little Tyler say?

He's like a little spaceman, Mrs Frey.

Yes. A little naked spaceman. Floating all alone, out there in space. But I couldn't say that, could I? I mustn't say anything stupid, not here, not now. So I kept my eyes open and my mouth shut. If only the floor would stop moving.

Rob's face was fixed on the screen, and there were tears glistening in his eyes. Was that happiness then? Or grief for the babies we'd lost? Was this just like a normal baby scan for him? Or something strange and alien, the way it felt to me? I used to be able to read him, but I wasn't so confident anymore. And a darker thought, creeping into focus: Did he have any idea what this was like for me? Was he even curious?

And suddenly, unexpectedly, those other babies were here with us now, the nameless ones, as tiny and strange as this little boy, and with them their big sister, Ellie. I wanted to gather them all up and hold on to them. Comfort them, poor ghosts. I wanted to tell them all how sorry I was for letting them down.

I looked back at the baby on the big screen. He looked so calm there, so – so self-contained. My first thought: he didn't need anything from me. He had everything he needed right there, in his neat white box, feeding him, giving him oxygen. And Dr Mansfield was here, and this lovely team of bright young people watching him and seeing to his needs around the clock. And he was safe here, wasn't he? Safer than he would have been in me. He had his box, and this building to protect him, the CCTV in the corridors, the security guards on all the entrances.

But in a flash I saw that I was wrong, thinking he didn't need me. I'd been so silly, fooled by the machines, the computers, and the cameras in the corridors, the photographers out there on the doorstep, Carole at work asking her silly questions. All the nonsense that made everything seem so unreal.

That was why I'd been feeling lost. Sometimes it was as if I'd been set up to fail: first off my body wasn't good enough to hold him, and then not even my eggs were good enough. And even after all of that, the world was waiting for us to make a mistake, waiting to judge us, waiting for there to be something wrong with him, between the journalists who used words like *Frankenstein*, the photographers who followed me to the supermarket, and the people who asked insensitive questions and secretly thought we were selfish to do it. No wonder I'd been struggling.

None of that mattered now. I could see through all that. I could see him for what he was.

My child. My little boy.

Yes, Dr Mansfield and her team were looking after him. He was safe here for now. But someday soon this little scrap would have to leave his uncomplicated, quiet haven and be born. He was strong and healthy, sure. But it was a big scary world out there, a world of playground taunts, of people who didn't mean to hurt you with their stupid questions but hurt you all the same, a world that could be tough on anyone who might be seen as different.

And everything shifted. My first glance had shown him floating there in his bubble, serene, sleepy, suspended. But now I saw him differently, a tiny person in freefall, naked, vulnerable, hurtling towards the surface of the planet.

Somebody had to be there to catch him.

22

Alex

Now, Sussex

No sleep. X is crying. All night long the rain lashes the house and I watch the room turn from pitch black to mushroom grey. Now light is beginning to seep in through the heavy curtains, touching everything with grubby morning. Meanwhile, X is crying, crying, crying.

Nothing I do calms him. So far, I've tried: changing his nappy; feeding him until he swoons; putting on an extra layer of clothing in case he's chilly; stripping him down in case he's too hot; turning off the light so we're in the dark; switching on the light again in case he's afraid of the dark; swaddling him in a blanket, in case the tightness comforts him (it does not); holding him upright against my shoulder; holding him cradled in my arms; lying him on his back; holding him belly down along one of my arms, his small face turned sideways in my palm; holding him tightly; holding him loosely; patting his back; patting his bottom; patting him between his blunt little shoulder blades; feeding him until it all comes back in a torrent of sick (yes I know, maybe not my best call); rocking him from side to side; swinging him while twisting at the hips; holding him whilst bouncing my knees; speaking, crooning, singing, humming; multiple combinations of the above.

Nothing is working.

In the lab, we knew what X needed. Or at least, we

thought we knew, occasional puzzling wobbles over cortisol levels notwithstanding. But now we're here, out in the big wide, complicated world, my feet planted squarely in the rubble of empirical method, and blown about on all sides by the chill winds of my own ignorance. My mind darts about, looking for solutions, even considering half-remembered anecdotes and old wives' tale.

What would Fiona do?

All this time, it turns out, X has been packing a sophisticated sonic weapon. If terrorists succeeded in unleashing something of this magnitude on, say, the London Underground, the country would be brought swiftly to its knees. I'm sure I can feel the waves of sound passing right through my tissues, muscles and ligaments, shaking my bones, jangling my nerves and disabling my higher brain functions.

Downstairs, Ted is slumped against the pipes in the back kitchen, his wrists tied with gardening twine and tea towels. Can he hear this incessant wailing? Does it affect him? Or is it target specific, this terrible weapon X carries, tuned to my brainwaves, calibrated to create maximum suffering in me alone? I've heard babies cry before, and I'm sure I was never affected like this. Perhaps Ted is sleeping peacefully through all this noise. Or perhaps he is using this valuable time to loosen his bonds and wriggle free, to creep upstairs and kill us both.

My imminent grisly murder glows bleakly; at least it provides the possibility of release from the terrible racket X is making.

But this is normal, right? It's something newborn babies do. An adaptation, a survival mechanism for a creature so dependent. I'm sure I've heard new parents complain about it. *We're not getting any sleep; she cries all night.*

I never thought they meant it literally. I dredge up a word from my memory: *colic*. Such an insignificant little word, a tiny cough, or something to be swallowed, with aspirin.

But at some point, it occurs to me that X's crying is of another order. This is something else. It has to be. This cannot be *ordinary colic*, the sort that *ordinary babies* suffer from. There is something terrible, inconsolable, pathological in his persistent rhythmic wail. Something is wrong with him, horribly, terribly wrong, and I am not doing the right thing to soothe him. He will tip himself over into a dangerous state, he will vomit blood, his head will spin around, he will mutter devilish words, unless I can figure out what it is he needs and cure him.

The responsibility is terrifying.

Later still, I wonder if something about the specifics of X's gestation has altered him, made him more difficult to soothe? (Nonsense, right? The kind of rubbish those maniacs on the internet were peddling, which I scoffed at, and ordered my lab team to ignore.) But what if his high cortisol levels have damaged his capacity to accept love and consolation? (Don't be ridiculous, Alex. His cortisol levels were never, really, very high.)

Sometime later, I ask myself, what if this isn't about X, at all? What if this indicates some failing, some deficiency in me? What if I was never built to comfort a baby, even this baby that I love? I was never meant to be a mother. I'm not maternal. I've said it myself, more than once. Other people have said it too. Ex-boyfriends. Those people online, and in the newspapers.

I'm not womanly, not feminine. Surely my milk must be bad; the mastitis is testament to that. My cuddles are not comforting. I am a hard woman. I am a bitch. I have a pathological desire to control everything around me. I have been unsexed by my career in science. I have relinquished my nature to follow the cold, hard road of my ambition.

It turns out, finally, that every cruel, ridiculous thing anyone ever said or wrote about me is true.

The crying goes on, and on, for a long time. In the end, it takes me to a place where there is no working hypothesis to draw upon, no computer-based model, no statistical analysis, a place beyond paranoia, and panic, and half-formed dark thoughts. In the end – and believe me, it's a long, long way down that grey-black road – there isn't even any language to form thoughts with.

Despite myself, I see that this is a good place. X has brought me here for a reason.

I stop thinking. I stop trying to figure it out. Instead, I just give him my body, its milk, and warmth and movement. I give him the non-verbal matter that comes out of my mouth, all of it nonsense.

I give him love. It's all I've got in the end. And for a long time, even that doesn't work.

And then finally it does.

23

Dolly

Yesterday, Newcastle-upon-Tyne, police interview

Come and sit down, Dolly. Now listen, we're recording this interview, but you aren't under any suspicion. You're just helping us – helping the police to find Dr Mansfield. Is that clear?

Yes.

You could request a lawyer, but that's only going to slow things down, and what we want is to find Dr Mansfield and the baby as quickly as possible.

That's what I want too.

So let's kick off. We don't know what's happened yet, not exactly, but we suspect Dr Mansfield removed the baby – the foetus? – okay, the baby – from the AU late last night. Do you have any idea why she would do that?

She wouldn't do that. No way.

You seem very certain.

I am. One hundred percent. Look, you don't know what she's like, how committed she is, how precise about everything. Obsessed even.

Obsessed?

She's been here day and night, watching over him. Like, this is her life, you know? She's been a nightmare about it. But, no, don't take that the wrong way. I see what you're both thinking. I don't want to make her sound... The thing is, I'm just saying she wants this to work. More than anyone. Apart from the parents, of course. And she's been super careful, about everything, all the way through. And taking X out of the AU, without medical back up, and then removing him from the building – and it's so bloody cold out there at the moment – well, that would be dangerous, right? She wouldn't do that.

Okay, Dolly. I'm going to share something with you. We have CCTV footage of Dr Mansfield walking out of this building at nine p.m. last night, carrying a bag which we believe contained the baby.

That can't be right.

That's the hypothesis we're working on. Based on your knowledge of her, why might she do something like that?

She wouldn't. Not unless someone had a gun to her head. And even then. She'd take a bullet before she'd let anyone hurt X. Unless –

Unless?

Unless she believed – I mean, the only way she'd take him out of here is if she believed he was in danger.

And was he in danger?

No. But look, you know what it's been like. Some nutter's been sending me dead mice, for God's sake. What I'm saying is, there are people out there with a grudge against us. What if one of those crazies wanted to hurt X? What if Alex discovered something, and had to get him out of there? But, no – that's bonkers, isn't it? I mean, people kept saying he was in danger. Under threat, I mean. But he wasn't. Not really.

*

'Coming to bed, Dee?'

Aimee wasn't the sort of girlfriend to sit around waiting for attention, but I wouldn't blame her for feeling neglected. To be honest, I could've done with some downtime myself, but here I was, up to my neck in papers, papers all over the table, papers all over my lap. Hair slicked back wet after a shower, shabby trackies on. Coffee steaming, my cup shoved in to the only space on the table available. The coffee would help me work late into the night; I was in this for the long haul.

'I've got to go through these.'

She slid onto the sofa next to me. 'What's up?' Her small warm hand on my neck.

I resisted the urge to shake her off and let the papers rest against my knees. Perhaps it would help to talk it through. 'Can you keep a secret?'

'You know I can.' The tips of her pink toes were resting against the table top.

'If I tell you – seriously – you mustn't breathe a word to anyone.' Her face was grave as she nodded. 'You know there've been these rumours. About X. That there's something wrong with him.'

'You told me that stuff was bullshit.'

'It is. People make stuff up and spread it on the internet. Other people repeat it as if it's true. The next thing you know, the mainstream media start commenting on it. Between the online rumours and the papers, the story is kept current, which means there's this low-level rumble in people's minds that there's something wrong with Baby X. And none of it's true, okay, but it's a worry all the same. Because how's it going to affect this poor kid's life, all this stuff about him out in the world, and he's not even born yet?'

'You can't worry about all that,' Aimee said. 'You just have to do your job as well as you can.'

'Yes, I know. But.' How to explain it? 'See this line here? The numbers jump. And then over the next six hours, it tails off?'

'Yes.'

'That spike there, see.'

'I can see the line goes up, but –'

'That's X's cortisol level. Well, to be precise it's the level of corticosterone in X's umbilical cord blood, that's what we're actually monitoring. But it's a good enough proxy for cortisol, under the circumstances.'

Aimee sighed. 'You've already lost me, Dee.'

'Look, the point is, we've all got cortisol in our bodies. The level fluctuates naturally, it runs our circadian rhythms, wakes us up in the morning. We couldn't function without it.'

'X has too much?'

'Not exactly. Cortisol's also part of the body's fight or flight mechanism, it's released in response to stress.'

'Okay –'

'And all babies are subject to stressors in the womb, because of the stresses their mothers are under, at work, at home, in daily life.'

'But X's cortisol is higher than that? That's why you're worried?'

'No, not really. It's within the normal range.'

Aimee sat back on the sofa, pulling her feet up underneath her. After a long pause she said, 'I'm sorry, Dee. I don't see what the problem is.'

'Look, this additional corticosterone in X's cord blood. Where the hell is it coming from?'

She sighed. 'But I thought you just said we all have it.'

'Yes, we do, but –' I tried another tack. 'Look at this line. Distinct spikes. Like something *happened*. You might see these sort of spikes in other babies, but other babies are subject to stressors in the womb.'

'So – ?'

'The question is, where is X's stress coming from?'

Aimee bit her lip. 'I'm sorry, Dolly, I don't understand.'

'It's a *locked* box, get it? In a *locked building*. A perfectly controlled environment. And we manage *all* the inputs. There's no maternal stress to factor in, no environmental toxins, no loud noises even. Nothing. So why this spike? Why then? I mean, what could have happened to freak the little guy out like that?'

'But it's not hurting him?'

'No, but −' I was starting to wish I'd never told her. 'That's the thing about *proper* science.' Not like your social science nonsense, I could have added but didn't. 'You can't see something like this and just ignore it. Okay, we don't think X will be damaged by these raises in his cortisol level, but we can't afford to take the risk. We need to understand what's going on.'

I saw her notice the "proper science" bit and choose to ignore it. 'And you have a theory?'

'Nothing I've looked at explains it. But I know what Alex is worried about,' I added darkly. 'What if there's something dampening X's ability to regulate cortisol. Something − how can I explain this − something in his environment causing his cortisol levels to run high.'

'What would that mean?'

'It would be a weakness in IVG babies. Something we hadn't anticipated. It would mean the end of the programme.'

She stretched and stood up. 'But X is all right, right?'

'Yes, I think so. I'm sure X'll be fine.'

'Then come to bed, Dee. All this will be here in the morning.'

*

127

But X is all right, right?

X.

Alex had freaked when we first started using it, but now everyone called him that, even her. It sort of just happened. First, *Baby X*, and then it got shortened. Strange in a way, when we'd resisted the whole 'Baby X' thing for so long. But 'X' was worse wasn't it? A mark, not a name. Like the way illiterate people used to sign a contract. Or else a maths problem: *Calculate the value of x.*

A problem. A nothing.

But somehow when we started calling him X we'd changed what the word meant. Or, weirder, like *he'd* changed it. Because when Alex said, *What did X get up to in the night?* she wasn't talking about a problem, or a nothing. All of a sudden it was the name of the most important person in the room.

He was having an effect on all of us, but Alex most of all. For all her talk of professional distance she was the one who sat up half the night watching him. I'd seen the system logs, time and date stamps from her sleepover shifts. She'd told me she suffered with insomnia, and it was worse recently, she said.

I could imagine her, sitting alone in the dark, in her pyjamas and that ugly knee-length cardigan she kept hanging in the dorm room wardrobe, her slippered feet tucked up on her swivel chair. Just watching him. Watching him swimming around.

24

Alex

Now, Sussex

When X wakes me for his next feed, something has changed. He latches on to my right breast, and I grit my teeth through the pain as the milk starts to flow. I look around, trying to work out what's different. The wardrobe door stands slightly ajar, empty save for clotted shadows. Our bags, thrown together at my flat or pilfered from Fiona's, are open on the floor near the foot of the bed. No sounds from downstairs. Is Ted still tied up in the back kitchen? Is he asleep? I strain to hear, and pick up nothing.

And that's when I realise: it's stopped raining.

When X is finished feeding, I carry him over to window, open the curtains. It's about nine, I think, judging by the light.

The end of the rain, the quiet and peace of it, is like a small miracle. I can just about see the beach in the aftermath of the storm – bits of wood, seaweed flung around, the stones disturbed. But there's a gentle flatness to the sea now. The air is cool and clear, light with possibility.

Despite the pain in my right breast, it feels good to hold X close. He's hot, like a poultice. I imagine the heat of him drawing out the infection, making me strong. And suddenly I've got this faint, raw optimism – they say things always look brighter in the morning. I can't deny the situation we're in. But as I stare at the sea and the sky, listen to the gulls wheel and shriek, feel X's heat against my body, I realise I'm not quite ready to give up.

Not yet.

I'm going to have to find some antibiotics. But, you know what? I'll manage it somehow. If I have to rob a pharmacy at gunpoint, I'll find a way. And then I'm going to get X and myself away from here and on to the next place, somewhere we can change our identities, somewhere we'll never be found.

And that's another thing: my head feels a little clearer, clearer than it has for weeks. I didn't take a sleeping tablet last night, I haven't taken them for two nights in a row. Those sleeping tablets couldn't have made me so fuzzy-headed, could they? Whatever, I feel as if I'm emerging from a fog, like I'm finally capable of coming up with a proper plan.

But there's something else I have to do. Ted did something to X *in utero*, and I still don't know what. Before we leave this place, and I lose this opportunity forever, I have to find out.

And if I'm being honest, I need answers for myself too. I need to know what Ted did to X, and what he did to me.

*

I remember sitting back in my office chair, eyeing my visitor with scepticism. The documentary maker, Matilda Gunn, sat opposite me on the other side of the table, her eyes owlish behind thick glasses.

'I'm sure you'll understand my caution,' I'd told her. 'We're doing our best to keep our patients out of the spotlight.'

'Not very successfully, by the look of things.' Her grin

was starting to irritate me. 'Anyway, I'm not here to cause trouble,' she said. 'Perhaps you've seen some of my work? *Concealed Maternity*, about women who don't know they're pregnant until the point they are ready to give birth.'

'I haven't –'

'It won an award, you know. And my film about breastfeeding was shown on the BBC last year.'

'Sorry, I didn't catch it.' I shuffled in my chair. The sooner she got to the point, the sooner I could get rid of her.

'Fascinating subject, breastfeeding. It's the combination of physical, social and psychological that interests me. Did you know, women who adopt babies are sometimes able to breastfeed them, even without using hormones to kick start the process?' She brought her hands together, steepling her fingers in front on her face. 'And in some places where maternal mortality is high, other family members – aunts, grandmothers – have been known to step in and breastfeed infants whose mothers die in childbirth. In Papua New Guinea, for example –'

'Of course this is all very interesting,' I interrupted, 'but perhaps you could tell me why you're here?'

Matilda smiled. 'Fertility triangles, Dr Mansfield. Yes, I think that could be the title of the new piece. Good, don't you think?' More enthusiastic nodding. 'I've found some fascinating cases. It starts with infertility. People find themselves in these triangular relationships to bring a baby into the world. Surrogacy, egg donation. Recent cases of babies with three biological parents. What's that called again?'

'Look, I'm sorry,' (I wasn't) 'but I can't help you.' (That much was true.) 'I only deal with the clinical aspects of infertility. And you know, we're very careful about the ethics of egg donation here. And we offer psychological counselling to all our patients –'

'2012, Wisconsin, United States,' Matilda interrupted, raising her hand. 'A thirty-one year old mother of two, Nancy Martin, donated eggs to her infertile twin sister, Mary. Following IVF, Mary successfully fell pregnant, and carried the baby to term. A little girl, Martha-Jane, quite adorable.' She paused, fixing me again with that glinting stare. 'But here's the thing. Nancy swears she experienced the whole pregnancy. Got sick with her sister through the early months, craved sugar like a demon, felt the baby kicking her in the night. Even had contractions while her sister was in labour.'

'Sympathetic pains,' I said, dubious.

'Nancy's husband says she gained thirty pounds while Mary was pregnant.'

'Well, you did say she was craving sugar –'

'He sat up with her, mopping her brow with a wet flannel, the night Martha-Jane was born.' She paused, the smile still on her lips, 'And that's not all, Dr Mansfield. 2014, Norfolk, U.K.. Donna Jamieson agrees to be surrogate mother for an infertile couple, May and Richard Mosse. Anonymous donor egg, Richard's sperm. You with me? Donna's had four babies before. Three of her own, and one previous surrogacy. Says she just loves being pregnant, wants to help the Mosses out.'

I waited, resigned.

'But all the time Donna's carrying the child, May's having pregnancy symptoms. Sickness, hunger, and check this out, says she was horny as anything right the way through.'

'Hardly scientific,' I said, 'you're talking about very subjective material.'

'Then take a look at this, Dr Mansfield. Taken in the

ninth month of Donna Jamieson's pregnancy.' She dug into her bag and passed a photograph over the desk.

A couple standing in front of an ordinary, suburban red brick house. The man's arm draped around the woman's shoulders, the woman dressed in summer clothing, her pale hands folded into the horizontal channel between her large breasts and the top of her huge belly. Despite the smiling eyes, her face was tired.

'This is Donna?'

'No,' she said, grinning in triumph. 'This is *May*. She's a big girl, Donna. A real earth mother. Total physical contrast to May who's usually as skinny as a bean pole. And look at that belly!' Matilda laughed out loud with glee. 'Sticking out like a torpedo.'

Claiming to feel sympathy pains was one thing, but this was something else. A shiver ran through me.

'Extraordinary though, isn't it? May's doctors were completely baffled. I've got dozens of photographs like this, Dr Mansfield. May was so intrigued by the experience she decided to document the whole thing. She's more than willing to take part in the film.'

'It is interesting,' I conceded, 'but why come to me?'

'You aren't aware of any cases –?'

'None, I'm afraid. I'm sorry you've had a wasted journey.' I started to rise from my chair.

'Would you give me access to your patients? With their consent, of course.'

I took a deep breath. 'No, that wouldn't be appropriate. My patients have already put up with too much media intrusion.'

'But even if the Freys didn't want to participate. I expect your work here will turn up some stories sooner or later.'

I was standing now, hoping my visitor would pick up on my cues and leave. 'I very much doubt that.'

'Oh, I don't know. Babies gestating separately from their parents? And then there's the doctors and researchers, looking after the foetuses, potentially forming attachments.' She raised her eyebrows at me. 'An emotional minefield, wouldn't you say?'

*

I can't remember how I got rid of her, but I managed it in the end. Now I move over to the corner of the room, and open the door of Grannie's wardrobe, angling the full length mirror on the inside to take in my reflection, examining myself with a scientists' eyes.

The woman I see is dishevelled, fortyish, although she could be older, which I'm guessing is explained by the exhaustion on her face, her greyish pallour, the deep purple smudges under her eyes. She's got her hair scraped back in a scrunchy, and her body is heavy, lumpy-looking, her hips and thighs tight in those leggings. And goodness me, her breasts are enormous. I notice the stains on her sweatshirt (milk? vomit?) and I notice her stance, her weight unevenly distributed between those lumpy hips, giving her poor posture and a crumpled, sloppy demeanour. She's holding a tiny baby against her chest, holding it one-handed, its legs bunched up underneath its body. An outsized plush peanut, a blob of heavy-headed softness.

Nothing about this image says, 'Alex Mansfield' to me. Not the Alex Mansfield I remember: scientist, clinician, pioneer, nor even the Alex Mansfield the press loved to hate: maverick, hard-case, Frankenstein. I stare hard at the woman's face, and her eyes stare back at me.

I'll admit she has my eyes.

25

Karen

Four months earlier, Market Harborough

Between them, the photographer and the journalist had changed the angle of the sofa, placed a small table alongside us and positioned a lamp (not ours) on top, along with a vase of fresh flowers. They'd even swapped pictures from one wall to another. It was confusing; they said they wanted to see us in our own home, but when they got here our home wasn't good enough, so they had to change it. Earlier they'd wanted photos in the baby's room, and that had been worse, because we weren't ready, not even close. But then, who gets a baby's room ready so many months in advance? We'd done our best to organise things on the spot, clearing away boxes, setting up the borrowed cot – Claire's – under the window. Rob had even dashed out to buy bedding, all in cream, with an embroidered border of brightly coloured dumper trucks and fire engines on the cot bumpers.

The feature writer was a woman called Jo Miller, a few years younger than me. She looked like something out of a magazine herself, with her dark hair in glossy ringlets, a burnt orange suit nipped in at the waist and a skinny black belt that matched her heeled ankle boots. She'd stood in the middle of the baby's room, hands on hips, and said, 'I don't know,' twisting her mouth to the side. 'A little too bare, don't you think, Benny?'

Benny was the photographer, young, skinny, with

gentle eyes and a raggedy beard. It turned out he had a baby himself – a six-month-old called Jakub – and he'd brought some bits from home. As I unwrapped the bedding and made up the cot, Benny retrieved a box from his car. There was a mobile to attach to one side of the crib, four jungle animals that rotated around a central plastic palm tree to a tinny tune. And a large stuffed monkey with an ironic expression and buttoned up waistcoat. Benny placed it on a shelf near the crib.

I wasn't sure about the monkey. It didn't look like the sort of thing *our* baby would play with. Part of me wanted to say something, but I didn't want to be rude, especially after Benny had gone to such trouble. So he took some photos of Rob and me standing there smiling in the faked-up baby's room with our arms around each other, then we went back downstairs and Benny set up a large silver umbrella to direct light onto our faces, while Rob and I sat on the sofa feeling awkward.

This morning, Rob had said to me, 'We don't have to go through with this, Karen. We can tell them to piss off and leave us alone.'

He was only trying to protect me from the stress, I knew that. But I was trying to protect us too. All of us, Rob, me and the baby as well. Because it didn't matter how many times you said no, or how politely you said it, there was always someone popping up to ask the question again. It'd got to the point where we were getting phone calls every day, asking us for an interview, an exclusive. And once they realised we weren't interested in money or publicity every one of them promised the same thing: it would go easier for us if we went along with it. Maybe they never meant it to sound like a threat, but that was the effect: if we co-operated, the papers would tell our story the way we'd want it to be told. Because there was a flipside, wasn't there? Unspoken, but there all the same: if we didn't co-operate, who knew what they might write about us.

Then, one day, it wasn't just phone calls. I'd left work after five and the car park was empty. There was a man, quite a big man actually, in a black leather jacket, standing near my car.

'Karen,' he said, as I got closer.

'Please,' I said to him, as politely as I could, though my heart was going. I'd guessed he was a reporter, but still, I was on my own, and he was bigger than me, and standing by my car, almost, but not quite, blocking my way. As I approached he took a step towards me. 'How's the little one doing?' he asked. 'Bet he's getting big now. Won't be long, eh?'

I pushed past him, opened the door, and slid in.

The man leaned against my window. 'Having second thoughts?' he sneered.

I kept my mouth shut and concentrated on starting the engine. What were you supposed to say? *No comment.* That sounded false, silly. Like I was a corrupt politician, or a common criminal. As I drove home my hands were shaking.

Then a Sunday, a few days later. Rob was doing some tidying in the back garden, cutting back the plants that were finished for the summer. I heard him shouting. 'Get off my bloody property before I call the police!'

Rob wasn't the sort of bloke who lost it, but I could see he was getting close to the end of his rope. Sooner or later he'd punch someone, and then where would we be? That night, I couldn't sleep for worrying. I spent the whole night going over and over it, but in the morning I had a plan. Although Rob was sceptical, he didn't try to stop me. After he left for work, I picked up the phone. I'd chosen a national newspaper with a good reputation. I explained we weren't interested in money, and we didn't have a cause to promote. All we really wanted was to be left alone. But we understood the public wanted to know about us, and about our baby too. There were rumours I said; we thought we should set the record straight. We hoped, if we made ourselves available this one time, then everyone would just leave us in peace.

The girl I spoke to was very understanding. She said I was doing the right thing. We arranged a time for the journalist and the photographer to come to the house. The story would appear in the weekend magazine, and be reproduced on the website too. They were very nice about it. I remembered thinking that these weren't the same sort of people as the ones who'd been harassing us. I'd made the right decision when I chose that paper.

The day before the interview, Rob and I sat down together to work out what we wanted to say. If we got our message clear, it would be easier to stay on track. This is what we came up with:

He's healthy.

He's well looked after, and he's got everything he needs.

We're just ordinary people.

We'd like to be left alone.

There. That was fair, wasn't it?

Now Benny was moving around us, clicking his camera, giving instructions. He kept telling us to relax, to look this way or that, telling Rob to put his arm around my shoulder, or his hand on my knee. He told us when to smile, and when to stop smiling. I kept thinking: at least it's not telly. Newspapers and magazines, it turned out, were strange enough. Horrible enough. But telly would be worse. I offered up a silent prayer, *Please God, protect us from television. Don't ever let us become the sort of people who appear on TV.*

'There,' said Jo Miller finally, her smile reassuring. She was sitting opposite me, her knees bent and folded to one side, legs crossed at the ankles. 'That's all over with, now for the easy bit. Don't look so worried, Karen. Just be yourself.'

I nodded, and made an effort to relax my face.

'So, tell me, what does it feel like?'

I took a deep breath, remembered the messages we'd discussed that morning. 'We're very happy,' I said. 'We're excited at the thought of bringing our baby home.'

'You must miss him terribly,' Jo said. 'All alone there in the lab, so far away.'

'Not really,' I said. 'We've never had him with us after all. We know he's safe. But yes, we're looking forward to bringing him home, and getting on with a normal family life.'

'It must be a strange environment,' said Jo. 'Sterile.'

'Well, it's all very clean,' I said. 'He's very well looked after. He's got everything he needs.'

Jo frowned. 'No, by "sterile", I meant clinical. Impersonal.'

Rob cut in, 'The staff at the Centre are all very kind. They've been good to us.'

'And Dr Mansfield. What's she like?'

'She's great,' I said.

'Interesting. Some people report finding her a little –'

'No,' I said. 'She's lovely.'

Jo leaned forward, her eyes locking with mine. 'I want to ask you, Karen, about those miscarriages. I'm sorry. I know it must be painful to talk about.'

'There isn't much to say really. You've got all the facts, right? From the information we gave your researcher?'

'Still, when you lost that last baby −' She glanced at her notes. 'At twenty weeks −' I nodded. 'That must have been devastating.'

I looked down at my knees. I'd known it would come up, I was ready to answer questions. But I hadn't expected her to press me for a reaction. What did she want me to say exactly?

Rob came to my rescue, 'Well obviously, it was devastating for both of us,' he said. 'We were seeing a specialist by then, you see. We thought the treatment Karen was having might fix the problem.'

'But it didn't.'

'Unfortunately not.'

'You must have felt quite desperate at that point, Karen.'

Honestly, she wasn't interested in Rob at all. She didn't even pretend to be interested. It wasn't Rob's fault, but I couldn't help the flash of resentment that ran through me. Why did all of this have to be about me? 'It was a very difficult time,' I said. 'For both of us.'

'It was a tough time,' Rob echoed. 'But we stuck together, didn't we, love? We got through it. And now we're looking forward to bringing our baby home, just like any other, ordinary family.'

'Just like an ordinary family,' Jo echoed. She tilted her head to one side. 'Did you consider adoption? Or using a surrogate?'

'We did talk through the options early on, with a counsellor at the Centre. But this was the way we wanted to go.'

'So you decided on this path,' Jo said, tapping a long orange fingernail against her notes, 'Even though in doing so − at least, this is what some people have suggested − you've denied your baby a normal gestation.'

I froze, uncertain at the turn things had taken. Benny was looking uncomfortable too.

'We'd've loved to give our baby a normal gestation,' I said. 'But it wasn't an option for us. I mean, it wasn't an option for *me*. Because of my medical problems.'

'You could've used a surrogate though, couldn't you?' Jo continued. 'Rather than this?'

'Well,' I said, 'We could. But we –'

'Or you could have adopted, or chosen not to have children at all.'

I could feel Rob bristling beside me and I slid my hand onto his arm. He said, 'Look, this is the safest way for us to have a baby. Safest for Karen, safest for the baby too.'

'Safest, yes. Except –' She paused again, the sympathetic smile back in place. 'What about all this speculation that the baby isn't healthy after all?'

'Those are just rumours,' Rob said, his voice rising. 'People just make things up. He's perfect.'

'Perfect.' Jo paused before turning to me. 'Is that what you wanted, Karen? A *perfect* baby?'

I didn't know what to say. 'We wanted him to be healthy.' I remembered Dr Mansfield phoning me, the morning she was certain our embryo had implanted. 'They picked the strongest,' I said. 'Out of all the embryos. To give him the best chance in the AU.'

Jo Miller nodded. 'Was that why you'd opted for the pre-implantation genetic screening?'

'We were having such difficulty conceiving,' I said. 'And Dr Mansfield wanted to find out what was wrong. We knew why I kept miscarrying. Or at least we thought we did. But then, all the months of egg harvesting, and we were still failing to conceive. And Dr Mansfield thought –'

'If you selected out the imperfect embryos –'

'Come on, now,' Rob said, 'you're twisting what we're

saying. Everyone wants their child to be healthy, don't they?'

Jo Miller tilted her head again. 'O brave new world,' she murmured, 'that has such people in it.' She turned back to me. 'I suppose what I'm asking, Karen, is what you'd do if your baby turned out to be less than perfect?'

I stared at her. 'I – I haven't thought about it.'

Jo Miller raised her eyebrows slightly. 'I mean, what if one of those chromosomal abnormalities you screened for was missed? What if he was born with some developmental disability?'

I couldn't speak. I was telling the truth: I hadn't thought about it, only, not in the way she was implying. Of course I worried about him, I worried about him all the time. But I'd been so focussed on me being the faulty one, the one who couldn't get pregnant properly, or carry a baby to term that I'd never seriously considered the idea of our baby being ill.

And there was something else too: I'd never thought about it, because it wouldn't change anything. I knew I'd love him anyway. If anything, I'd probably love him more. Was that it? Was that what I meant? I opened my mouth to express this somehow, but it all seemed too difficult, too tangled, and nothing came out.

'Hmm,' Jo said, leaning down to her dictaphone and clicking a button to end the recording. 'You know what,' she said, 'that's probably enough to go on.' She looked up at Benny, who was still looking uncomfortable. 'Did you get everything you needed?'

'We're not judging anyone else's choices,' Rob said, his voice uncertain now. 'We're just doing what's right for us.'

Benny packed up his equipment, and passed us each a form to sign, to give our permission to use the photos in the magazine. 'I'll get the stuff from upstairs,' he said.

After they'd gone, I went back to the baby's room and stood there looking around. Somehow it felt even less real than earlier, when I was putting the sheets on the mattress and attaching the cot bumpers to the crib. Rob came in and put his arms around me.

'I'm sorry I put you through all that,' I said. 'I wasn't expecting her to be so...'

Rob balanced his chin on the top of my head. 'It's all right, love. It's all over now.'

That was so like him, always telling me not to worry, telling me everything was going to be fine. I knew he meant well, so why did his reassurance set my teeth on edge?

'I hope so,' was all I said, leaning back against him, even as I wondered how far I could trust him to support my weight.

26

Alex

Now, Sussex

I'm sitting on the ladder-backed chair, my back straight, my socked feet flat against the cold floor. X is resting in the valley between my thighs, his head at my knees, his curled feet pointing in the direction of my belly. One of his purplish hands is raised, elbow cocked, fingers lazily uncurling. The other hand rests lightly on his sternum, rising and falling with his breath. He is both relaxed and poised, conked-out unconscious and charged with vitality. Even with my fever spiking and the pain still throbbing in my right breast, I'd happily sit here all day and watch him.

But I don't have time to sit around gazing at my baby. I raise my eyes to stare at Ted, slumped, tied, defeated. He stares back at me.

'The problem,' I say, 'is that I still don't believe you.'

He sighs. 'I'm getting that,' he says, his voice thick.

'So why don't you tell me the truth?'

'I've been telling you the truth.'

I shake my head. 'The whole truth.'

He shrugs his arms against the ties. 'I need to pee.'

'Tell me first. After that, I'll – I don't know – I'll get you a bottle or something.'

He takes a deep breath then looks up at me, resigned. 'Okay,' he says. 'I give in. I'll tell you everything. But get me that bottle first.'

I feel myself softening towards him. 'Once we're safely

144

away,' I say, heading back towards the kitchen, 'I'll phone someone and tell them where you are.'

*

I'd never given much thought to the Frey's egg donor. The National Gamete Service had taken care of the selection, providing a donor matched to Karen Frey's ethnicity, build, and colouring. I'd set the medical parameters, then left them to it. But recently I'd wondered if something in the donor's health profile might shed light on the anomalies in X's cortisol levels. No particular reason to believe I'd find anything; to be honest, I was clutching at straws.

I'd called up the egg donor's record on my system: a lot of the personal information was hidden from us clinicians to protect the donor's anonymity, but there was relevant health screening data, along with a donation date, the donor's age at the time of harvesting, her date of birth. Not that any of this was especially relevant to my inquiry, but I found myself staring at the dates.

I mean, you notice your own birthday, don't you?

It had to be a coincidence. Except, it wasn't just the birth date. Sure I couldn't remember the exact date of my extraction, but that was the right year, I was sure of it. And the right month too, possibly? About the right month, I remember the heat on the day of the procedure, my bare arms, the harsh light through the consulting room window.

Could it be? What were the chances of this sort of coincidence? I ran a quick calculation in my head. How many other young women had donated their eggs that summer, as part of that research project? Surely many of them would have been about my age; many of us were

145

graduate students on the same programme, women in their mid-twenties.

But my *birthday?* How many of the women donating their eggs that summer shared a birthday with me?

Was it possible that when the National Gamete Service selected an egg donor from the experimental pool available to the Centre, they'd unwittingly selected the woman at the head of the programme?

That night, staying over in the tiny dorm, I couldn't sleep. I was too hot under the duvet, too cold without it. I kept getting out of bed – another glass of water, another trip to the tiny en-suite bathroom – then climbing back in, re-plumping the pillows in a futile attempt to get comfortable. Eventually, giving up on the idea of drifting off naturally, I'd pulled a cardigan on over my pyjamas, and padded along to the lab.

I pressed in my key code, and waited for the green light. As my computer booted up, I woke the big screen. X was often busy at this time of night, kicking and somersaulting, enjoying all that space inside the AU, lashing out at the soft walls of his bubble, flexing his arms and legs. I pitied any poor woman with an active foetus like this one inside her, no sleep for her.

Meanwhile, I wasn't doing much better. So I brewed a cup of chamomile tea and enjoyed the show. I'd always loved watching X's night time antics, but tonight they seemed even more special, even more precious. He seemed – if this was possible – more perfectly adorable than ever.

I had to consider the question, alarming as it was. Was I X's biological – I baulked at the word mother, forced myself to reframe the question – could X be related to me?

And what would it mean if it was true?

I wasn't foolish enough to jump to wild conclusions.

For a start, I reminded myself, they probably weren't my eggs at all. Some other girl, donating that same summer, happened to share my birthday. Most likely, this was nothing.

Nothing.

Don't get me wrong. I knew he wasn't mine, not really. I was looking after him for the Freys. That had been the deal all along.

I didn't even want a baby. Wait – did I? No. No, I did not. But somehow there was a pleasing sort of symmetry to it. The Freys had come to me to have a baby, and I, like their fairy-godmother had waved my magic wand and made it happen. And, when it turned out that Karen's eggs were not going to provide them with a child, I'd provided them with the missing piece of the puzzle. Only, it turned out I'd already given this, years and years earlier, never knowing how important it would turn out to be. And my eggs had just been waiting there, in storage, this whole time.

Had anyone at the National Gamete Service spotted the connection? But that was a terrible thought. And – come to think of it – I did feel uncomfortable at the thought that anyone might find out? It wasn't as if I'd done anything wrong, donating my eggs to the Centre a decade before. But if I had – inadvertently – discovered myself to be X's – no, not *mother*, that wasn't right – if I was X's *egg donor*, did I now have a duty to declare this information to someone in authority? Would keeping it to myself at this point constitute professional malpractice? I could imagine what the papers would say. It would be a national scandal. There would be questions in the House of Commons. And some people would speculate that *I'd* engineered this situation all along, although exactly what I had to gain from the arrangement was a mystery to me.

Except I hadn't *discovered* it, had I? Not really. I still didn't know for sure. It was only a couple of dates on the record, and I needn't have checked those. No one need ever know.

I felt a fluttery sort of excitement, as if I'd discovered something rare and precious, something I could get out in private, to look at and enjoy.

But no. Most likely this was just some odd coincidence, leading to a strange, late night fantasy. Better he was the product of someone else's egg, some other, anonymous twenty-five year old woman who strangely shared my birthday.

But there was a problem: now the possibility was in my mind, could I cope with not knowing for certain? And if not, how could I find out the truth without alerting anyone to my suspicions?

In a flash I knew who I would ask: Ted. Yes, that was it. I'd visit him in the National Gamete Service offices tomorrow, ask him to call up the details of the Frey's egg donor, pass me a couple of key facts. Sure, it was somewhat unethical, breaching donor confidentiality. But I didn't really want to know about the donor's identity. It's not like I was planning to leak her details to the press, or contact her, or – I just needed to know enough to exclude the possibility that those eggs were mine. And once I knew for certain, it would be out of my mind, and I'd be able to stop worrying and get a decent night's sleep.

*

'I'm sorry to ask this of you,' was what I'd said, turning up in Ted's office the following morning, feeling bad about taking advantage of our relationship to ask him to break the rules. Apart from anything else, I'd been making a

148

habit recently of turning up unannounced. Often too busy to meet, I didn't always return his calls and sometimes his texts went unanswered. Then sometimes I'd pitch up at his office door to say, *Are you free now? Let's go out*. He never seemed to mind, at least, he never complained. Perhaps it suited him better this way.

Sometimes we'd have a drink, and afterwards we'd go our separate ways. More often than not we'd end up at my place, or at his, and in the morning I'd get out quickly, claiming I had somewhere to be. Of course, given what he was actually up to, I'm not surprised his tender feelings weren't hurt. With hindsight, I wish I'd wasted less time feeling guilty.

'Run this past me again,' he'd said, and I did. I wanted information from the National Gamete Donor Register. I needed some details about the egg donor we'd used to create X.

Ted frowned at me. 'What's this about, Alex?'

I sidestepped the question. 'I'm sorry to put you in a difficult position.'

'You're worried you missed something. In the donor's profile,' he offered, clearly fishing for a reason to go along with my request. 'Something that might affect the health of the baby.'

And in a way he'd guessed correctly. At least that was why I'd started looking into the donor, although the cortisol issue had receded into the background somewhat in the last twenty-four hours. 'Just something I need to check,' I told him. 'I'm sorry I can't let you know more.'

He hesitated for a moment, then called up the system and logged on.

I joined him on his side of the desk and jotted down the donor's NHS number. I couldn't tell immediately if I recognised it or not; I'd had to wait until I was alone, in private, before I could get my own NHS ID card out of my wallet to check.

Before I left, Ted had turned to me and asked, 'Do you trust me, Alex?'

I'd looked at him, wondering. Did I trust him? I was starting to; I'd trusted him enough to come to him for help. I didn't think he'd mention my digging to anyone else. But what if I did turn out to be X's donor? What then? Would I trust him with something like that?

Not bloody likely.

27

Dolly

Yesterday, Newcastle-upon-Tyne, police interview

Are you close to Dr Mansfield, Dolly?

I work with her every day. I mean, not close exactly. Not friends. She's my boss.

A good boss?

Most of the time. She's been a bit –

A bit what?

Oh, I don't know. Stressed recently. Emotional. You know.

How about you tell us.

*

I can't remember where Alex was that day. Not in the lab with us, and that was unusual. Anyway, whatever the reason, when Laura discovered the problem, she came to me.

'Dolly, have you got a minute?'

'Sure.' I looked up from my desk to see Laura fiddling with her long plait of cherry-black hair, her standard tell for anxiety or discomfort. 'What's up?'

She flicked the plait back behind her shoulder. 'Can you come over to my monitor? There's something I want to show you.'

I followed her to her desk, rolling my swivel chair across the space between us.

'Okay so look.' She turned to face me, and I had the feeling she'd been thinking this through for a while now, working out how exactly to share what she wanted to show me. 'So Alex told me to go back and trawl through the system records? Focussing on the days before the corticosterone spike? She wanted me to see what correlations I could find, give us something to work around.'

'And you've found something.'

'It doesn't make a lot of sense to explain it. Looking at the numbers it took me a long time to work out what I was seeing. See here, I plotted a graph.'

I stared at the brightly coloured line-graph on Laura's screen, the rising and falling line, the colour-filled area underneath. Time ran along the horizontal axis in ten second chunks, and there were numerical values along the vertical axis, tiny numbers, parts per million. I glanced at Laura. 'What am I looking at?'

'Here's the level of corticosterone in X's umbilical cord blood. And see here, over a twenty-four hour period, there's a line, like a wave, up and down, up and down.'

I looked at the wave she'd plotted, the regular rise and fall of the line. 'Yes, I see.'

'But look here. A few hours before the last spike? Look what happens to the graph.'

Presented as a graph, the anomaly was unmistakable. Instead of a smooth curving wave, there was a rigid break in the line, a sheer cliff edge. 'That can't be right, can it?' I said.

'I've checked it and checked it. Those are the readings I have. So I thought about it, and in the end – '

Laura pulled out a A4 jotter pad, and I saw she'd re-sketched the graph from her computer screen onto the lined paper. I saw the neat little pencil marks where she'd reproduced points on the line, and where she'd drawn in the curve between the points, shading the area underneath in diagonal stripes of grey. But instead of copying it out directly, Laura had left a wide gap in the middle of the paper, a gap which began with the top of the cliff and then picked up again where the curve resumed its normal course. And between these two points, Laura had drawn a dotted line, following the expected gradient of the curve.

'You've stretched out the timeline, to account for the change in values.'

A small nod. She was looking at me intently now, checking to see if I'd come to the same conclusion. Not wanting to lead me to it, not wanting to spell it out.

'You've extrapolated from the expected curve,' I said carefully, 'but in order to make it work, you've had to add time.' I hesitated, my brain working overtime. 'You're saying this timeline, this one here, the one you've drawn – you're saying that's what really happened?'

'I think so. It's the only way it makes sense.'

'But hang on a minute. You're saying there's some *time missing* from the records? Like the system clock just what – ? Stopped recording for a couple of minutes?'

'Two minutes and forty seven seconds. If those minutes exist, the numbers makes sense. Without them, our data is garbage.' She reached round and pulled the plait to the front of her shoulder again, started fiddling with the ends of her hair. 'Can you think of another explanation?'

I stared at the floor, then back at her. 'But the system clock can't just – stop.'

'I know. But if it isn't that, then what?' She looked at me, her mouth a thin line. 'And there's more,' she said. 'After I drew this graph I went looking for similar anomalies. And I found two other instances.'

'Honestly?'

'I think there are – let me get this straight – seven minutes and fifty six seconds missing from the record.'

'But that's not possible.'

'It's got to be salvageable, right?' Laura said. 'We'll just have to track back through the data. Work out where the jumps are. Reconstruct the timeline, the way I did here. I mean it's going to be a ball-ache, yeah? But it's not impossible.'

She was thinking about her research, about her career, and okay, so maybe if you're not an experimental scientist you probably won't understand what a big deal this was. A couple of minutes here and there, what did it really matter? But everything we did was date and time stamped – everything – it was essential to the accuracy of our data. If anyone got wind of anything being even slightly dodgy about all those readings, we might as well give up any pretence of doing any proper science, give up on the papers we all hoped to publish.

But honestly, Laura's research profile was the least of my worries. If she was right, that meant what exactly? The system had just, like, switched itself off for a couple of minutes? No, that wasn't possible. If the system had failed, X would be dead. Anyway, there was backup power, not to mention alarms, emergency systems. If anything had gone wrong, even for a moment, we'd all know about it.

So, no, the system hadn't switched off, but somehow the internal recording of those minutes was missing from the record. And the two sections of time, either side of the break, had been stitched together, as if the section in the middle had never happened.

It didn't make any sense.

But X was just fine, developing perfectly, now half way through his period of gestation. I glanced at him on the big screen. He was levitating upside down now, his legs crossed, serene as a miniature sadhu. A strange looking sadhu these days, more like a little werewolf, or maybe a baby chimpanzee, his body covered in fine, black hair, shifting this way and that in the amniotic currents, hennaed by the pink glow from the light source.

Lanugo. All human foetuses had it, and any day now X would shed his into the soupy interior of the amnion, then suck into his mouth, and swallow it, washed down with the warm, sweet tea of his amniotic fluid. The downy lanugo would collect in his bowel, forming a soft, dark, hairball, where it would remain until he was delivered into the world, when he would pass it as a green-black tar called meconium. And just as his first cry would prove his newly working lungs, his first shit would prove his bowel, and with both ends working he would be kitted for the world.

'What are we going to tell Alex?' Laura asked.

How would Alex take this? She was already wound pretty tight, this might tip her right over the edge. And practically, what could be done about it right now? Christmas was coming, and soon after that the baby would be born. That had to be our priority. Sorting out the mess this made of our research findings could wait a couple of weeks.

'I'm going to have to think about this,' I said. We'd need to tell Alex eventually, it was just a question of timing. Like Daniel kept telling me, Alex needed someone looking out for her, watching her back. And sometimes that meant keeping information from her until she was ready to hear it. Right now, she didn't need anything else to worry about.

28

Alex

Now, Sussex

Here's a memory that comes back to me. This time I'm not the doctor, but the patient, lying on the examination couch, my smart black trousers unbuttoned, my blouse hitched up. The GP seemed young to me, Dr Layton, if I remember her name correctly, fine, mousy hair secured in a tortoiseshell clip, pointy little face. I hear my voice saying to her, 'Go ahead and check if you like. But I'm definitely not pregnant.'

'You'd be surprised how many times I've heard that,' Dr Layton said, smiling.

Oh really. In all your many years of practising medicine?

Dr Layton started palpating my abdomen, feeling around the edge of my hip bones, digging into the bowl of my pelvis with her long girlish fingers.

'When I said it's not possible,' I said, 'I didn't mean, my boyfriend and I have been very careful. I meant, it's really not possible. And I haven't missed a period.'

She tried to hide her smile. 'Some women don't.'

All right, young lady, let's not forget who's the world-renowned fertility specialist.

She stopped digging and looked me straight in the eye. 'You know what?' she said, 'I can't tell. Have you done a test?'

'No. Because I'm not pregnant.'

But of course there was a part of me that thought: *A baby? Could it be?* Despite myself, the image in my mind was of X, all oversized head and sweet little toes.

But I couldn't have a baby now. *Not now.* I had X to look after, complete, deliver. I had my project to finish. And besides, it was early days with Ted. Very early days. We were still feeling our way through the idea of being together, and neither of us knew where this fling of ours might lead. He'd run a mile if I suddenly announced an unplanned pregnancy? Wouldn't he?

But I couldn't quite squash the thoughts that rose up in me: A baby, what about it? What if this was my last chance?

Bloody hell.

A baby.

I took the plastic pot into the toilet, peed carefully and left the pot on the edge of the basin while I washed my hands and unwrapped the dipper. Was this how my patients felt, waiting in the bathroom for an answer? This sense of standing at a crossroads, on the cusp of a great revelation, one which might change your life forever.

Calm down, Alex. Ridiculous woman.

It was negative, of course.

'False alarm,' I'd said brightly, stepping back into the consulting room. I couldn't help noticing Dr Layton's disappointment, now I'd burst her only working hypothesis like a soap bubble.

'So what is going on with me then?' I asked, reminding her of the nausea, the fatigue, the back pain, the worsening insomnia.

'Might you be a little stressed?'

No shit Sherlock. What with the most important project of my career underway, the Frey's identities leaked, the Centre under attack, my staff harassed by maniacs, the press daily at my throat. And then, to top it all, the revelation that my eggs had been used to create X. I kept stumbling over the size of that coincidence (utterly unbelievable, it couldn't be), but I'd seen my NHS number there, in black and white on Ted's screen, and checked it and checked it countless times since against the card in my wallet.

And so what if I was X's biological mother? What did biology have to do with anything? I'd donated those eggs to the Centre in good faith, for use in research. I'd never imagined a child being created.

I'd always known I needed to protect him, but now that sense was stronger than ever. And my secret felt like a bomb I was carrying, something that could go off any minute. So, yes, I was a little stressed.

Perhaps I should have confided in someone, but I didn't know how to. It would have been unprofessional to burden Dolly, and while I'd been able to go to Ted for information on the donor, I couldn't explain my findings to him. The person I came closest to telling was Daniel. We'd been meeting in his office recently, first thing in the morning, for a strong cup of coffee and a comradely debrief before the battles of the day ahead. I talked to him about everything else going on, and he listened sympathetically, and gave sound, level-headed advice. But I couldn't share this with him. Not this. Sympathetic and level-headed as he was, he'd think I was going crazy. So I carried my bomb around, feeling it ticking inside me.

'I could write you a prescription for some sleeping tablets,' Dr Leyton suggested.

I hesitated, not sure I wanted to go that route. But hell, if I was going to survive this, I needed to get some sleep.

29

Karen

Three months earlier, Market Harborough

Things quietened down after the interview. We still got the odd phone call, but once we told them about the exclusive we'd given they backed off and left us alone. I stopped feeling so nervous when I was out and about, and Rob went back to working in the garden without glaring at strangers over the fence.

I wouldn't say we were looking forward to reading Jo Miller's article but I thought, we haven't done anything wrong, what's the worse she can say about us? By the time that weekend came around, I'd almost convinced myself that I was right.

On Sunday morning, Rob went out early to get the paper, promising not to look until he got home. Then we sat on the sofa together, just as we'd sat with Benny circling us and taking our photographs. The first thing we saw was the picture, a great big one, Rob and I in the baby's room, complete with all the faked up props and Benny's baby's monkey. Another smaller picture showed us sitting on the sofa. We barely looked like us in either photograph, more like a couple of actors, people pretending to be us. But there wasn't any point getting upset about that.

The headline was 'Brave New World' and underneath it said, *Jo Miller talks to Karen and Rob Frey, the parents of Baby X about infertility, the desire for a perfect child and life in the media spotlight.* Which was weird for a start, because I don't remember that being what we'd talked about.

The article started off with a story about a disabled baby girl born to a surrogate mother in India. When the commissioning parents decided they didn't want a disabled child, the baby was abandoned in an Indian orphanage. Which was horrible, obviously, but what had it got to do with us?

We read on, about the "alarming trend" in society — parents who see themselves as "consumers buying a product".

And when that product turns out to be faulty, the article continued, *the impulse is to complain, sue even, and ultimately send the "product" back.* The article quoted me then, saying, *Karen Frey is clear about her rights as a consumer. She says, 'We told Dr Mansfield we wanted our baby to be perfect. And Dr Mansfield has promised us he is. They screened the embryos for every conceivable genetic disease, and picked the strongest.'*

'That's not what I said,' I said to Rob. At least I didn't think it was what I'd said. It didn't sound like me.

What many parents fail to understand, the article continued, *is that life is not perfect, and no child is perfect. What if your child, like millions of children in this country, develops a minor illness, asthma, for example in infancy? Or doesn't get A*s in all of his A Levels? Will they decide then that their child is not quite perfect enough, and send him back? Sue the Centre for Reproductive Medicine? Life is a process of imperfection, and parenting is an exercise in unconditional love. Until today's perfection-seeking parents understand this, we risk raising a generation of insecure children who see themselves as only worthy of love if they meet their parents' ludicrously high expectations.*

Jo Miller went on to talk about genetic disabilities, which would be eliminated in this new world of "perfect children". She had a niece with Down's Syndrome, she said, and found this "new eugenics" to be "utterly chilling".

We folded up the magazine and put it, along with the rest of the newspaper, into the recycling box in the kitchen. I think we were both in shock. We didn't really understand what had just been done to us, at least not immediately. Over the next few days some of the issues in the article were repeated in other newspapers, in comments sections, and then in editorials, not blaming us exactly, but often citing us as an example. Then the journalists came back, standing on our doorstep first thing in the morning and last thing at night, calling through the letterbox, banging on the window of the car as we tried to leave our driveway.

'How do you respond to accusations that you –'

'What do you say to people who criticise –'

By the following Sunday things had calmed down again, and my older brother Ian came over for lunch, bringing his wife Carrie and their two little kids, Grace and Nathan. I made a roast chicken, with apple pie and custard for pudding, and afterwards the kids went out to play in the garden. Grace tore up the lawn in her tatty bubblegum-coloured princess dress ('She won't go anywhere at the moment unless she's wearing it,' Carrie had confided) and Nathan pottered about, toppling onto his padded bottom on the decking. Carrie went outside to supervise and after a while Rob followed her, leaving me alone with my brother in the kitchen.

Ian stood beside me at the sink, wiping off the roasting tins with a tea towel as I lifted them out of the soapy water. 'I can't decide if I should tell you this or not, Karen,' he said.

The sound of high-pitched squeals leaked through the patio doors. I could hear Carrie laughing, and Rob pretending to be a monster chasing the children.

'Tell me what?' I asked.

'Carrie says I shouldn't bother you with it. But if it was me, I think I'd want to know.'

That sinking feeling, familiar now. Oh God, what was it this time? 'Go on then,' I said.

So he told me. There were more rumours, apparently, about us and about our baby on social media. About his poor health, how he would be born sick or disabled somehow, as a result of his unusual gestation. More of the same then. But this time with the kicker that we'd abandon him if he wasn't perfect.

'What can we do?' I said. 'We just have to ignore it, don't we? Rise above it.'

Ian hesitated. 'There's something else, Karen. Maybe you two should go to the police.' He explained that some of these so-called "trolls" had been actively wishing us harm, threatening to hurt us.

'It's all talk,' I said, staring into the soapy water.

'Of course it is,' Ian said. 'But some of these characters are proper nutters. It's better the police deal with them.'

After Ian and Carrie and the kids went home, I went online to see what he'd been talking about. I set up a fake Twitter account with an anonymous name, no point drawing more fire. I searched the way Ian had explained, using hashtags and keywords, and felt my heart sink, realising there was a whole corner of the internet devoted to discussing us and our inadequacies. I was a hardened career woman who'd "left it too late", apparently, and now, desperate for a baby, and selfishly insisting on "having it all", I didn't care who I hurt to get what I wanted.

I'd heard about men giving women a hard time online,

but most of my attackers were women. Why were they so angry? What had I done to them? *I hope you die of cancer, you selfish bitch,* one woman said. Another claimed she was going to find out where we lived, and set fire to our house.

Rob said, 'I knew we shouldn't have done it. That interview was a mistake.'

'They were talking about us before the interview.'

'But we've made it worse.' I heard the accusation in his tone, even though he didn't say it out loud. *You've* made it worse.

We spent the rest of the evening in silence, not speaking to each other. The world suddenly seemed a scarier and sadder place. Did we really want to bring a child into this? We watched a bit of telly, Rob staring straight ahead at the screen the whole time, not even glancing at me.

I wanted to reach out to him, to stop him being angry with me. We hadn't created this situation, it wasn't our fault. There might even be worse, further down the line. We might have to explain all this to our son someday, perhaps after some ugly incident at school. But you didn't crawl into a hole and hide, did you? You just had to be yourself, do the right thing, stand up straight and get on with it.

More than ever, he needed us to be strong. And we weren't about to let him down.

30

Alex

Now, Sussex

I remind Ted of our bargain. 'You promised to tell me everything, remember. Then I'll get you some food, and X and I will be gone. Once we're away, I'll call someone to come and get you.'

He looks at me, mouth set, eyes resigned. 'Okay, Alex. You win.' He shifts his weight, trying to get comfortable, and I have a flash of sympathy for him. But I can't let myself be distracted.

'I was working as a researcher for Verlaine, at the lab in Bristol,' Ted begins. 'But you know that already, right?'

I'm not about to reduce my advantage by revealing my hand. 'Go on,' I say.

He blinks. 'I was part of a team who were testing a new drug Verlaine was developing for the autoimmune market. A nonsteroidal anti-inflammatory. Cairox.' My eyes must widen because he pulls a face. 'I'm not surprised you've heard of it. Given what happened later.'

X has started to squirm in my lap. His hands, which were relaxed, begin to stir the air in front of his face. Any minute now, he'll wake, and start to cry. In anticipation, my breasts gain weight and heat. I hold him close, pat his nappy-padded bottom. He's wearing the blue sleepsuit I bought, just before Christmas. I should be listening to Ted, but my mind drifts as I let my hand play across the downy fuzz of X's hair, remembering the day I bought him this sleepsuit.

I'd made my way through the Christmas crush of the department store, the confusion of sounds, lights and colours, a garish window display of animatronic carolling mice. In the children's department I stopped to stare at the racks of clothes. Babies, apparently, came in three colours: pale pink, pale blue and a sort of porridge-beige. I selected a pack of pale blue vests, another of pale blue sleep suits, and held them limply, unconvinced. Would these do? I took a deep breath and then headed in the direction of the toys.

I didn't have to buy Karen and Rob Frey a present. In too many ways to mention, I was already giving them enough. But then, I'd be fooling myself if I thought this was a present for them.

Okay, I wasn't exactly behaving rationally. X wouldn't remember his baby clothes, and any toy I bought him would be irrelevant until months after his birth. But I couldn't quite shake the impulse that I needed to give him something. Something precious, to take with him into his new life. Something to remember me by. I carried a vague notion, deliberately unexamined, that if I chose carefully enough my gift might become grubby with love, sucked, thumbed, infused with a familiar smell. The sort of thing he'd miss if he dropped it, and cry to have returned.

Ever since that article had appeared in the weekend newspaper, I'd been struggling with complicated feelings about the Freys. Okay, so I'd guessed Karen Frey must have been misquoted; I knew her, if only slightly, and that didn't sound like her at all. The journalist obviously had an agenda, and she'd moulded the Freys' answers to fit it. But there was something about the photograph of them in the baby's bedroom that didn't sit comfortably with me, and I'd found myself staring at it, wondering what was wrong.

Rob and Karen's stiffness was just nerves, wasn't it? The result of the awkwardness and unreality of their situation, topped off by pressure from the press. All the same, I kept looking at that picture, wishing it was different. They just didn't look happy. More like a couple of puppets, posed and manipulated. Passive, too, like they'd found themselves trapped in something and didn't know how to get out. Was this simply the media pressure getting to them? A worse thought came to me: were they starting to have doubts about X?

So there I was in the toy aisle worrying about the Freys, surrounded by soft things stuffed to near-stiffness or left limp and baggy, hard things that rattled, scrunchy things, bobbled things, animal-shaped things with small bells sewn deep into their torsos. Unable to choose, I picked up a pale blue cloth rabbit with black beads for eyes and long ears in some impossibly soft fabric. Then I just stood there, rubbing the ears between my fingers.

'When's your baby due, love?' A middle-aged woman, stout in her overcoat, her smile gentle.

'January,' I answered, truthfully, without thinking. But January was barely a month from now. The woman's eyes flicked towards my belly, confusion spreading across her face. 'Oh, no,' I said quickly, attempting a light laugh. '*I'm* not pregnant. I mean, he's not mine.'

Not mine. The words could have stuck in my throat. The woman's eyes narrowed, but her mouth was still kind.

'I'm buying something for my sister's baby,' I clarified. The woman was still giving me that gentle, quizzical look, so I did the worst thing possible and attempted to cover my odd behaviour with too much information. 'They found out the sex. They've got two girls already. They're going to call him Oscar.' And finally, I'd stopped speaking. Thank heavens for that.

The woman hesitated, then put out her hand and placed it on my arm, where it rested, surprisingly light. 'I'm sorry, love,' she said in that soft voice. 'I didn't mean to intrude.'

'Don't apologise –'

'It's just that you've got that look about you.'

The hairs stood up on the back of my neck. 'What look?'

'You know,' the woman said. 'Distracted. A bit dreamy. Like you're only half here.' She paused for a moment, but I didn't answer, stuck for anything to say. 'I'm sorry,' she said again. 'Take no notice of me.'

I headed in the direction of the till, and escape, good intentions of carefully chosen gifts laid to waste, purchasing, in my confusion, the things I had in my hands: a pack of pale blue sleep suits, a pack of pale blue popper-gusseted vests and the very soft, pale blue cloth rabbit.

Something was happening to me, that was certain. Something that led people to mistake me for a pregnant woman, that was changing my body, changing my mind too, my *thinking*, in subtle but unmistakable ways. Turning me into the sort of woman who stood around in department stores feeling emotional about soft fabrics, the sort of woman who no longer felt competent to carry out simple mathematical calculations in her head, who'd recently had trouble reversing her car into one of the narrow parking spaces in the basement of the Centre. Who was this woman? Myself, or some imposter? A heavier, slower, softer version of myself.

Who are you? And what have you done with Alex?

I'd been taking the sleeping tablets Dr Leyton had

prescribed, and yes, I had been sleeping better. But if anything I felt more tired, more fuzzy-headed, more in need of the strong coffee Daniel made for me when I stumbled into his office, bleary-eyed, every morning.

*

'We'd been given a short timescale on the Cairox trial,' Ted tells me. 'A competitor was developing a similar product for the same market. It was a race to the finish line.'

I'm dragged back into the room by the sound of Ted's voice, and glance down at X. His face scrunches and smoothes, scrunches and smoothes, as he surfaces out of his deep sleep.

'It was a large scale, randomised, controlled trial with a group of arthritis patients,' Ted continues. 'I administered weekly injections at the clinic. I never made up the syringes – those were done by a different team.'

'To keep the trial double-blind,' I say. X mews softly, and I lift him to my chest, hold him upright. His head wobbles on his neck, then comes to rest against my collarbone.

'That's right. I had no idea who was getting the active ingredient, and who was getting the placebo. Every week, we'd run through patients' symptoms using a checklist, ask them to rate severity. And I'd monitor side effects, keep an eye out for anything serious.'

'So what happened?' X is awake now, and is gently head-butting my collarbone, a signal I recognise as *milk, milk, milk*. I should start feeding from the left breast, keep it fair, take it in turns. I don't want to end up lopsided. But the urge to relieve the pain in the right breast is overwhelming. I reach around my back with the hand that isn't holding X, unhook my bra, lift my t-shirt.

Ted's watching me the whole time, and I resist the urge to tell him to fuck off. 'Nothing you haven't seen before,' I mutter.

'Is it supposed to be that colour?' he asks, frowning.

'Mastitis,' I hiss.

'Does it hurt?'

A hard stare, all he deserves. I've never been a very patient person, and pain is destroying any patience I once had. 'Tell me what happened with the Cairox trial.'

Ted looks down at the floor. X is having trouble getting his mouth around the engorged mess that is my nipple. But we persist.

'To start with,' Ted says, 'things went well. A lot of patients found their symptoms improved. But after a while, I started to realise the improvements must be happening in the control group too – virtually every patient recorded feeling better.' He looks up at me again. 'This was my first large scale trial. I didn't know then that most patients will show some improvement, just from being offered new hope. And then, after a few weeks, I started to get worried about some of the side effects. Dizziness, headaches, gastric problems, that sort of thing, even a case of gastrointestinal bleeding.' He pauses for a moment, and then goes on. 'Then a patient in my group was hospitalised. Flank pain –'

X is struggling, coming off, going back on. My nipple is getting mashed in all this ineffectual half-latching, and it bloody hurts. Still. Look at me, calmly interrogating my enemy while struggling with the early days of breastfeeding. Look at me following this conversation about research methodology without getting distracted. Look at me multi-tasking, picking up his reference to flank pain. 'An early warning sign for kidney failure,' I say.

Oh yeah. I still got it.

'That's right,' Ted says.

'And?'

'The patient was removed from the trial.'

'Rightly so,' I say, my gaze dipped towards X.

Ted is quiet for a moment, so I glance at him just in time to see him shake his head. 'Yes, of course, he had to stop treatment,' he says. 'But when I say he was removed, I mean, I was asked to completely remove his *records from the trial*. So the side effect wouldn't show up in our results.'

I wonder if he's lying. To manipulate the results like that, brushing a serious side effect under the carpet, surely no one would have risked asking Ted to do that. 'You didn't object?'

X is making another valiant attempt to latch on, but now he's getting frustrated. He's only managed a couple of decent gulps of milk, and he's hungry. In desperation, I turn him around and switch him to the other breast. Milk drips from my right nipple, falling on to X's babygro-clad feet. A minute ago I was competently multi-tasking; suddenly I'm making a complete hash of this. A split second of self-consciousness: Ted is a former lover and here I am, in front of him, sick and dishevelled, flashing my bulbous tits, failing to feed my baby.

But Ted's not watching me. Eyes on the floor, he says, 'I took it to my supervisor. He seemed to listen, but then the next thing I knew, I'd been moved out of that study and into another one, also Verlaine funded, but nothing to do with Cairox.'

'You should've complained.'

'I tried to. But, look, Alex, you know how beholden you are. Several months of work already wasted. And I didn't want to piss off my supervisor.'

'And the other study?'

'They moved me into Dekker's team.' He looks at me, gauging my response to the mention of Dekker's name. 'But you know about that, right?'

Well now... I do and I don't. I know Ted worked on Dekker's research, and that this was the project where he messed up, big time. I know Dekker's earlier work provided an important component of IVG, even as he failed to produce the groundbreaking treatments he envisaged. What I don't know is what Ted worked on with Dekker, and what happened next. If I understand this, I'll be closer to knowing why Ted came to Newcastle, and what he wanted from the IVG project. I'll know why he targetted me, and what he did to X.

So, yeah, there's a lot I don't know yet. But I know I'm getting close.

I help X to get a better latch and then sort out my bra to cover myself up on the right. 'Tell me about Dekker,' I say.

31

Dolly

Yesterday, Newcastle-upon-Tyne, police interview

Let me tell you what I'm hearing, Dolly. Dr Mansfield's behaviour has been increasingly erratic over the last few months. And you had your own personal safety to worry about, given you'd received threats –

Not threats exactly. Mice –

You received a series of dead mice – at your home address – which would make a lot of people feel uncomfortable –

Yes, but –

But you didn't go to Dr Mansfield with these problems because you didn't trust her reaction? Who exactly was in charge around here?

*

We'd all piled out of the gig at around midnight, clouds of misty drizzle almost pretty in the streetlights. It had been my mate Jez's birthday, and he was even drunker than usual, singing loudly and tunelessly, insisting on his inalienable right to a kebab with onions, chilli sauce, the works. But, yeah, it was his birthday, and we'd had a good night, one of those nights you want to carry on for longer. So when Hamish suggested a final drink in this late night place tucked away on a side street, I didn't have the heart to argue.

'Only the one mind,' I told them. 'I'm at work tomorrow.'

'It's *Saturday* tomorrow.'

'I know. But I'm on duty.' It was going to be quiet in the lab, deathly boring, most likely. Alex popped in most days, even on the days she wasn't working. But she wouldn't be there tomorrow, she was travelling back from her nan's funeral. It would just be me and X. I'd check he was all right, pull off some data, then maybe I'd go for a nap. How hard could it be?

'We should come and see you at work, Dolls,' Jez slurred. 'In the Frankenstein lab.'

'Yeah, right. Like that's ever going to happen.'

'You could show us the nipper.'

'You've got to be kidding. There's no way I'd let you lot in there.'

'She won't even let me in,' Aimee said with a lopsided smile, her hair all frizzed up in the mist, a big blonde afro framed by the hood of her fur-lined snorkel parka. 'I look like a terrorist, apparently.'

'I never said that,' I corrected. 'But yeah, I'd never trust you lot in there. Jez's so clumsy he'd lean on a keyboard and launch the birthing protocol four weeks early.'

The late night drinking hole was busy, we weren't the only damp losers in town not yet ready to go home. Hamish got a round in, and we crammed onto a little table in the corner. It was like I'd broken some sort of a seal by mentioning work, because Hamish and Jez carried on talking about it. They both had all these questions, like they'd been storing them up, but hadn't known if it was okay to ask. Weird that, since we'd all been friends for years.

'Is it true about the – you know – the marks on his head,' Jez asked. 'From the clamps?'

I nearly choked on my lager. 'Clamps?'

'There are clamps right? Holding him in place in the machine?'

'God, Jez, you are such a loser. Of course there aren't any clamps. He just floats about.'

'I read it on Wikipedia.'

'And here endeth the lesson,' I said raising the bottle to my lips. 'Never believe *anything* you read on the internet.'

'I don't know what all the fuss is about,' Hamish said. 'I wouldn't have minded being an IVG baby.' He'd started constructing another roll up, long fingers busy. 'I reckon it's nice in there. You've got everything you need. I'm sure my mum was chain-smoking and drinking the whole time she was pregnant with me.'

'And look how you turned out,' Aimee said, but gently. We'd heard plenty about Hamish's mum in the time we'd been friends.

'It *is* nice in there,' I said. 'Clean and safe. Uncomplicated.'

I caught Aimee's eye. Ever since I told her about the cortisol I'd been worried that maybe she'd tell someone else. Maybe this would be one of those situations, a leak, where someone tells someone else who maybe tells another *someone*, and pretty soon it ends up online.

But no. I could trust Aimee, couldn't I?

'Anyway,' I added, 'don't talk to me about mums. Mine's been giving me untold grief.'

'She just cares about you, Dee,' Aimee said.

'Yes, but she's being such a *lunatic* about it. Ever since the last bomb scare. Calling me every day virtually, *begging* me to pack it in.'

'That's mothers for you,' Hamish said. 'Not that mine would notice if I got blown up at work.'

'See it from her point of view,' Aimee said, ignoring Hamish. 'Those mice are pretty creepy.'

'Mice?' asked Jez.

I shook my head. 'Someone's been putting dead mice through our letter box. Wrapped up in tissue paper and stapled into jiffy bags.' I give Aimee a sharp look. 'And I can't believe you told my mum about that.'

'I was freaked out about it myself. When she phoned she asked me what was up so I told her.'

'But she'll be more anxious than ever now. You know what she's like.'

'Hang on a minute,' Jez said. 'Who's been sending you dead mice?'

'We thought it might be the Animal Liberation lot,' Aimee said.

'Why would they kill mice?'

'Who knows what they'd do.'

'But why send them to you?'

'IVG was tested on animals,' I explained. 'We're a high profile project, there's been a lot of publicity. We attract some – shall we say – *fringe* opposition.' I took another swig from my bottle.

'The police took it seriously,' Aimee told the boys. 'They even tested the mice, in case it was an actual, you know, an act of biological terror.'

'Yeah, mouse terror,' I said, shaking my head. 'Anyway. No toxins. Nothing. Just mice.'

But I felt uncomfortable, as the memory of how I'd got all riled up about X's cord blood, and how Verlaine was going to own it, surfaced suddenly. I hadn't done anything about it, apart from moan to Alex, and look where that had got me. I was turning out to be a right wimp. It was the same with the so-called "educational" touchscreen displays in the Centre lobby, which annoyed me so much, but I'd never actually put in that complaint to the Education Department.

'There is something that bothers me,' I told my friends now, and explained about the cord blood.

Hamish stared at me. 'They're taking his *blood* to use in developing new medicines?'

'That's sick,' Jez said.

'They aren't actually taking his blood,' I clarified, half wishing I hadn't said anything. 'I mean, it won't be removed until after his birth, and it's not as if he needs it then. If it doesn't get used, it'll just be thrown away.'

They all looked at me, confused. 'So what's the problem?' Hamish asked, after a moment.

'I don't have a problem with anyone using the blood,' I said. 'It's just that the medical developments that potentially come out of it will be owned by a private company. Do you get me?'

My friends shook their heads.

'Which means that in the future, when you get sick, you'll need to pay Verlaine for treatment.'

'Or the NHS will,' said Aimee.

'But that's what I mean. The NHS will have to pay whatever Verlaine demands for this resource, whether it can afford it or not. If the blood was held in a public bank, nobody would have to pay a company to use it.'

'But someone's got to fund research though, right?' Hamish said.

Did the non-disclosure agreement Alex'd mentioned apply to me? Should I even be talking about this? If it got out there'd be trouble. Trouble for me, and worse for Alex. For a moment I enjoyed the dull ache of satisfaction at the thought of Alex getting her knuckles rapped, and then immediately afterwards, there came a sharp backwash of guilt. Alex wasn't the bad guy here, was she?

I needn't have worried. Jez was too pissed to follow what I was saying, and Hamish didn't get why it mattered. And I didn't think Aimee was going to go to the papers.

Later on, as Aimee and I were walking back to our Heaton flat, she said, 'I know you're all looking after him. But you hear stories, about animals in labs. About people doing horrible things. I know you keep talking about how safe he is, but he's vulnerable too, isn't he?'

'It's okay,' I said. 'All the people looking after him are nice people.' I took her arm. 'People like me.'

'But if it was done on a bigger scale – an *industrial* scale. If a lot of babies were – were –'

'Gestated,' I supplied.

'If a lot of babies were gestated like that. It might be different. I know most people wouldn't deliberately hurt a baby. But they might make mistakes, treat it like a job, you know. Slack off a bit.'

'I slack off all the time,' I said, leaning into her. She looked so shocked it made me laugh. 'Look,' I said. 'It's not like you have to do anything most of the time. I'm mainly crunching data. And sometimes I'm in the dorm reading a book, or watching a DVD.

'Blimey,' Aimee said. 'And I've always thought of you as conscientious.'

'I am.' I paused, trying to work out how to explain. 'I do take it seriously. But a lot of the time, there's nothing to do. When I do anything to X, I'm careful, I check and double check what I'm doing. But you're right, it's a job.'

'So someone could make a mistake?'

'Well, I suppose. But that's why we have systems.'

'Okay,' she said, snuggling closer. 'That's reassuring.'

'And like Hamish said, it's not like natural gestation is perfect. At least none of us is smoking in the lab.' I sniggered. 'Sorry. Just imagining what Alex would say if someone lit up a fag and poured a measure of gin into the interface.'

Was that funny? Not funny? Sometimes these days I couldn't tell.

32

Alex

Now, Sussex

X is feeding happily now so I can relax, despite the glowing, pulsing pain in my right breast, and my roiling fever. But at least I'm getting somewhere with Ted. He's going to tell me about his work with Dekker and how this led him to the Centre. I'm close to finding out what I need to know.

'Dekker's immune research amounted to nothing,' Ted tells me. 'So he was given another project to mind. Something small, insignificant. And I was shifted across to assist him. I knew I'd been demoted, punished for making a fuss. But I kept my head down and got on with it.'

I say, 'Tell me about the project.'

'It seemed innocuous enough. Another randomised controlled trial, a vitamin supplement this time, for pregnant women. We were focussing on the outcomes for the women and their babies, improved Apgar scores at birth, that sort of thing. And all the women signed up to a small sample of cord blood being taken at the birth, and tested. Oh, and then the babies were scheduled for a second blood test after birth, performed as a heel prick.'

'A randomised trial on pregnant women? Isn't that a bit – unorthodox?'

'It was only a vitamin supplement. Considered risk-free.'

'And nobody thought it was strange for Dekker to be involved? Hardly his field.'

'Dekker had taken the failure of his synthetic immunology research hard, professionally and personally. I think he'd been given something simple to do, to get him out of the way, allow him to lick his wounds. We'd both been sent to the research gulags – for failure in his case, for making a fuss in mine.'

'So what happened?'

'About a year into this new position, I heard Cairox had been licensed.'

Everyone knew the Cairox story. The drug was withdrawn seven months after hitting the market, although by then, Verlaine had already netted millions of dollars' worth of sales. Even counting the damages paid out to victims' families, it had been a profitable drug.

'I was pretty sore about it,' Ted says, 'given my experience on the trial. Then one day – this was after the drug appeared on the market, but before the scandal – I was talking to another researcher who'd been involved in the study, that's how I knew her. I told her I couldn't believe they'd licensed the drug, given the side effects we'd seen. She was surprised and we ended up arguing. I couldn't remember all of the original measures, but she still had some copies left over in her office, so we went back to look at them. And guess what?'

I shake my head.

'Someone had changed the measure.'

'Honestly?'

'It was subtle, but yeah, they'd changed it all right. Using the new measure, and with aggregated data, the side effects were less noticeable. Someone was hiding dangerous, potentially fatal, side effects, to push a new drug out before it was ready.'

'You were angry,' I say, careful to keep my reaction neutral. I'm not sure I'm believing a word of this, but I don't want him to know that. I have to act impartial. Keep him talking.

'I was furious. I couldn't believe anyone would do something like that. I went home and talked to my girlfriend about it. Together we tried to work out what I should do to expose them. I knew I couldn't trust my supervisor. I barely slept that night, but I went into work the next day. I didn't have a plan. I just thought, I'll bide my time, give it a week or so, work out what I'm going to do.' He hesitates. 'It's not easy being a whistle-blower, Alex. You wouldn't wish it on anyone.'

So this is it: Ted's motive, his reason for hating Verlaine.

Now we're getting somewhere.

33

Karen

Ten weeks earlier, Market Harborough

I got back from the chemist about five o'clock, white paper bag in hand. Rob was in the kitchen. Chopping onions apparently, from the tang in the air. He looked up at me, his eyes following the bag as I placed it on the kitchen table.

I switched on the kettle. 'D'you want a brew?'

Rob said, 'You don't have to prove anything to anyone, Karen. It doesn't matter what those idiots say.'

'I know, love.' I did know. 'This isn't about them.' It really wasn't. 'Ordinary tea?'

He put down the knife and looked at me, his face sad. 'He's gonna love you anyway.'

I opened the cupboard door, reached for the mugs. Of course our baby was going to love me. Love was what babies did. They didn't grade you against a checklist to work out if you were good enough. They didn't assign you a mark out of ten based on whether you'd conceived them without help from doctors, or carried them to term, or for that matter, birthed them naturally. And you know what, they didn't hand out extra marks for doing it without pain relief.

Which was lucky, in my case.

'What are you making?' I asked.

'Vegetable soup.' No relaxation in his shoulders. I was still in the doghouse then.

'That's perfect. Thank you.'

He turned back to the chopping board, paused, then said. 'Please Karen. I haven't tried to stop you doing anything before. But I can't watch you go through it again.'

'Go through what?'

'The disappointment when you fail.'

I glanced at the paper bag on the kitchen table. It contained boxed blister packs of birth control pills, and another drug, domperidone. It did feel strange, a backwards step almost. How had I ended up back here, with a bag full of tablets on prescription?

We'd started to receive letters, you see, some forwarded from the newspaper, some sent on to us from the Centre for Reproductive Medicine. I'd been nervous about opening them, but for the most part they weren't from people wishing us cancer, or threatening us with violent death. Most of them were heart-breaking. There were tales of infertility, some with happy endings, plenty without, but they all had a common message: *I know something about what you're going through. Don't let others judge you.*

We'd had this one letter, from a woman called Kate who'd adopted a baby and wanted me to know she'd breastfed him.

Yes, *breastfed.*

She didn't want to tell me what to do, she said, only she'd read the article in the paper, and been thinking about me ever since. She thought I might like to know about her experience. You know, just for information.

When I first read that letter I thought, *What?* And once I'd googled it, and worked out it was possible, I was left with a nagging sense of, *Oh, brilliant, yet another thing I can't do properly. Another way I've fallen short.* I put the letter in a drawer and tried my best to forget about it.

Then a couple of days later, I was watching telly when this advert came on. An advert for follow-on formula milk actually, but it didn't start off like that. Before they advertise "moving on" to formula, they have to give you the line, you know, that breastfeeding is best for your baby. And the thing that struck me was that the "mother" in the advert was very young, and very beautiful, a model of course, probably just a teenager and not a mother at all. Between the look on her face, and how pretty she was, and probably the lighting too, she looked like an angel, her shirt open and thrown back on one side, baring more of her shoulder than was strictly necessary, the beautiful plump baby held at an artful angle to her body, light coming in from the windows and falling onto her golden hair, a small, smug smile on her face. And the house, my God, you should have seen the house! A sofa in this very pale colour, not a colour you'd want in a house with a baby in it, and so clean it was luminous, everything luminous, ordered and clean, not a speck of dust or dirt anywhere, not a cushion out of place.

I couldn't help it, but I wanted to cry. What about me with my dodgy eggs and blood clotting disease, what about me with my hormones that barely functioned and my uterus that couldn't carry a baby to term? And for that matter, what about women who tried to breastfeed their babies and couldn't?

All of a sudden there I was, glaring at the telly, clenching my fists, grinding my teeth. And honestly, I'd held it all together so well, hadn't I, through miscarriages, the unsuccessful treatment, the rounds of egg donation. Not to mention the press intrusion, and the weirdness of IVG, and all the nasty things people had been saying about us. Then one silly little advert and I lose the plot completely.

I had to get up off the sofa and walk around the house. I found myself fantasising about writing to that adoptive mum who'd sent me that letter. I wanted to give her a piece of my mind.

Who do you think you are telling me what to do? Have you got any idea of what I've been through to get here?

Well, have you?

I'm glad to say it didn't last long. The thing was, she *did* have an idea, didn't she, of what I'd been through. I mean, she'd read the article about me, and the reason she'd cared enough to write was that she'd been through a journey of her own. Four rounds of IVF, nearly broke her marriage, she said, before they'd agreed to adopt. And that, she'd told me sadly, was only the beginning. And she wasn't really telling me what to do, was she? Not really. She was just offering up her experience, no strings. As a gift.

The next morning I'd woken up, padded into the toilet for a wee, and while I was giving my hands a quick rinse in the sink I caught sight of my face in the mirror. Sleep-creased and dozy, hair a mess, no make-up. Just me, my face.

And I thought to myself: *Why the hell not?*

I'd seen plenty of women breastfeeding their babies in the park, and they never looked like that gorgeous young woman in the advert. I'd seen Claire breastfeed her two, and she never looked like she was receiving the Holy Spirit in sunlight through the windows. And her house was nothing like the house in the advert, any more than mine was.

And that woman, Kate, the adoptive mum who'd written me that letter, she'd failed too. What was it she'd said? Something about –

I went downstairs and got it out of the drawer, and stood there reading it again.

The thing I wanted to share with you, Karen, is that somehow, after all the years of treatment, doing this has actually made me feel like my body is my own again. Isn't that strange? But I believe it gave me my body back. I'm not talking about that silly thing they say in the women's magazines, about "getting my pre-baby body back". I don't mean that. I mean, when all is said and done, doing this made me feel strong.

My body had never done what I'd wanted it to, and it hadn't done what the doctors wanted it to either. Was I just beating myself up by trying again?

And in the end it wouldn't matter if I failed, we'd hardly let him starve. If no milk came, we'd feed him on formula. I'd look on it as an experiment. But this time, not an experiment run by doctors, conducted in a hospital. Not an experiment where I'd get poked and prodded by strangers, however kind and well-meaning those strangers were. An experiment I was in control of.

What was the harm in trying?

I googled it again, printed out the information I wanted. Then I went to my GP and talked it through. He wrote me a prescription, and here I was. And okay, so Rob didn't understand why I was doing it and wasn't going to support me, well, so what? Maybe I'd just do it *all by myself.*

I thought of our baby all those miles away in the lab, floating in his funny little tank.

And here I was, getting ready for him.

34

Alex

Now, Sussex

X has fallen asleep. His head has dropped back, mouth open. He's snoring softly.

Ted's story might have bored X into submission, but I've been listening. I'm letting him spin this thing however he likes, making sure I don't put him off. I don't want him to flinch from the next chapter, the one where he explains the scandal from the inside. Not the Cairox scandal, I know about that already. No, the scandal Daniel alerted me to, and Miles remembered. The one that will explain why Ted ended up in Newcastle spying on the IVG programme.

'So there I was, asking pregnant women health questions, filling in the scales, noting their answers, hearing them talk about various pregnancy symptoms. Administering the vitamin injections. All very standard, all very boring.'

'And what happened?'

'There was this one patient,' Ted says. 'A woman in her mid-thirties, mother of two, pregnant for the third time. Maggie her name was. Maggie Barnes. An interesting case because she had rheumatoid arthritis. It wasn't severe, the symptoms weren't affecting her life too much.'

'You must've checked that drug for contra-indications with the vitamin.'

'Of course. All above board.'

'So what happened?'

'The morning after I'd found out about the Cairox measure, I'd gone into work in a daze. I gave Maggie Barnes the injection in her upper arm, same as I'd done a million times before. The following day, she was brushing her teeth and noticed her gums were bleeding. She carried on getting ready for the day, thinking she'd phone her nurse later that morning, but she collapsed leaving the house. Her eldest son phoned for an ambulance, but she was dead before she reached the hospital.'

I've been anticipating this, haven't I? In his tired, overwrought state, Ted made a mistake, and Maggie Barnes paid the price. All the same, I hardly know what to feel. I keep expecting my hatred of Ted to harden around this fact, but instead I'm strangely empty.

'At the inquest, they said I'd mixed up the syringes. They said I'd given her something different, not a vitamin supplement at all, but a powerful drug which reacted with her arthritis medicine. There was even a suggestion I'd done it on purpose, that it was murder, rather than medical negligence. Although in the end the Crown Prosecution Service couldn't find enough evidence against me, so they dropped it. Thank God.' He looks up at me, and for a moment, he almost smiles. 'Although, it has to be said. If I was in prison for murder right now, at least I'd never've met you.'

I ignore this last comment. 'You made a mistake,' I say, keeping any judgement out of my voice.

He shrugs. 'Maybe I did. I was a mess that day. I'd been up all night raging against Verlaine. I should have taken the day off, but I didn't. I went into work that day and injected that woman with something that killed her. But Alex –'

'What?'

'I don't think I made that mistake.'

I shift X's weight in my lap. 'In that case, what happened?'

Ted looks down at the floor, then up at me, eyes blazing. 'At first I thought someone inside Verlaine had framed me.' It's a struggle to hold his stare without giving away what I feel. 'Hear me out, Alex. I know it sounds crazy. I'd discovered something damning about Verlaine's testing of Cairox, and was planning to blow the whistle. The next moment, something happens to discredit me. I was immediately suspended and there was an investigation into Maggie Barnes's death.'

This is crazy talk, isn't it? Massaging figures is one thing, but killing a patient, just to get at Ted?

'So during the investigation I made my accusation against Verlaine.'

'Did the judge buy it?'

Ted laughs. 'I was accusing someone within the company, an unknown person I should add, of deliberately endangering – no, *killing* – a pregnant woman in order to discredit a, let's face it, very lowly, potential whistle-blower, who didn't have any substantive evidence. The lawyer destroyed me. I mean, who exactly did I think I was?'

Just as I suspected. No sane person would have believed Ted's story.

'After that, my life was in tatters. I lost my job of course, but it was much, much more than that. My career was finished. I was lucky not to face criminal charges. Worst of all, I had to live with the likelihood I'd been responsible for Maggie Barnes's death, and the death of her unborn baby. I was depressed. And after a good eighteen months of trying her best to live with a self-pitying, furious, conspiracy theorist, Sue finally left me.'

There's something here we're still not getting to. 'But I don't see what any of this has to do with –'

Ted cuts me off. 'I'd been trying to accept my guilt. At some point I decided I needed to investigate further, see if I could come up with a better explanation for what happened. I started reading again. I went back to my biochemistry textbooks, and I could still access medical journals via my university account. Eventually, I discovered something.'

I blow out a lungful of air. 'What did you find?'

'The trail led me back to Dekker. Several years earlier, Dekker had made an application to carry out an immune-therapy trial on pregnant women.'

I raise my eyebrows at him.

'He was never given permission, of course. But the point is Dekker believed pregnancy might provide the necessary delivery mechanism for his therapy. His theory was that if a dose of his immune-product reached a developing embryo during pregnancy, the embryo's immune system would be modified, and as a result, stem cells from the foetus's cord blood could be primed for a particular therapeutic role.'

'I don't know, Ted. That sounds pretty far-fetched.'

'I came to the conclusion that the trial I'd been working on was a cover. Dekker wasn't testing a vitamin supplement at all.'

'You're saying the syringe you gave Maggie *had* been switched, but by someone else, and for Dekker's immune-serum?'

'Dekker never intended to kill her. He wanted her to go on and give birth to the child whose cord blood stem cells would cure her arthritis.'

I sit back, astonished at the intricate web of fantasy Ted has constructed to vindicate himself.

'I went looking for Dekker. I wanted to confront him, but he'd gone to ground. Then I heard about IVG, and how Dekker's research, and the Ig240 immune-product, was being used to support the foetal immune system during gestation.'

'It's unconnected. It's a coincidence that Dekker's ideas had an alternative application. These sorts of accidental discoveries happen all the time.'

'Unconnected? Are you sure about that? Verlaine was funding yet another piece of research based on Dekker's theories in a setting eerily close to the one he'd planned all along. But this time, guess what? No pesky pregnant women to get in the way.' I shake my head at him. 'I know Dekker's been using IVG as a cover this whole time. I just had to get close enough to the project to find out more. When the job came up in the National Gamete Service I applied for it.'

'And they gave you the job? With your history?'

'I disclosed everything. As the job had no clinical or research element, they were happy to have me.'

I sit quietly for a moment, running over what I know. Ted believes his intrusion into the IVG system was justified. He was protecting X, and other poor vulnerable foetuses, from the evil corporation, Verlaine, and from mad scientist, and possible murderer, Dekker. Unfortunately for Ted, I know something he doesn't. Something that will blow his crazy theory out of the water. I don't want to play my trump card quite yet, so I say, 'Talk me through how it works.'

'You target the immune system of the foetus during gestation, and this primes the umbilical cord blood for use in stem cell therapies. Specifically – do you want to know the details? – it's to do with creating the requisite concentration of trained lymphocytes in the foetus's cord blood, which has major implications for transplant recipients.'

X is rousing again. I lift him to my shoulder.

Ted continues, 'Who's going to put their own infant forward to test this stuff? No one. To get it off the ground, through the first few stages of development, covert testing was needed.'

I'm shivering again. The quicker I get out of here and get some antibiotics the better.

'Verlaine knew Dekker was crazy enough to go ahead with this research, and they let him get on with it, hoping he'd discover a safe form of genetic engineering, resulting in harvestable stem cell products. Of course, later on, the corporation would be able to distance itself from Dekker, and from any scandal. From there it would be easier to develop the technology.'

I stand up, knees bouncing softly, X resting against my shoulder. Let's get this over with, shall we? Then X and I can be on our way. I don't quite know where to start deconstructing Ted's outlandish conspiracy theory, but I do have the killer piece of evidence that proves he is wrong.

'Ted,' I say calmly, 'Dekker couldn't have been involved in IVG. He's been seriously ill – well, actually he has been for years – he's had Parkinson's disease. He hid the symptoms from his colleagues for a long time, but eventually it got to the stage where he couldn't hide it anymore. He's virtually paralysed now, and being cared for in a private nursing home. He's been there since before the IVG programme was underway.'

'How do you know this?'

'I already knew there was a connection between you and Dekker, and I did some digging of my own. Dekker's a very private person apparently, he didn't want many people to know about his illness. But I made a call to a family friend, who'd known him slightly, years back. He told me what he knew about the deterioration of Dekker's health.'

I see Ted's face fall. And that's when I know he's been telling the truth. At least, his own, utterly ridiculous, insane version of the truth.

The crazy bastard.

35

Dolly

Yesterday, Newcastle-upon-Tyne, police interview

How has Dr Mansfield been these past weeks?

Okay, well – she's not been on great form to be honest.

Can you be more specific?

She's had some problems in her personal life. A family bereavement. And also, she'd been in this – erm – relationship, but it turned out the man was using her. He was spying for one of Verlaine's competitors.

We know all about Ted Hayward.

Yes, of course. But you see, for a while there, we were all worried he might have done something to – to the baby. Because there are people out there who've wanted to hurt us, and some of them want to hurt X too.

So Dr Mansfield took it hard, breaking up with her boyfriend?

No, not exactly. I mean, she was angry with him. But she wasn't like – she wasn't moping around after him, if that's what you mean. It was more about X. And I didn't mention this before, because it's really not relevant, okay? But there are some things in the results, his cortisol levels, or – not his actual levels, which are fine, really, but there are anomalies. Things we can't explain, and as a scientist, that's always unnerving.

Dr Mansfield was worried too?

She cares about him. I mean, we all care about him, but she cares about him more. These last few weeks, it's been sort of – obsessive. You know, like it's gone way beyond professional concern.

Obsessive?

She was here all the time. And I don't think she was looking forward to the birth.

Why would that be?

I don't know. It was like she was dreading it. Like she was going to miss him or something.

You think she was planning to take him?

No. I know people will say that, especially after – but, no, I don't believe it. It doesn't make sense. If she'd wanted to have a baby, she would have just had one, right?

*

The day after Jez's birthday I had a bit of a hangover. Not a bad one, I hadn't had that much to drink, but I didn't want to be at work. Still, I spent an hour diligently checking the systems to see how X was doing (corticosterone readings normal, nice one), pulling data off the system for analysis. After that, as the data started to look a bit fuzzy round the edges, I stopped working. I was well into my third game of Spider Solitaire when there was a buzz from the lab door.

Could that be Alex, back early? But Alex wouldn't buzz. I went to the door, checked the intercom camera. Daniel Hall stood there, his body foreshortened by the camera angle, his pale freckled face outsized and convex.

'Morning!' He couldn't see me, but smiled winningly into the camera. 'Do you mind if I come in?'

He always asked so politely, as if he was a visitor, rather than part of the team. He didn't even have his own key card, which was silly when he was so close to the project, and helped us so much. Alex had explained it to me once: according to the strict terms of our licence, only named clinical staff were allowed in the lab unsupervised.

I pressed the key pad, waited as the door swung open. 'I didn't know you were working today.'

'I've got some paperwork to do. Do you mind if I sit in here with you?'

So that was the end of my Spider Solitaire marathon. I couldn't just muck about with Daniel in the lab. And didn't he have his own office? I'd have killed for my own office.

Perhaps he guessed what I was thinking, because he laughed and said, 'Yeah, I know it's a bit weird, but I like it in here. I like being near him, watching him on the big screen.'

Okay then. I liked that he felt the same way about X as I did. 'We all do,' I said.

'I figured one of you would be here today, so I thought I'd come and hang out. You don't mind, do you?' I shook my head. 'Well, don't let me stop you working.' He glanced up at the big screen. 'But he's a fascinating little thing, isn't he?'

'Some friends of mine have been asking to see him. They're interested too.' Oh hell. I was coming across as completely flaky, unprofessional. 'I'd never bring anyone in here though, you know.'

'Of course you wouldn't.'

'I'm not sure I'd be able to,' I babbled, 'even if – you know – I wanted to. How would I get them past the security desk? And then there's all the CCTV.'

'What?' Daniel said, smiling. 'Surely a clever girl like you, operating on the inside, could find a way round the CCTV.'

'A way around it?'

'I don't know. A way to override it or something.'

I blushed. Override the CCTV? I'd never even

considered it. But I didn't want to leave Daniel with a bad impression, so I said again, 'I'd never do anything like that.'

'Course you wouldn't,' Daniel said. He made us both some coffee in the dorm and carried it back through, before sitting at one of the desks and unpacking some papers from his briefcase. I called up the analysis I'd been working on, and pretended to look at it again while I sipped my coffee. I didn't get far though, because before long we were chatting. It was good to have someone other than Aimee to talk things through with. It made me realise how much I'd been missing the chats I used to have with Alex. I ended up telling Daniel what had happened with Dr Morvan, and the Cord Blood Bank, and how excited I'd been about our chance to work together. When I got to the bit about how Verlaine – *your* lot, I'd said – had refused the Centre the opportunity to co-operate, Daniel had wrinkled his nose.

'It *is* a shame,' he said. 'But look, you have to see it from Verlaine's point of view. The investment in this place –' He gestured around at the lab. 'Honestly?' he said, 'human being to human being, I can understand why you're disappointed. Don't be too hard on Alex though, this isn't her fault.'

'I just wish she'd been willing to fight for – for the principle of it.'

'Maybe there's someone I could go to,' he said. 'Maybe we can come up with a solution that suits everyone.'

'Do you mean that?'

'Maybe we can work out some sort of sharing arrangement. Verlaine gets access to the stem cell supplies it needs for research, but agrees to make an annual donation to the public bank. It'd be good PR for Verlaine, and Dr Morvan would get what she wants too. I'm not senior enough to push something like that through. But I could have a think about who to approach. Maybe there's a board member who'd be sympathetic.'

'That would be amazing, Daniel. Wow. Thanks very much.'

'What's your interest, Dolly? You seem very fired up about this. You aren't just angling for a job with Dr Morvan, are you?'

'I'd love to work in stem cell research,' I said. 'But mainly I just want to believe in it.'

'I can relate to that,' Daniel said. 'You want to make a difference.'

I felt shy then, like I'd given too much of myself away. 'I'm getting the impression you feel the same,' I risked.

'Me? Yes, I do.' He paused, looking at me. 'I've got my own reasons for caring, I suppose.'

'Have you?' I said, and then felt embarrassed. 'Sorry. I don't mean to pry.'

'It's okay. I don't mind talking about it. The thing is, my mum had Multiple Sclerosis. She was diagnosed with it when I was very little. She died when I was nine.'

'I'm sorry,' I said lamely.

'My dad was always telling me to be careful, be gentle. I worried I might break her if I was too loud, or too rough. And then I think when she started to get worse I felt guilty, as if it was something I'd done, by not being careful enough.'

'That's awful,' I said.

'It's all right. You don't have to feel sorry for me.' He looked at me again, a slight smile around his eyes. 'You can probably tell I've had a lot of therapy, the way I talk about it. Anyway, that was a long time ago; I'm all fixed up now.'

'That's why you're interested in medicine.'

'Nowadays, the doctors would've been able to help her. Even now, the available drug therapies could have transformed her life, as well as my childhood. And your Dr Morvan and her stem cells, well, they might even have cured her. So, yeah, I get the idealism thing.' He looked down at his knees, then back up at me. 'There,' he said, stretching back in his chair. 'Now you know all about me.'

I yawned. Daniel's personal revelations had only added to my exhaustion, and I suddenly wanted to be by myself, to nurse my hangover in private. 'I'm not going to get much more done today,' I said. 'I might just crash out in the dorm.' I looked at him again, feeling awkward. 'I shouldn't really leave you in here on your own.'

Daniel started gathering up his papers, packing them away in his briefcase. I felt bad about it. He'd said he liked being in the lab with X, and it was a bit insulting, given how lovely he was, and how helpful, and how he'd just confided all that stuff to me, about his mum and everything. If he wanted to work in here on his own, what was the harm? It wasn't like he was going to touch anything. It wasn't like leaving Jez in here. And it was sweet, wasn't it, the way he wanted to be near X?

'You know what,' I said, 'it doesn't matter if you want to hang out.'

'Are you sure? I don't want to get you into trouble.'

'Look,' I said. 'Why don't I leave you my key card? You can drop off the card in the dorm before you leave.'

'Thanks, Dolly,' Daniel said. 'I'll only be another hour or so. Then I'll be out of your hair.'

36

Alex

Now, Sussex

Ted is watching me carefully. At any moment, I'm expecting him to recognise his elaborate conspiracy theory for the fiction it is. Dekker wasn't involved in IVG, and that means he wasn't involved in an illegal research project in Bristol either. Ted is responsible for Maggie Barnes's death. He tracked Dekker to Newcastle on a misunderstanding; he tricked me and used me for nothing.

I'm bouncing X against my shoulder, and he's grizzling quietly. I almost feel sorry for Ted, with his pathetic fantasies, but I'm not about to let him off the hook. Ted's the reason we're here, isn't he? Maybe he never intended to hurt X, but that doesn't mean he didn't hurt him.

'It's over,' I say. 'You might as well tell me the rest.'

'The rest? I've told you everything: I broke into the control system. I was looking for evidence I could use against Dekker. There's nothing else.'

'There's no point keeping it from me now,' I press. 'Tell me what you did to X and why.'

'What I did to X? I never touched him.'

'If not you, then an accomplice.'

'No, Alex. I wasn't working with anyone else.'

I know he's lying. I saw the mark on X's leg. I saw it with my own eyes.

*

I was working late, alone in the lab, when I took the call from Laura. She told me about the readings she'd been taking, how she'd deduced that minutes were missing from the system clock record, how she already discussed it with Dolly and how the two of them had decided not to tell me straight away. But then she'd felt bad, she said. She'd been stewing on it and decided she needed to let me know.

I didn't stop to think about Dolly's poor judgement. There was no time for that. Instead, I got to work, trawling through the system to locate the breaks Laura had found in the timeline. This new evidence raised a horrifying possibility: had our cyber-attacker somehow erased part of the system record? And what if there was a connection between this latest anomaly and the corticosterone spikes we'd already observed?

I worked systematically, focussing on the sections of the record Laura had highlighted. It took me hours, looking at the numbers, and examining the live video feed from the AU, running it backwards and forwards, searching for anything to account for X's stress, or explain those minutes missing from the clock. The correlation with the corticosterone spikes was strong: I was certain that there was a connection, but I couldn't find it. By nine o'clock I was getting frustrated.

That's when it struck me. I'd been so focussed on a cyber-attack that I'd been searching the system for signs of tampering. But what if the attack hadn't come via our computer systems?

I got up from my desk and crossed the room to the stout, white box of the AU. Two weeks from now, the Freys would be here. We'd drain the fluid from the inside, open the front door and simply lift X out into the world. I leaned forward to examine the door, the three chrome catches, each as big as my fist.

What if someone had opened the AU? I pulled back the first of the catches, heard it release with a hiss. Then the second, then the third. I pulled hard on the heavy door. As it swung open, the thick rubber lining of the interior bulged towards me. I was so used to watching X on the big screen it was a shock to see him so small. I put out a hand out to hold him steady, my palm flat against the warm plastic of the fluid-filled outer bag. He flinched away from the lights of the lab, then relaxed. Was that flinch enough to trigger a stress reaction?

No. There had to be something else.

X slid towards my hand and I felt the warm weight of him, his heart beating against my palm. Supporting him as gently as I could, I examined the plastic sections of the seal, developed to allow a needle into the inner bag, should it ever be necessary. But I couldn't tell if anything had passed through the seal.

Very carefully, I turned X's little body, inside his cushioning bag of fluids. If I was going to inject, or take blood even, from a foetus, where would I place the needle? I brought X's body up to the clear plastic, flush against it, examining his skin.

And there it was: a tiny red mark on his thigh.

At his birth two weeks from now this mark would be healed. No one would ever know that someone else had stood here, holding him as I was holding him, pressing a needle through the seal, and into his body.

I stroked his knee gently with my thumb. All I ever wanted to do was keep him safe. My first instinct was to pick up the phone to Jim in security but something stopped me. I thought about the complex layers of security around the Centre, the protocols, the locked entrances, the key system, the CCTV. How could something like this have happened? I couldn't ignore the possibility that Jim was a part of the conspiracy. Until I knew how far this went and who was involved, I couldn't afford to trust anyone. Not even my own team. Even Dolly was keeping things from me.

I'd call the police, wait here with X until they arrived.

And then what? I'd insist on a round-the-clock police presence, to keep X safe until he was born. Would they give me that? Would they believe me? What if they had another interpretation of the marks on X's leg? I imagined the exchanged glances, the eyebrows raised behind my back.

Looks more like he's scratched himself with a fingernail, Doctor. I'm sure it's nothing to worry about.

Stress getting to you, Doctor? Your colleagues have mentioned you've been quite – emotional – recently.

Are you sure you're not misinterpreting this situation, looking for the worst?

My heart beat fast. What if someone came to the conclusion that I wasn't to be trusted? That I was the threat to X? Dolly had been giving me sidelong looks all week, they all had. And now I had to face the possibility that one of my own staff had done this. Daniel was my closest ally, and even he was losing patience: I'd noticed the note of calm tolerance that crept into his voice when he spoke to me. I couldn't risk getting locked out of the Centre, leaving X at the mercy of whoever was hurting him.

And then I thought, what if I've already tripped an alarm by opening these doors? What if the conspirators have already been alerted? What if they're on their way here now?

I would stand and fight. Anyone who wanted to hurt X would have to get past me. But could I really protect him?

Whoever controlled the system had the power to destroy X at a key stroke, simply by starving him of oxygen. What if they were out there now, monitoring my actions?

I knew what I had to do: the only way to keep X safe was to take him out of the AU.

Could I do it? It was only a matter of days until his planned birth date, he was already, technically, at term. I'd be taking some risks carrying out the birth unassisted but hell, I knew what I was doing, and I trusted myself more than anyone else right now.

I'd remove X from the AU, smuggle him out of the building, and take him somewhere safe. But where? A police station? Could I turn up at a police station in the middle of the night with a newborn baby? That wasn't going to work. If I couldn't trust the police to listen to me in the lab, I'd hardly be able to vouch for my own sanity once I'd taken X.

I'd take him to the Freys. Yes, that was the thing to do.

*

'Come on Ted,' I say, 'the game's up. I saw the mark on X's leg. I know someone opened the door of the AU, to take blood, or else inject him with something. Now I'm guessing your plan was to take blood, to confirm your theory about Dekker's research.' Ted's shaking his head. 'I know it wasn't *actually* you,' I say. 'There was no way you could've got back into the Centre after you'd been caught. So you must have been working with someone else. I want you to tell me. Who was it?'

'Alex,' Ted says. 'Haven't you been listening to anything I've been saying? I was trying to find out what Dekker was doing with the IVG programme. I did break into the system and I was downloading files. But I never did anything to X. And I wasn't working with anyone else.'

'So who then? Who opened the AU and stuck a needle in through the seal?'

Ted shakes his head. He knows he can't blame Dekker now.

'You aren't much of an investigator,' I say, 'chasing a conspiracy with a paralysed man at its heart.' This isn't working. X is hungry again and I'm sick. We need to get away. I try another tack. 'Okay, let's talk about what you did to me.'

'I'm sorry about that,' he says, and for a moment there he really does look sorry. 'When I first asked you out, I admit, I was using you to get close to the programme. I thought you must be in on it, the conspiracy with Dekker, and I wanted to find out what you were doing. When I was at your flat I accessed your laptop – that's how I got into the Centre's systems. Your personal security practices are terrible by the way, Alex. You never log out of accounts you access at home on your laptop, you use the same passwords across different systems. If I'd have wanted to I could have cleared out your bank account too.'

I glare at him. 'I'm supposed to be grateful you didn't rob me too?'

'But then I realised you weren't in on it. The number of times I almost confided in you –'

'Why didn't you?'

'I didn't think you'd believe me. I was worried you'd tell someone else what I'd told you.' He sighs. 'It's bloody hard work keeping up a front like that.'

'But you managed it. Even in bed.'

'Yes.' He looks down at his knees. 'At the beginning, I thought, it'll only take a couple of dates for me to find out what I need to know. But you know, we got on.'

'You're a sneaky, lying –'

'No, Alex, that was real.'

'You expect me to believe you?'

'Yes. And after I was arrested and locked out of the Centre, I had my laptop confiscated. And then they let me go, but I was told to stay away from you. Then, the night before last, remember?'

How could I forget?

'I thought, Alex is smart, she'll work it out for herself sooner or later. So I decided to risk it, even though I wasn't allowed to contact you. I drove over to your flat, I was going to tell you everything.'

'But I wasn't there. I was at the Centre.' I was removing X from the AU.

'When I got to your flat, your car wasn't there. I parked a little way off, and waited. And then, you came back. I watched you walk in through the front doors of your building. You had what looked like blood on your clothes and there was something about the way you were carrying that bag.'

I look at him steadily. I can just imagine what I looked like.

'I saw you go into your building. I wasn't sure what had happened, but I knew something was wrong. You looked crazy, Alex, absolutely batshit crazy. It spooked me. So I sat out in my car for a bit, trying to work out what was going on. Why the blood, and what the hell you had in the bag.'

'You called me.'

'You didn't look like you'd react well to me showing up on your doorstep. So I phoned your mobile.'

'And when I saw the caller ID –'

'You came to the window. You thought I was spying on you.'

'You *were* spying on me.'

'Well, yes, I was. But what I'm trying to tell you, Alex, is I never meant to hurt you. I know I lied in the beginning. I'm sorry for that. But coming to your flat that night, and following you here, all I wanted to do was protect you.'

He's not going to tell me about X, but there's still information we haven't got to. I change tack. 'Ted,' I say as calmly as I can, 'I need to talk about what you've done to me.'

'I'm sorry, Alex. I keep telling you I'm sorry.'

'I'm not talking about you tricking me into sleeping with you to give you information, although that was shitty enough. I'm talking about what you've *done* to me.' I look down at my heavy body, my ridiculous outsized breasts. 'You arranged it so it was *my* donated egg used to conceive X for the Freys. Only you could have fixed that up, with your position in the National Gamete Service. And you've been getting something into me, right? What is it, some combination of hormones that's tricked my body into behaving as if it's pregnant? And come to think of it, the confusion, the fuzzy-headedness. I know I've been taking sleeping tablets, but they wouldn't make me feel like this.'

He looks genuinely confused now. 'What are you talking about? No, hang on, back up, Alex. What makes you think it was *your* egg?'

'I came to you, remember. You showed me the donor's NHS number.'

He's staring at me blankly, and for the first time it occurs to me that I might have got this all wrong.

Just then, the sound of tyres on the gravel outside.

Ted looks up, 'Who else knows you're here?'

Fiona knows. Maybe she decided to turn me in after all. Or else the police have managed to trace the car; there must be CCTV footage of my stops en route.

Ted nods at X. 'Do you want me to hold him while you go check? You could untie me.'

Yeah right. I stop bouncing, still holding X against my body. Outside the house, I hear a car door slam and then I turn in the direction of the kitchen.

'Alex,' Ted says, and I glance back at him. 'For God's sake, be careful.'

37

Karen

Six weeks earlier, Market Harborough

At first there was the feeling of being dragged up, out of a deep sleep, of trying to ignore the sound of the alarm clock and failing. I opened my eyes and found the lights of the clock in the dark. Two o'clock. Right then.

I leaned across, found the switch of my bedside lamp and flooded the bedroom with yellow. Rob groaned, throwing his arm across his eyes. 'Seriously? Don't you have to get up tomorrow?'

'I'm getting my body clock into training,' I said. 'When the baby comes we'll both be up in the night.'

'We're both up in the night now.' But he rolled towards me, his face in my side, a warm hand sliding onto my leg. There were moments like this, when he was distracted, or groggy with sleep, when he almost forgot he was angry with me. I was tempted to slide back down under the covers and into his arms. Almost, but not quite.

I'd left all the kit at the side of the bed. I'd already connected the sterilised bottle to the electric pump and left it sitting where I could grab it, so I wouldn't have to faff about with bottles in the night.

I pulled up my t-shirt, fitted the plastic nozzle to my breast, flipped the switch on the pump.

Rob moaned again at the rumbling sound. 'Can't you go into the other room?'

'It's too cold. I want to stay here.'

He rolled away from me, pulling a pillow over his head.

I felt the squeezing sensation, strange but not unpleasant, as the pump started to work. I sat in the dark waiting. The adviser at the hospital had told me I needed to stick at it for at least ten minutes at three hourly intervals during the day, with a session during the night as well.

Rob shifted next to me. His scepticism was understandable, I suppose. It's not like I was producing very much. Milk was the point of all this, and it wasn't exactly gushing out of me. But the lactation consultant had said this was normal, there wasn't much at the beginning, some women only got a few drops before their baby arrived, but that *every single drop was precious* and all that preparation would pay off in the end. *Laying the groundwork* was the phrase she'd used.

The other day I'd told Claire about the letter from the adoptive mum, about the hormones and the electric pump. She'd looked at me sidelong. 'You don't have to do all that, Karen.'

'I know,' I snapped, irritated that someone else was going to try to talk me out of it. 'No one's making me.'

Claire pressed her lips together. 'No, I mean. You don't have to make yourself do this. To compensate or something.'

'That's not why I'm doing it.'

'Then why?'

'I know it sounds strange. But I think I'm doing it for me.'

Claire had laughed and said, 'Then in all honesty, I think you're bonkers.'

I'd always cared so much about what people thought of me. Too much probably. But so what if Rob thought I was setting myself up for another failure. So what if Claire thought I was punishing myself? I mean, *so what?*

After those first few letters, they'd just kept coming. Letters, sometimes cards, and parcels too, little gifts for the baby, small soft things, clothes, toys. Corporate gifts as well, asking us to endorse their products. 'We'd be delighted if you would try our nappy rash cream.' Baby food samples. Nappies. The works.

We stored the gifts in the baby's room, but it soon became clear we couldn't use it all. I asked around at work if anyone knew of someone needing baby stuff. Then Claire had the idea to get on the phone to Children's Services, and they agreed to accept a donation for a Women's Refuge nearby. The location of the refuge was secret, so Claire and I drove over together to the Council offices, the boot of my car loaded with boxes. A round-faced woman met us in the car park, and between us we lifted the boxes from the back of my car and shifted them into hers.

'You won't believe how useful this will be,' she said, all smiles. 'We're a pauper service, you know. Operating almost in secret, no one knows where we are and no one cares. Could get closed down any minute, and then where would my poor girls go?' She told us lots of the women at the refuge were pregnant, a higher proportion than you'd expect, as pregnancy was often a trigger for worsening domestic violence.

'We only hope we can hang on to them for a bit, help put them back together so they've the strength not to go back to their abusers. If they do go back, their children can be taken from them,' she added with a frown, 'and no one wants that. But they're so fragile, these girls, no confidence – all the brio knocked out of them. They can hardly look after themselves, let alone care for a little one.'

We drove home in silence, our initial elation at doing something useful dulled by the conversation we'd had in the car park. Eventually, Claire said, 'I'm sorry I put you through that, Karen. You've got enough on your plate.'

It was the sort of stupid thing I might have said – apologising to someone else for the world being so full of violence and meanness. Because more than anything the conversation with the woman from the refuge had made me feel grateful. Because yes, we'd lost those babies, and yes, some people were choosing to misunderstand us and our motives, and yes, that was hard. And okay, things weren't exactly plain sailing between Rob and me at the moment, but we'd be all right, wouldn't we, once the baby came?

I'd found myself reaching out more these last few weeks, I mean, to those beyond my family and immediate circle. It had started with chatting on the internet, to mums and wannabe mums in the infertility and adoption forums. I'd been nervous at first, because after my experiences online, I thought they might judge us for our choices. But it was okay, you know? Most of the time the other mums were supportive and kind, once you got past the weird acronyms and shorthand: *dh*, darling husband, *lo*: little one.

And what if I was hardly speaking to my own dh? Connecting with other women really was the best medicine. I'd always thought of myself as defective, incomplete, a woman whose body didn't do what it was supposed to, even with whole teams of doctors and nurses lining up to help. But it turned out *everyone* had some sort of struggle with this complicated business of making, birthing, feeding, and raising babies.

I'd become a little braver recently, saying what I actually thought, disagreeing even. I always did my best to be polite but I didn't bite my tongue as much as I used to. And funnily enough, people liked my input. Yes, that's right, little old me.

Claire and I were even running again, and I was feeling less worried about reporters and photographers following me around. One time recently, someone had taken a snap of me in the park – we'd spotted the man hiding behind one of the big sycamores. I just ignored him. Kept my chin up, kept running.

I kept in regular contact with Dr Mansfield, and she gave us updates on our baby's progress. He was fine, she said, happy and healthy. But I couldn't help noticing the strain in her voice, the way she sounded distant, as if she too had a lot on her mind. I didn't think she was hiding anything from us, only that she seemed tired, and stressed. What it was like for her, all that responsibility? I bet she'd be glad to have it all over and done with.

I switched off the electric pump, and stared down at the meagre drops of yellowish milk collecting in the bottom of the tiny bottle. How much was that, a teaspoon, maybe two? He was going to need more than that. Then I heard the lactation consultant's voice again: *Every drop is precious.*

Time was ticking by. It would be Christmas soon. We'd do lunch here this year, our last without him, for my mum and dad, Ian and Carrie and the kids. And next Christmas, our baby would be coming up for his first birthday. I imagined him fat and healthy, a big laughing boy, astonished by his presents and all the Christmas food he could dip his chubby fingers into. I pictured him with bright cheeks, apple red, laughing at everything, crashing out on my lap after all the excitement while the family settled on the sofa to watch the Doctor Who Christmas Special. Perhaps he'd even be toddling by then, or if not, crawling, or dragging himself about on his nappy-clad bottom.

Okay, maybe my fantasies were a little rose-tinted. Maybe I'd be ragged with sleep deprivation, and our little boy would be cranky, and Rob and I would pass him between us over the dinner table while our turkey got cold.

But whatever, he was coming, and we were going to be ready for him. Nothing anyone could say or do to us would change that. No nasty comment online was going to bother me. No stupid journalist. If I couldn't make enough milk myself, it would be okay, there were alternatives.

And if Rob and I barely saw eye to eye these days, it didn't matter, because as soon as our baby was here we'd be a family, a proper family, and the distance between us would melt away and be forgotten.

38

Alex

Now, Sussex

A door slams and then a voice calls out, 'Alex? Are you in there?'

I recognise the voice immediately: Daniel.

Relief floods through me. How clever of him to find me here, how ever did he manage it? All these months we've been meeting and talking, and Daniel's always had my back. And now, somehow, he's worked out where I would come, and he's followed me, and found me.

I make for the front door, flick the latch one handed, tug the door free of the frame. I've still got X hooked against my chest with my left arm, and I step back into the hallway to let Daniel in.

Daniel will help me work out what to do. He'll help me get some money, some antibiotics even, at the very least some better painkillers. Maybe he can get me a passport. If anyone could do it, it would be him. He probably already has a plan to help us escape, to spirit us out of the country to somewhere safe. I wouldn't put anything past him. For the first time in a long time I don't feel quite so alone.

*

My mind darts back to that night. Two nights ago; a lifetime ago. I can see the front door of the AU hanging open in front of me, I can feel the warm weight of X's body against my open palm, swaddled in layers of thick rubber, cushioned by the amnion.

Was I endangering X taking him out of the AU early and without medical back-up? I risked throwing away my career, my reputation, everything we'd achieved so far. But if I couldn't guarantee X's safety in the AU, I had to get him out. Someone had been tampering; I'd seen the needle mark on X's leg. I couldn't trust the police to keep him safe, I couldn't trust my team, couldn't even trust security. Thinking through all the available options, I knew what I had to do.

Very carefully, I pressed X back inside the AU and closed the heavy door. I checked X's oxygen levels and counted his steady heartbeat, feeling my own heart quicken. A deep breath, then I hit the button to initiate birthing.

Calm down, Alex, concentrate.

We had planned a longer process: the slow release of hormones into the AU to ready X for birth. But there wasn't time now to follow the full protocol. I set the timer for ten minutes: that would have to do. Another quick check of X's oxygen, then I hurried out into the corridor, hearing the lab door swing shut behind me, the locking mechanism sliding into place.

Just along the corridor, on the same floor as the lab, we had a room set up with everything ready for the Frey's arrival. It was a comfortable space for them to unpack their things, relax and wait, and afterwards, a space where they could rest a while, and bond with their baby, until we were satisfied he was safe to go home. I cast my eye over the small bed and the easy chair, then grabbed the plastic bassinet on its trolley, and wheeled this over to the locker, stocked with sheets and cellular blankets, fresh towels. I wheeled the lot back to the lab, my hands shaking as I pulled out my key card to let myself back into the lab.

A strange, clearheaded calm came over me as I took the cellular blankets from the plastic bassinet and folded them in a stack on the bench, then lined the bassinet with fresh towels. I washed my hands, pulled on thin plastic gloves, located the clamp and scissors in their sterile packaging, peeling back the seals so the implements were to hand.

X's ten minutes of preparation was up: the gentle shushing of the pipes had been replaced by a new sound now, a rushing, as the amniotic fluid drained away.

I watched X on the big screen, the inner lining of the AU shrinking back to hold him. A human baby, near full-term now, vacuum packed in plastic. The image was unsettling, but the placenta would maintain his oxygen supply for several more minutes.

Then it was time to act fast. The placenta was degenerating, X needed to draw breath through his lungs. I grappled with the catches on the front panel of the AU, heard them release with a hiss. X was already wriggling and kicking inside, bucking and twisting his spine, turning his head. I grabbed the tear-cord, and with a whoosh the air rushed in, the bag loosening. The smell was strong, sharp and metallic: placental blood, rich and viscous. I lifted X out of the interior cradle as the placenta slid wetly away from its moorings and came to rest at the bottom of the empty bag.

Now he was in my arms. His skin was a mottled purple, overlaid with streaks of greasy yellow vernix. I stared at his little face, crumpled, sceptical almost, his eyes scrunched against the light, the corners of his mouth turned down, lips wobbling. For a moment, I almost didn't recognise him. He'd seemed larger on the screen, smoother, and in the water, so graceful. Beached, this little scrap was tiny, and bad-tempered, barely bigger than the span of my blue-gloved hands.

X lay quietly for a moment, and then opened his mouth wide and let out a howl. I held him against me. He'd been like an eel in my hands, all tense muscle, but as I held him close and murmured gently he quietened to the sound of my voice and I could feel his body relax.

I needed to clean him up, cut his umbilical cord. I placed him carefully in the bassinet, and he lay still, looking up at me, eyes wide, dark and deep. I attached the clamp to his umbilical cord, then took the sterile scissors and snipped through the solid yellow rope, blood spilling onto my fingers. That smell again: blood. Blood everywhere. Blood from the inside of the AU had pooled in the base and was now spilling over the walls. Why hadn't I anticipated so much blood? But then, I was alone, without a team to clean up around me as I worked. We'd envisaged Verlaine's operatives harvesting the placental blood, someone else vacuuming out the base of the AU while the baby was being washed and weighed.

I breathed out hard. No time for those thoughts now, X and I had to get out of here. I had to deliver this boy to his parents, deliver him to safety. I pulled the edges of the towels up around him, wrapping him warmly, all the while speaking nonsense in a soft soothing voice I barely recognised as my own.

Then I pulled on my coat, slung my bag across my body. I was just about to lift X from the bassinet, towels and all, when I remembered the CCTV cameras guarding the corridor outside, lining any possible exit from the building. But next door in the dorm there was a soft, deep sided beach bag; I'd used it to once bring clean clothes from home. If I packed the bottom of the bag with towels,

X could lie comfortably inside, resting on his back, and I'd be able to walk straight out of the building, carrying him beside me.

Just as long as he didn't start to cry.

*

It's been hard, taking difficult decisions by myself, operating entirely on my wits, improvising. Hard, and lonely too. But now Daniel's here, things are going to change. I don't have to face all of this alone, not any more. Daniel will find a way to get us out of this mess. If anyone can do it, he can.

I'm so relieved my smile makes my face hurt.

39

Dolly

Yesterday, Newcastle-upon-Tyne, police interview

Thank you, Dolly. You've been very helpful. The most important thing now is to work out where Dr Mansfield's gone.

Really, I'm more confused than anyone.

Try Dolly, please. Rack your brains for anything Dr Mansfield might have told you. It could be something that didn't seem significant at the time, but might give us a clue about her next move.

There's nothing. She spends all her time here, and if she's not here she's at her flat.

Officers are there now, examining the place. There's evidence that she did go there, late last night, but she's not there now.

Then I don't –

Did she ever talk about somewhere special to her? Somewhere she might go?

No.

What about friends, family?

She has a sister. I can't remember her name.

We'll find her. Who else?

She didn't really talk about friends.

Any boyfriends?

Not since Ted. Oh no, has he got something to do with this? What if he's kidnapped Alex, and X too?

Given what we saw on the CCTV footage, that doesn't

seem likely. But we're considering every possibility, don't worry.

So don't waste time talking to me. You need to find Ted.

We will. In the meantime, can you think of anything that might help us work out where Dr Mansfield is?

I'm sorry, I don't know.

Then go home, and have a think. If you think of anything, you'll call us?

Yes. If I think of anything.

And Dolly? Don't go anywhere. We might need to get hold of you.

*

The last few weeks of X's gestation were turning out to involve a lot of waiting. There were readings to take, and systems to monitor, but increasingly those days it felt as if the system was running itself. Once the baby arrived, it would be a different matter. We were expecting a flurry of activity: results to polish and send out, papers to publish, press calls to field. But until then, it was time to sit quietly, and watch him lay down a little fat on those skinny thighs.

I remember the day Alex took the call from her sister. We all listened to her, murmuring in a low voice into her phone. We were wondering what had happened. I know it's rude to eavesdrop, but it was hard not to in the lab, you know? When she got off the phone she told us her grandmother had died.

'The funeral's the day after tomorrow,' Alex said. 'But I can't possibly go, not now. Another way to let my family down.'

'Of course you should go,' I'd said. 'We can look after X.'

It took us a while to persuade Alex she could leave us in charge of X for a day or two. Daniel even offered to drive her down to the place where her family were gathering, her gran's house, she said it was. Somewhere isolated, near a beach, somewhere on the South Coast. A tricky place to find, she'd said. She worried about getting a decent mobile reception.

'Just write down the address,' I said. 'We'll send a helicopter for you if we need to.' I was surprised to see Alex begin scribbling something onto a yellow sticky note; I'd been joking about the helicopter, obviously. But if Alex felt better knowing we could find her, maybe it was worth it.

I stuck the yellow note to the corner of my monitor. 'But listen, Alex, what could possibly happen?'

I saw her glance up at the big screen where X was floating, head down, legs crossed.

'You'll only be gone a day or two,' I said. 'Everything will be fine.'

40

Alex

Now, Sussex

Daniel follows me into the kitchen. He's carrying a black briefcase which he places on the table.

'How on earth did you find me?' I ask, although when he smiles I know I don't need an answer. This can be another mystery, just like all those times he got us the lab equipment we needed, or funding for extra staff, or support, and I didn't need to know how he'd done it.

'I'm going to get you out of this mess, Alex,' he says. 'You can trust me.'

A sudden flash of panic: 'You can't make me give him back,' I say. 'He's mine.'

Daniel takes a step towards me. 'Alex, he says, his voice gentle. 'It's going to be okay. We're going to take him home.'

'No.'

'You're confused,' he says, his voice softer now. 'You know that, don't you.'

I am confused, he's right about that. I've been confused for a while now. I stand in the kitchen doorway, dazed, trying to remember the sequence of events that led me here.

*

I remember carrying the deep, soft beach bag, crossing the

car park, hearing the blip of my key fob over the sound of the rain. Inside the car, I wedged the bag upright in the foot well of the passenger seat. A quick glance inside: X was awake, alert, but quiet.

It wasn't ideal, but it would have to do.

I couldn't drive the hundred and eighty or so miles to the Frey's house with a naked and bloodied baby wrapped in blankets in a bag on the floor of my car. And wouldn't he be hungry soon? So, I needed a plan. I'd go back to my flat, clear my head, grab some clean clothes, for me and for X too. I still had that pack of blue sleep suits and vests, all wrapped up and ready to give to the Freys. If I got a move on, I could get X fed and dressed and back into the car by ten, and with a full belly and a bit of luck he'd sleep for the rest of the journey. I had the Frey's address in my phone, I shouldn't have much trouble finding them. I'd be arriving late at night, but under the circumstances, that wasn't important. The main thing was that I'd be there long before Dolly arrived at work tomorrow morning, long before anyone noticed we were gone.

We stopped at a petrol station for supplies, a few streets from my flat. X was in his bag, wedged into the foot well of the passenger seat. As I leaned across I saw that his blue black eyes were open, watching me. I couldn't leave him in the car, but if I took him inside with me, would he give us away? I opened my door, got out and went round to the passenger side, retrieving X, bag and all. As I walked across the petrol station forecourt I swung the bag in time with my steps, glad of the cover of the corrugated roof that protected us from the rain.

The petrol station had a small supermarket attached, almost empty. There was one man at the till, buying cigarettes by the look of things, his back to me. I walked up and down the short aisles, trying to look normal, calm, unhurried. I selected a pack of the smallest nappies I could find, along with cotton wool balls, nappy sacks, a couple of plastic baby bottles, and a pack of small cartons of ready mixed infant formula. At the till, the bored-looking attendant barely registered my face.

Back in the car, I glanced at the CCTV camera mounted onto the roof of the petrol station. So, okay, this looked bad. I'd taken X from the Centre, walked him out of the building past security. But before anyone looked at that footage, before the police came looking for us or anyone tried to piece together my movements, I'd be at the Freys, explaining what I'd done and why.

Very soon X would be safe, and all of this would be over.

*

I lean with my hip against the kitchen table, staring at Daniel, feeling the slight weight of X in my arms.

I was taking him to the Freys, I remember that now.

He isn't mine, not really. He never was. Daniel is right: I have to give him up. I have to give him back to his parents.

'Come on, Alex,' Daniel says. 'You look a mess. Let's get you sorted out, shall we?'

41

Karen

One week earlier, London

I stared across the busy station concourse. The week before Christmas, the space under the high vaulted roof churning with people, all wrapped up tightly in coats and scarves, their heads dipped against the cold.

Would she be here already, waiting for me? Would she have changed her mind?

Several days ago, Rob made me a sign which he then tacked to the back wall above the computer in the spare room. The sign was made of red card and he'd written in thick black marker, block capitals: 'DON'T FEED THE TROLLS!!!' He'd even added a picture of a troll. It was a ridiculous creature with wonky teeth and outsized claws.

It was the sweetest thing he'd said or done in weeks.

Okay, so I hadn't exactly been following his advice. I understood his point of view: Don't reply, don't wind them up. If it upsets you, step away. But that didn't make sense to me. I thought, why should the bullies be allowed to take control of the playground? Why should the haters and harassers be the only ones who get to tell their stories? Believe it or not, I'd even gone back to Twitter. I'd set myself up with a proper account this time, my real name, and a photo.

I'm not sure how exactly I got talking to her. AngelBaby she called herself online. It didn't suit her. Ever since the Jo Miller article, she'd been abusing me.

People like #KarenFrey shouldn't be allowed to have children

Selfish bitch #KarenFrey No right to be a mother

If something happens to that baby it will be her fault #KarenFrey

She wasn't interested in Rob, of course, or even the baby, not really, though she sometimes claimed to be; she liked to pretend that all that hate and bile was inspired by concern for him. But I knew better: this was about *me*. I was the one she named in every comment. I was the focus of her hatred. Once you stopped taking it personally, it was sort of interesting.

Rob didn't think it was interesting. He thought AngelBaby was just plain nasty and should be ignored.

It was me that made contact first. I don't know why I did it. Maybe AngelBaby was the straw that broke the camel's back, and I wanted to understand what it was about. I sent her a message, on a whim. I sent, 'Why are you doing this?'

I didn't expect her to message me back. But she surprised me. 'What do you want?'

'To talk.'

We went back and forth. The funny thing was, she did want to talk to me, I could sense it. Despite all that hate and fury, she was as curious about me as I was about her. Which was how I found myself on St Pancras station that cold December morning. She'd mentioned she lived in London, so I suggested travelling down to meet her. I'd already finished work for the Christmas holidays; I could combine it with a shopping trip.

Rob thought I was crazy. 'It's going to be amazingly awkward, Karen. She's a total nutter.'

'What's she going to do, attack me in the middle of St Pancras Station?'

227

'I just don't know why you're doing this.'

'I want to understand.'

'You don't find out why someone hates you by asking them to their face. She won't tell you the truth.' He turned to me, exasperated. 'At least let me come with you.'

And have him sit beside me in silence all the way there, stewing in his resentment at this latest crazy errand I'd dragged him into? That sounded like fun.

'Two of us turning up together might scare her off.'

I reached out to touch his arm, felt him tense and pull away. 'Look, don't worry about me,' I said. 'I just want to meet her.'

We agreed to meet in a café on the main station concourse. I walked in to see a woman looking up at me. Was that her? I'm not sure what I'd been expecting, but this woman was younger than me, late twenties I'd guess, and pretty too, with curly light brown hair and a smattering of freckles across her nose.

I ignored her while I queued for my herbal tea, and then I walked over to her table, extended my hand. 'Karen.'

She nodded, but didn't take my hand. 'Stacie.' She had a soft American accent. Or Canadian maybe, I couldn't tell. I took the seat opposite her, wrapping my hands around my steaming mug.

'You probably hate me,' she said.

That made me laugh. 'Not as much as you seem to hate me,' I replied.

To my surprise, she smiled. Not at me, down at the table, but still. 'It's weird,' she said, 'seeing you in person. You aren't what I expected.' She stared into her empty coffee cup. 'I've been obsessed with you for such a long time. Whenever I read about you, in the papers or online, I'd just feel this – this rage. I'd never really questioned it.

But then, when you got in touch, it made me ask myself why.'

'Have you figured it out?'

She shifted in her chair. 'You're getting what you want, aren't you? And you don't care who gets hurt in the process.' That didn't seem fair, but I bit my tongue. 'Look,' she said. 'I know about these things, okay? Five years ago I was at college, back home in the States.' I nodded. 'I was racking up debt, working two jobs on top of my studies. Then I saw this advert for egg donors online. They were looking for college educated women under the age of thirty who wanted to help people. And I thought, that's me, that's me exactly. I'm working on my college degree, I'm twenty-three and I want to help people.' She held my eye. 'They were offering up to ten thousand dollars.'

'That's a lot of money.'

'You're telling me. The clinic ran through the risks as quickly as possible. It was clear their priority was to sign me up. But look, I'm not stupid, all right? I did some research, found out everything I could. There were women out there talking about bad experiences, but also lots who were positive about it. One of them said it was the most rewarding thing she'd ever done.'

Sadness welled up in me, and that old, familiar feeling of inadequacy. I would've loved to give an infertile couple the chance for a family. If only my body would cooperate. I wouldn't have cared about the money.

'I decided to go for it,' Stacie said. 'I injected myself daily with the hormones, and yeah, it was okay, it wasn't that bad. I got bloated, you know? But not too cranky. When they took out the eggs, fourteen of them that first time, I got some cramps, but it was okay.'

I nodded at her, remembering my egg harvesting sessions at the Centre.

'The clinic placed my eggs with a couple, and I got

paid. A couple of months later, the clinic phoned, asking if I'd do it again.'

'And did you?'

'Of course I did. For that sort of money? It had been a walk in the park.' She looked away from me again, her hand closed in a fist. She said, 'I did it four times in total. The fourth time I got Ovarian Hyperstimulation Syndrome. I phoned the clinic and told them I was ill, but you know what? They couldn't give a shit about me. I'd outlived my usefulness to them and they just wanted to get rid of me.' She looked up at me, her eyes ringed with red. 'I messed up my ovaries with that last donation,' she said. 'I've ruined my chances of having my own family.'

I resisted an impulse to reach across the table and touch her arm.

'The clinic sent me a letter, a year later, to let me know that two babies had been born, as a result of my eggs. I must have ticked the box at the time, so they would tell me. The times I wished I never ticked that box.'

I pressed my lips together. Anything I could say would come out sounding trite and insensitive. So I just sat quietly, and in the end, she worked it out for herself.

'I know it doesn't make any sense, the way I've been attacking you. I know you're not to blame.' She looked at me, and her face hardened again. Whatever softening there'd been in her attitude towards me had passed. 'That photo,' she said. 'You and your husband in the baby's room. You looked so fucking smug, your perfect house, your perfect marriage.'

I snorted at that. I couldn't help myself.

Perfect marriage? Well, that was a joke.

42

Alex

Now, Sussex

'Why don't you sit down?' Daniel says. 'Let me make you a cup of tea.'

God yes, tea sounds good. But I say, 'What I really need are antibiotics. I've got mastitis. It's horrible. The most painful thing I've ever –'

'Shssh,' Daniel says. 'Plenty of time for that. Tea first.'

*

I made it back to my flat, leaving my car in my usual parking space at the back of the building. Once inside, I placed X in the middle of my double bed, still wrapped in towels, still greasy with blood and vernix. Then I went to the dresser and took down the parcel, wrapped in blue and silver paper, and carried this over to the bed. X turned towards the rustling as I ripped open his present.

Inside there were two further packages, each wrapped in clear plastic: one set of pale blue sleep suits, one set of vests. And the soft cloth rabbit, I'd forgotten that. I laid this next to X on the bed.

I found the carrier bag from the petrol station, pulled out the nappies. I gathered cotton wool and fresh towels, and a plastic bowl from the kitchen which I filled with warm water.

'Just clean you up, eh little boy?' My voice was soft,

unfamiliar, crooning. 'Then we'll get you fed and be on our way.'

I unwrapped the towels from X's purple-mottled body, dipped cotton wool in warm water, and started washing away blood from his body before drying him carefully with the fresh towels. His legs flopped open froggily from his hips, his belly broad and flat. I lifted his legs to slide a nappy underneath him, fastened it: too big, but it would do. Then I pulled a vest over his head, bending his sapling arms to find the holes and fastening the poppers, and shimmied him into a long-legged sleep suit, bending in his arms and legs.

I'd hardly any experience with infants, and handling Fiona's babies had always made me feel awkward. I worried I might accidentally hurt or upset them, not support their heads correctly, or else somehow, through some unknown mechanism, they might sense my discomfort and disapprove of me, wanting to be back in the arms of a properly maternal woman. But with X it was different. I felt the tension and resistance of his muscles against my fingers, and he seemed to respond to the dance, letting me lead.

I fastened the poppers that ran down the front of the sleep suit, from his neck all the way to his toes. There. He looked respectable. Properly dressed, in the soft pale blue jersey fabric, printed with the ghosts of pale teddies. A normal, newborn infant.

'That's better, isn't it?' I said. 'More comfortable.'

He stared back at me. I was so disoriented I half expected him to smile, or even speak. I picked him up off the bed, felt him fit comfortably into the crook of my arm. 'I couldn't leave you there,' I explained. 'And I couldn't take you to the police.'

X rolled his eyes.

'I know,' I said, 'but how are the police going to look after you? A police station in the middle of the night is no place for a newborn.'

He was starting to squirm now, turning his face towards me, arching his back and curling his tongue, opening and closing his mouth like a fish. It took me a second to work out what was going on.

'You're hungry. Of course.'

I carried him into the living room, laid him gently on the sofa, where he immediately started to cry. The sound started up a kind of panic in me, and I dashed back into the bedroom to grab the bag from the petrol station, taking out bottles and cartons of formula. With every passing second, X's cries increased in pitch and volume, sending painful vibrations through me, like the sound of a dentist's drill. At the edge of my consciousness I was aware of my breasts, hot and uncomfortable.

'All right,' I called, working to keep my voice calm. 'I'm coming.' I stared at the label on the carton of formula milk.

Always give baby milk in a sterilized bottle.

Sterilized bottle. Fuck.

Suitable from 6 months. Infant formula is not a substitute for breast milk.

Hang on a minute. Suitable from 6 months.

Stupid, stupid. Crushed under the weight of my unpreparedness. The sound coming from X now was awful, dangerous, as if he would tip himself into some sort of fit or convulsion. Could I put him back in the car, screaming, then drive to the petrol station to buy the right kind of infant formula? And then what? Get him out of the car and carry him inside still howling?

What if they didn't sell newborn formula milk in late-night petrol stations? Perhaps people with newborns had the foresight to buy their formula at proper supermarkets, during the day. What else did I need? I had bottles, but no sterilizing equipment. How on earth did one sterilize a baby's bottle anyway?

If only he'd stop crying, I'd be able to think.

Lifting him off the sofa only brought the awful sound closer to my ears. Still I felt overcome with pity for him, so newly born and terribly hungry. He hadn't asked to be born – early at that – only to be cared for by this awful incompetent woman who hadn't considered how she would feed him. Considering the expertise, research and preparation that had gone into providing his nutrition in the AU, the lack of expertise and preparation in the room right now was shocking. I could have banged my head against the wall for shame.

But the sound was intolerable, and thoughts were quickly blotted out by the all-encompassing, pulsing wail. X slid to my shoulder where he proceeded to beat his small head against my collarbone, insistently, in rhythm with the terrible noise. Dazed and panicked, I sat down on the sofa and laid him across my lap. Then I pulled up my sweatshirt, adjusted my bra, and awkwardly guided X's mouth, still opening and closing like the beak of a baby bird, to my left nipple. There was a sharp pain as his jaws clamped down, but the sound had stopped, and the relief was so acute that for a second or two the pain didn't register. By the time it did, the sensation had become almost pleasurable, like scratching hard on a patch of itchy skin until it bled.

I looked down at X, champing away.

Now this was something new. I'd put a baby to my breast. And not my own baby, oh no, but a baby that a couple of hours earlier I'd removed, illegally, from a research facility.

How am I going to explain this to Karen Frey? The

question was so absurd it made me snort with laughter.

Undeterred, X sucked on.

I wouldn't tell them. Yes, that was the way. It wouldn't happen again. I just had to acquire the correct equipment, and then everything would be fine. It would be hours before X was hungry again, and by that time I'd be properly prepared. And once everything was under control, I'd deliver him to his parents.

I looked down at X's face, familiar and adorable. He was suckling intently, working his jaws like a monster. I was filled with a sudden and inexplicable confidence that my instincts would guide me correctly.

Just then, my phone rang. Holding X against me, a warm bundle of sweetness, milk and warmth, I leaned into my bag.

Ted.

Why was he contacting me? Had he worked out what I'd done? Of course, it made sense. Ted had been hacking into the AU control system, so maybe he'd somehow left a trace in there. When I removed X from the AU then he, or his accomplices, must have been notified. Were they on their way here now?

X had finished feeding and fallen into a doze. Lifting him carefully, I walked to the window. Outside the lights of the bridges were strung like beads across the river, buffeted by the wind and rain. And on the street below, there was Ted, standing next to his car, his phone against his ear, looking up at my window.

He'd come for us. We had to get away. If we avoided the lifts and the main entrance and used the stairs instead, I could sneak out the back of the building and head for my car. Then with any luck we could drive straight out onto the main road without Ted seeing us leave. There was no doubt Ted would follow us if we gave him the chance. He'd be after us soon enough anyway; we needed whatever head start we could get.

*

I sip the tea that Daniel hands me, and watch as, like the impossible magician he is, he opens his black briefcase and takes out two white plastic pill bottles.

'You've got one hell of a fever there,' he says amiably, laying his hand on my forehead. 'No wonder you feel like shit.' He shakes one of the bottles, opens the cap, hands me two white capsules. 'Here. These painkillers will bring your fever down. And this one,' he takes the second bottle, 'wide spectrum antibiotic. This should knock the infection on the head.' He hands me four of the bright blue pills.

I raise my eyebrows at him. 'Double dose to get you started,' he says. 'Old pharmacist's trick.'

'Are you sure these are okay?' I ask. 'I mean, I'm breastfeeding.'

'It's all right, Alex,' he says, and the tone of his voice is so calm, so authoritative, I feel myself relax. 'You don't need to worry.'

'But how did you –?' I begin.

'You know me. Always prepared,' Daniel says. He smiles as I swallow the handful of pills with my tea, deciding not to think too much about why he's carrying antibiotics in his briefcase. Let alone these painkillers, whatever they are, I don't recognise any of them. 'There,' Daniel says. 'You'll start to feel better now.'

I hold X against my chest while I finish off my tea.

'So this is a mess,' Daniel says after a while, 'but if you trust me I reckon I can manage it for you. You do trust me, don't you Alex?'

I nod, obedient.

'So, for starters, you've had some sort of breakdown.'

'Yes,' I say, although I'm not sure that's what I'd call it. 'You're right, I've been confused. Something's happened to my brain.'

'You imagined there was a problem in the lab, yes? You felt confused and paranoid. So you took X.'

'Yes,' I say. 'That's all true. Except I don't think I imagined all of it.'

'Alex,' Daniel says, his voice firmer now, 'I need you to listen, and to do exactly what I say. That's the only way I'm going to get this story straight for you.'

Explaining feels like a mountain of words I have to climb and I don't know how to find the energy for it. 'I think someone was messing with X. There was a mark on his leg. I opened the AU and I saw it.'

If I thought I was tired yesterday, right now I want to lie down on the floor and sleep forever. It must be the relief flooding through me; I've been running on adrenaline for days now, and now my system is starting to crash.

'What do you mean, a mark?' Daniel asks.

'A needle mark. As if someone took blood, or else administered an injection. And that's not all. The corticosterone spikes. The breaks in the recording.'

Daniel is shaking his head. Somehow I've got to convince him I didn't imagine this whole thing. But did I really create this ridiculous story all by myself? And how trustworthy am I, anyway? A crazy woman who stole a baby? And what if there's another explanation for the corticosterone spikes, the system clock? What if I imagined that mark?

I think about Ted, tied up in the back kitchen. Isn't he the final proof – if any were needed – that I'm the one who can't be trusted?

43

Dolly

Today, A1, just north of Scotch Corner

So, tell me again, Dee. Where exactly are we going?
We're going to find Alex. And X too.
I thought the police told you to sit tight at home.
Yeah. They did.
This is sitting tight?
Not exactly.
You know where Alex is?
I don't know. But I've got an idea.
Okay, but Dee?
What?
If you know where she is, why didn't you just tell the police?

*

After the interview, the police told me to go straight home.

I didn't want to go home without speaking to Daniel, but he was called in to his interview with the police directly after me. Which meant he'd be in there for at least half an hour, maybe more. I walked along to his empty office, let myself in, perched on his desk. I called his mobile, which went straight to voicemail, as expected.

'It's me. I'm in your office at the moment. Come and find me when you get out of the interview?'

And that was when I saw the yellow sticky note.

It was odd, seeing it out of context, on the middle of Daniel's desk. I'd got so used to it being on the corner of my computer screen, where I'd stuck it after Alex went away for her grandmother's funeral. It'd sort of become invisible to me and I'd just left it there. When had Daniel taken it from the lab? And why?

Unless.

An empty house, isolated, Alex had said. Where was it exactly?

I opened the map app on my phone and put in the postcode.

Bloody hell.

Where was that anyway? Sussex? Somewhere along the coast from Brighton by the look of things. And judging by all the green space around it, that building – the house? – was isolated. I made a note of the address on another scrap of paper, did my best to commit the mental shapes of the map to my memory.

The Centre was crawling with police. Someone was bound to come along this corridor at any minute, and I didn't fancy explaining why I was hanging around, looking shifty, when I'd been told to go straight home.

But what if this was my chance to find Alex?

I needed to talk to Daniel. Was he thinking what I was thinking? Is that why he'd taken the sticky note? Perhaps he'd come with me, drive down to find her. I'd rather not go on my own.

Or maybe Daniel would tell me to hand the address over to the police. But then again, he hadn't given them the sticky note either, had he? He'd taken it from the lab, and left it in here.

I was tempted to wait for Daniel to come out of his interview, but my nerves were getting the better of me. I went home.

That afternoon I paced my flat, waiting for Daniel to call back. When he didn't call, I watched the rolling news on the telly until Aimee got home, then we watched it together over a pizza. Neither of us could work out what the hell was going on, no matter what crazy theory we came up with, none of it made any sense.

I thought about the Freys, and hoped they were doing okay. I hoped Alex was all right, and even more than that, I hoped X was.

When we went to bed at midnight, Daniel still hadn't phoned.

I thought about the isolated house on the South Coast. Why would Alex go there? And why would she take X?

Maybe there was only one way to find out.

*

That's my phone beeping in my bag. Aims, can you grab it?

You've got a text.

Maybe it's Alex.

Sorry Dee, it's your mum again.

For God's sake. All right then, read it out.

She's worried sick. She needs to talk to you.

Not now, Mum. Honestly.

Oh look, and here's another one coming in. Your mum again. 'Please Samantha. Just call me. There's something I need to tell you.'

Put it on silent. I'll deal with her when this is over.

You don't want to hear what she's got to tell you?

That's the last thing I want right now.

What if it's important?

Believe me, it won't be. The thing is Aimee, I have to give her a chance.

Your mum?

No. Alex. I have to give her a chance to make it right. I had so much faith in her, and somewhere along the way I lost it all. Maybe I idolised her too much at the beginning, and that's why I got disappointed. But she's a good person, I'm ninety-nine per cent certain of that. Maybe I was right about her at the start, when I decided to take the job. Look, I don't know how all of this happened, but I'm pretty sure Alex is in deep shit right now, and I'm pretty sure she needs my help. If we can just find her, and find out what's going on. Maybe Alex can turn herself in before they catch up with her. Return X safely –

You think that'll make a difference?

It just might.

44

Alex

Now, Sussex

'It's a standard screening test,' Daniel explains, calmly unbuttoning the leg of X's sleep suit and working free his small, wrinkled foot.

'Couldn't it wait till we get to the hospital?' I ask, although to be honest I'm too exhausted to put up much of an argument. And for that matter I'm just so relieved Daniel is here, helping me, taking charge.

Holding tight to X's ankle, Daniel takes a needle from the briefcase and pricks X's heel. X howls in protest, and I stroke my boy's forehead, making small noises to calm him.

'Better do it now,' Daniel says. He looks at me. 'Besides, we're not leaving here until we've got your story straight.'

He squeezes a bubble of blood from X's heel into a small plastic bottle. He fits the stoppered bottle, now dark with X's blood, into the foam casing of his briefcase. He clicks the latches shut, and places the briefcase back on the floor.

'There,' he says, buttoning up X's sleepsuit, then reaches up to press his palm against my forehead. 'Still hot,' he says. 'Those pills should start to work soon.'

My fever might not be dropping, but something's happening. 'Are those painkillers supposed to make me drowsy?' I ask.

'A little,' he says. 'Perhaps you need a lie down. Just a nap before we go. I'll look after this one.' He takes X from my arms and I stand up. Too fast, apparently, as the room swims around me, and I clutch at the edge of the table for balance. 'Come on,' Daniel says, shifting X into one of his arms, and picking up his briefcase with the other. Then he leads me upstairs towards the bedroom.

*

As we travelled south, I lost all track of time. After a while X started to cry again, and it did seem odd, that he could be hungry again so soon. Perhaps something had gone wrong with time; it was affecting X as much as it was affecting me. I'd intended to be better prepared for this next feed: I had bottles, but no means of sterilising them. I had formula milk, but the wrong sort. I needed to deliver a baby to the Freys who was fed, clean, and comfortable. What was I going to do now?

For such a tiny baby he made an awful lot of noise, and it was difficult to concentrate on driving. Thank goodness the roads were almost empty. I drove on doggedly until we reached a motorway service station. By the time I pulled into the car park his cries were already at fever pitch, so I pulled him out of his bag and breastfed him again, there in the driver's seat.

Afterwards, I felt crushingly, inexplicably tired. I started to think, what if time worked differently for X, because he was so new? A day for him must feel like a whole lifetime. Perhaps I was tuning in to X's experience of time, being infected by it.

Except. Hang on.

Alex. Get a grip.

Then I thought, perhaps the reason I was so tired was

that time itself had actually gone wrong. It had become loosed somehow, from its moorings. Maybe this had something to do with the glitch in the clock in the AU system. If you couldn't trust the system clock, what could you trust?

Or maybe it did have something to do with X after all, something to do with the unusual nature of his gestation. He was like a black hole, immensely dense, sucking in matter, sucking in light, bending time around himself. That would explain his gravitational pull, the energy it took not to touch him.

Rain pelted the windscreen. I enjoyed the sound of it pounding the roof of the car, and a sense of wellbeing crept over me. This was all very strange, but at least I was thinking like a scientist, noticing connections, constructing a rational hypothesis.

A jolt, and I was bolt upright again, drenched in panic. X startled, then slumped. I must have been dozing. It was dark outside, a little after two. The car park was almost empty. I stared down at X, fast asleep in my arms. Funny to think of him now as that small creature howling for his milk, then suckling the life out of me, all taut muscle and working mandible. I lifted his small hand, let it drop. He was limp as a rag doll, all the tension smoothed out of his face.

I should put him back into his bag and keep driving. But the bright lights of the service station glowed invitingly in the dark. And I was *very* thirsty. A cup of tea. A nappy change. It need only be for an hour. Just to clear my head, reset my brain, be safe to drive. I'd still reach the Freys several hours before anyone arrived at the lab, long before anyone realised we were missing.

I lifted X so his cheek was resting against my clavicle, then inched out of the car, digging into the back seat for my coat and overnight bag. I pulled the coat around both of us, and dashed across the dark car park towards the yellow lights.

There was a small hotel at one side of the service station. I paid up front for the room, in cash, and used a false name for the form. Inside the room, I lay down on the bed next to X, curling my body around him, a crescent of protection, my arms at his back. I stroked his thin, dark hair, allowing my thumb to trace over the indent of his fontanel. His skin was plumper and less purple than it had been just a few hours earlier. He was already filling out.

As I drifted off to sleep, he seemed to change size, to grow bigger, until the room was full of him, everything else crowded out, pressed away. I wasn't alarmed, but lay very still, watching him. *How he is able to do it?* One minute baby-sized, the next room-sized, and then back to baby-sized again. I hadn't known babies were capable of such implausible feats of transformation.

Really, the things I *had* known about babies could be counted on the fingers of one hand. But still, this sort of information was surprising. Mothers must know, I supposed, but they had chosen to keep this information to themselves. It was a kind of insider secret. I'd ask Fiona, later on.

But – no, that wasn't right. Babies didn't suddenly change size, did they? It was only X who did this, and wasn't this really an optical illusion, caused by all those months of watching him on the big screen in the lab?

Babies couldn't really just –

I blinked, hazy and confused, then sat up, shrugging off my coat, kicking off my shoes and snuggling down under the heavy duvet, leaving X on the top of the covers, his thin cellular blanket laid on top of him. I would sleep for an hour, two max. Then I'd take a shower, and have a cup of tea, and we could be on our way. It was taking a long time to make this journey, but we'd still be there by morning.

I yawned. All would be well.

I woke to the sound of X wriggling around, making small, snuffling noises, turning his head back and forth. I wriggled down the bed until we were face to face.

His eyes were an unfathomable deep blue-grey, all iris and pupil. I felt a shiver run through me, an emptying out, like the sucking back of a wave as it draws away from the beach, followed by a deep crash of love that broke over me, bringing milk to my nipples and tears to my eyes.

How had he done this? He was some kind of magical creature, an entirely new being. Surely no mother had felt this for her child before now, not this. I melted into him, dissolved into elemental particles and then reformed, a new shape.

Until that moment I'd honestly believed I was taking him to Karen and Rob Frey in the Midlands. Now the idea was laughable. Why would I hand my baby over to strangers? What kind of a monster would do that? He needed me. He needed his mummy.

I pulled him close, pushing the heavy bed covering down so it wouldn't smother him, and putting him to my breast again, my mind emptying as he suckled. After he was finished and had fallen back into a milk induced swoon on his back, his arms and legs splayed, his body relaxed, I undressed and headed for the bathroom. I stood under the weak spray of the shower, wondering, if I wasn't taking him to the Freys, what next? I needed a plan. It would, no doubt, involve leaving the country, or going into hiding, somehow, for a long time. I towelled my hair, pulled on some clean clothes. Where could I go?

That's when I thought of Fiona. She was a mother herself. She would understand.

Besides, she'd probably have some old baby things she could lend us. She might even dig out an old car seat, to make sure X was safe and comfortable on the journey. So yeah, I'd keep driving south, head for Fiona's. I already felt so much better for having a plan.

I packed up our few belongings, and then lifted X who was still sleeping, off the bed. At the shop in the main building, I bought a croissant, and a big bottle of water, X wrapped into the fold of my coat, one arm clasped around him as I fumbled one-handed for change. Nobody seemed to recognise me. Most of the people around were single men, lorry drivers travelling through the night. Tired people too ragged to notice anything, the night staff at the coffee chain too bored.

I got back into the car, placed X back in his deep sided, towel-lined bag. He lay back, arms raised above his head in surrender.

I was going to have to get him a car seat. It wasn't right to cart him round the country in a beach bag. I gulped back water, then drank the coffee more slowly, and ate the croissant. I'd only been driving an hour when the sky began to turn silvery grey with morning.

45

Karen

Yesterday morning, Market Harborough

I'd woken with a jolt. There was a dream, just beyond reach now. Something about the baby. Was there something wrong with the baby?

No, just a dream. I ran through my usual mental drill. The baby was fine. We didn't need to worry about anything. The baby was healthy and well. Dr Mansfield and the team were looking after him. Just a couple more days, then we'd be together.

Rob was snoring gently on the other side of the bed. I wanted to snuggle up to him and be comforted, the way I used to. Instead I turned my back on him, swung myself into a sitting position, my bare feet on the cool carpet.

What was that dream? Almost every trace of it was gone, but I couldn't shake that faint sense of worry. It was nothing. Nothing. Just nerves as our big day got closer. Understandable, though, that I was feeling jumpy. Only a matter of days now, and I'd be able to hold my baby in my arms.

I'd already packed the bag to take with us when we travelled north. It was a leather holdall, the usual overnight bag Rob and I took when we went away for the weekend, but this time, in addition to our spare underwear, clean tops and pyjamas, there was also a carton of newborn nappies and a stack of neatly folded baby clothes.

Ridiculously early, I know. Silly of me. Because this

wasn't the sort of pregnancy where everything could change at the last minute, one second twiddling your thumbs and the next second action stations.

I decided that I might as well get up. There was no point sitting here on the edge of the bed. And goodness it was cold. I pulled on my dressing gown, wrapped it tightly around me, and opened the bedroom door as quietly as I could so I didn't disturb Rob.

We still had strings of Christmas cards hanging up by long red ribbons around the living room, and the Christmas tree was standing in the corner. I switched on the fairy lights as I passed, noticing the dry needles peppering the carpet. Perhaps I'd take everything down today, get it over and done with. That might make the days pass faster.

Strange to think I wouldn't be going back to work. This year, our staff Christmas party had been a joint do, Christmas for everyone, and a leaving party for me to boot. They'd had a whip-round, bought me a lovely basket of presents. Bath bombs, a slab of expensive chocolate, a book about running technique.

'Nothing for the baby,' Carole said, rosy cheeked after the wine. 'Although some of us were tempted. We thought it would be good to treat you for a change.'

It was sweet of everyone; I'm not ashamed to say I cried. Everyone hugged me when I left the restaurant, and Rob sat outside in the car with the engine running, waiting to drive me home.

I shut the kitchen door so the radio wouldn't wake Rob. I filled the kettle and made myself a cup of herbal tea. A lot of the usual nonsense on the radio. A politician had once promised something and had now done something else. A footballer was in trouble for bad behaviour. I was only half listening.

Then the male news anchor said, *We've got some dreadful, shocking news, just in. There's been an attack on the Centre for Reproductive Medicine in Newcastle upon Tyne. Our reporter Nancy Welford is at the scene.*

And then a woman's voice said, *That's right, I'm here now. It's still difficult to establish exactly what's happened, whether it's a kidnapping or some sort of terrorist attack. Police have told us they are not going to release a statement until they have spoken to the family.*

The family? They didn't mean us, did they?

They couldn't mean us.

And that was when the phone started to ring.

46

Alex

Now, Sussex

I slide under the covers, collapse against the pillows. 'Let me hold him,' I say. 'I want us to fall asleep together, one more time.' Daniel places his briefcase on the floor, then hands X into my arms. I hold my boy close, committing to memory every inch of his face, every detail of the way this feels.

'You know stem cell medicine is the future, don't you Alex?' Daniel says quietly.

I look up at him, confused, one hand resting on X's head. Why is he telling me this?

'IVG is going to make it possible,' Daniel continues. 'Stem cells from umbilical cord blood are already potent, but once we're able to support their delivery by modifying the foetus's immune system *in utero*, the sky's the limit.'

I try to sit up. My head is so heavy, and my arms are too. I can barely manage to shift X's weight against me.

'Of course no one would let us tinker with their unborn baby's immune system to test our hypothesis,' Daniel continues. 'Which is why we needed you.'

I try to speak, but something's wrong. My mouth is too dry; my tongue won't work properly.

'You think of this as fertility treatment, Alex, but you're wrong about that, you've always been wrong.' He smiles at me. 'Once this technology takes off, we'll have a perfectly optimised supply-chain. Of course, no one's going to *force* anyone to gestate their foetus in an artificial uterus. But you've got to understand the economics. The NHS is already close to bankruptcy. Ten years from now a couple will be able to choose to have their baby in some filthy, disease-ridden, understaffed public hospital, and risk mother and baby contracting some superbug while they're in there. Or, for a fee, Verlaine can grow their foetus in a state-of-the art, sterile environment, where it will get absolutely everything it needs. I can already picture the television ads.'

My head feels enormous, like it's too heavy for my neck.

'And if you can't afford the fee, you could offset the cost of your deluxe pregnancy by contributing to Verlaine's blood banks. You agree to have your baby's umbilical cord blood banked with us, that's a discount right there. You agree to have your baby produce one of the modified strains of umbilical cord blood we need to feed our stem cell industries, you'll get the whole service at a substantially discounted rate.'

I shift my weight in the bed, searching for the strength to interrupt. But Daniel's on a roll.

'Anything can be converted into a commodity,' he continues. 'Why have one, two, three eggs extracted for IVG, you have twenty, thirty per cycle, and donate the excess to the Verlaine's gamete bank for an additional discount on your bill? It's all in the marketing. Who wouldn't give their baby "the best start in life" if they could afford it?'

I can barely manage to shake my head at him. All this sounds more like extortion to me.

'The question is, when the world is reconfigured in this way, where do you want to be? Inside the shiny bubble where we can cure virtually any disease, or outside where these new treatments aren't available to you because of the cost? So what if I had to test it, illegally, in secret, without a license, or the consent of X's parents?' He shrugs his shoulders. 'I'm at the forefront of medicine. I'm ending the sort of suffering my mother went through, when no one was able to help her.'

I struggle to pull my body upright. Daniel doesn't seem to have noticed.

'Some people might say we've got women and babies taking unnecessary medical risks,' he says, 'all so we can make expensive new technologies out of their spare body parts, and sell these back to them at an inflated cost.' He smiles again. 'But just think about it. We'll charge them to stimulate their ovaries, then we'll charge to extract and store their eggs. We'll charge to gestate their babies, and if the parents want some of that precious umbilical cord blood banked for their children's future use, we'll charge them to store that too. And further down the line, when these women develop ovarian cancer from all the follicle stimulation hormone they've been taking, Verlaine will use banked eggs and the stem cells in the cord blood to create a tailor-made cure.'

'For a price,' I manage to say.

'Of course. But doesn't that sound like an incredible business plan to you?'

I wriggle one of my feet out from under the covers, find the floor. There's no way I can fight my way out of this, not now, drugged, with X in my arms. I'm not sure I could stand, let alone fight. But I'm getting control of my tongue. 'How did you do it?' I ask.

'Your lab team have been very accommodating. On one occasion Dolly gave me access, on another it was Laura. Unknowingly, in each case, but all the same. Your security protocols stink.'

'Was it worth it?' I croak, playing for time.

'Well, that's the question, isn't it? The night before last, the system alerted me to what you'd done. I got there just in time to take a sample of cord blood from the AU, before the police turned up and sealed the place off. It was already degrading, of course, completely useless therapeutically, but I was able to test the level of lymphocytes.' He shakes his head. 'It didn't work as well as we'd hoped. And the blood I just took from X's heel? I expect that will confirm X's immune system is less mature than we would want it to be, given the intervention.'

I'm trying to think straight, wondering if Daniel noticed it wasn't my car outside, but Ted's. My car's still hidden round the side of the house. If Daniel didn't clock it, there's a chance he doesn't know Ted is here. And that makes Ted my best chance of escape right now. If he could somehow wriggle free, he could surprise Daniel, overpower him.

If only I hadn't tied him up so tightly.

'You're probably wondering where this leaves my research,' Daniel says. 'Well, I'll tell you, I'm not sharing these results up the tree.' He shakes his head at me. 'If they found out it didn't work, they'd pull the plug on me and I can't allow that to happen. There's already too much talk about how much this is costing, how long it'll be before shareholders see a profit. Verlaine's been bankrolling Dekker for years on this, and the execs are losing their patience.' I stare at him. 'So, okay, it didn't work first time. That's research for you. I'm not giving up. Next time we'll have a battery of ten foetuses, we'll give them a range of immune serums. One of them has to work.'

I attempt to shift my weight, trying to regain control of my body, clear my mind.

'Oh, I know what you're thinking. After this disaster

will they let me do it again? The thing is, Alex, this disaster is on you, not me.'

'You knew I would take him,' I slur.

'No. I wasn't expecting that.'

'But my eggs – ' He shakes his head, amused. 'And these – symptoms. You messed with my head. You made me feel like I was pregnant, to –'

Daniel runs a hand across his face, exasperated. 'To do what, exactly?'

I don't know. 'To confuse me,' I manage.

'Jesus, Alex. In my entire life I've never met anyone so self-obsessed. What makes you think that any of this is about you?'

I don't answer. My tongue feels like dead meat in my mouth. But I know something's happened to me. I've changed. My body. My mind. And I've been so confused. About myself, about X.

Daniel laughs suddenly. 'You think this is all down to some deep biological connection between you and this baby? Come on Alex, I thought you were a scientist.' He narrows his eyes at me. 'Okay then, I'll tell you. When we started this project I had to establish whether or not you were going to be a problem. I considered recruiting you, at the beginning. But it didn't take long to realise that wasn't going to work.'

Recruit me to test this new technology illegally on X's immune system? Daniel's right I would never have done it.

'You're inflexible, Alex, that's your problem. You see everything in black and white. And you get mired in little details, miss the bigger picture.' He glares at me. 'We're the ones saving lives here, you know, we're the good guys. Still, it was easy enough to manage you. A bit of flattery, some help with resources and staffing. You rolled over, like the rest of your team. I only got concerned when Ted

Hayward showed up. I guessed he'd be cautious, would want to work out what side you were on before he showed his hand. Still, it was a risk. I had to make sure you wouldn't trust anything Ted told you.'

He certainly achieved that.

'Even with Ted gone, we've been worried you might work it out. I couldn't avoid leaving traces: X's cortisol levels, the breaks in the timeline. So these last few weeks, when we've been meeting for coffee in the mornings…?'

So he's been drugging me this whole time. I can't imagine the cocktail Daniel must have used to trick my body into believing it was pregnant.

Daniel's eyes soften as he smiles. 'Honestly, though, Alex. This wasn't the reaction I was expecting, with the small dose I've been giving you. But yeah, if you're interested, it's an antidepressant.' There's a glint in his eye as he adds, 'A new one. It's going to be a massive commercial success.'

I think about my jitteriness, my nausea and confusion over the last few weeks. I can't speak for my serotonin levels, but I don't think this new drug is going to cure depression.

Daniel must notice my scepticism because he adds, 'Admittedly, no competent psychiatrist would prescribe it in tandem with those awful sleeping tablets. And before you ask, I'm not in cahoots with your GP. That was just a happy coincidence.'

I look down at X in my arms. He isn't mine, I know that now. Has all of this been some kind of drug-induced madness, brought on by the sleeping pills I've been taking, in combination with the drug Daniel's been feeding me?

No. I know he isn't mine. But I also know I love him.

'You're wondering what all this was going to do to X's immune system? It's an interesting question. On the upside, it might've saved him from some mundane childhood illnesses. Then again, it might've resulted in him developing a more serious condition. Anyway, that's all academic now.'

I look up at Daniel again. Cold crawling fear prickles my skin.

'Like I said,' Daniel continues, 'I wasn't expecting you to run. But now you have, you've provided me with the perfect means of clearing up this mess and starting again with a clean slate.'

'No,' I croak, trying, and failing, to sit up.

'It's already too late, Alex,' Daniel says calmly. 'I reckon you've got about thirty minutes. I've given you just enough to knock you out, and I've got everything I need in here,' he taps his briefcase, 'to finish the job. I'll arrange you on the bed, the dead baby in your arms. Pills and whiskey on the bedside table, perhaps. I'll make it look like you smothered him first, then took your own life.'

'No one will believe I hurt him,' I slur.

'You think?' Daniel laughs, a harsh, explosive sound. When he speaks again his voice is smooth, concerned, the voice of our early morning meetings. I can almost hear him talking to police, reporters. I can see him on the sofa on daytime TV.

He says, 'It's tragic. Alex has been going through a personal crisis. She'd put the best years of her life into helping other people have children, and in the process she'd neglected her own relationships. Her own child-bearing years were behind her, and she regretted that. She simply never anticipated the strength of her feelings towards this baby. I've done my best to support her, to be a good friend. But Alex is a difficult person. She can be stubborn. I imagine the way she saw it: she loved the baby, but couldn't possibly keep him for herself. She was between a rock and a hard place.'

I detect movement in my peripheral vision. If I'm not imagining things, someone's already come up the stairs, and is waiting on the landing. Is it Ted? Or someone else? Whoever it is, I mustn't give them away. I make myself look down, concentrate my gaze on X's face. I've got to keep Daniel's attention.

'What would you have done?' I ask. 'If I hadn't taken him.'

Daniel laughs again. 'Honestly, Alex, I was in a bind. Ever since I got the results I've been scratching my head, looking for some way to spin this to the execs. And then you come along and provide me with the perfect way out.'

There's a sudden movement, then Ted rushes headlong into the room, throwing himself in the direction of Daniel's back. Daniel grunts and falls sideways off the bed. He catches himself on one arm, and is pulling himself into a standing position, when Ted barrels into him again, knocking him to the floor. I gather all my strength to drag myself up out of the bed, X in my arms. Ted is on top of Daniel now, pinning him to the floor, but Daniel is fighting back. I spot Daniel's briefcase on the floor by my feet and give it a sharp kick, sending it sliding under the bed, and out of Daniel's reach. But I don't hang around to help Ted further. It takes me a second to regain my balance, and tighten my hold on X.

And then I run.

47

Karen

This morning, Market Harborough

The Family Liaison Officer is called Sandra. She's got wiry, ginger hair, which she wears tied back at the nape of her neck, and a broad, flat face with heavy, hooded eyes. She's said she'll wait here with us, until there's any news.

She's in the kitchen right now, making more tea. I'm not sure how tea is supposed to help. A while ago, she put her hand on my shoulder. 'It'll be okay,' she said. 'They'll find him.' I looked at her hand, confused. I understand she's going through a series of planned moves, designed to comfort me, keep me together, but I can't make sense of any of it. Why isn't she out there looking for our baby?

Most of the time my head is buzzing with questions, broken, unanswered and unanswerable, running round and round in an endless loop. Where is he? With Dr Mansfield? Or has someone else taken him? Why? What are they planning to do with him? How could this happen? Why does nobody know where he is? Then for a while it all stops, and there's nothing in my head at all. Seconds later it starts up all over again.

Rob is making himself scarce. Right now he's sitting at the end of the garden on a tree stump near the compost heap. I get it, no really, I do. He's managed to put himself as far away from me as he possibly can, without actually leaving the house. And he wouldn't leave the house, not while we're waiting for news. When I stare out through the patio doors I can see him, and the thin curling wisp of grey smoke rising from his hand.

Rob is smoking? Rob hasn't smoked since his teens. Or maybe he started again recently, in secret. Maybe I just don't know him anymore.

I watch Sandra walk down the lawn towards Rob, carrying a steaming cup of tea. Rob stubs out his cigarette on the side of the tree stump, looks up at Sandra briefly, takes the cup. They exchange a few words, Rob holding the mug in both hands. He doesn't take a sip. I've no idea what they talk about, since Sandra is unable to answer any of our questions, the important ones anyway.

Is Rob cold, I wonder? It's frosty out there, and he isn't wearing a coat.

I wonder if he'll blame me now, for our child being taken. He won't ever say it out loud, but maybe this is one more thing that will end up being my fault. I've got so used to thinking we'll be okay again once the baby comes. But what am I basing that on, really? Having a baby never saved anyone's relationship. Marriages with children break up all the time.

And what if our baby never comes home?

But no, I mustn't think that.

Never that.

We weren't like this before, were we? Even through all the miscarriages. We grieved together. I remember us holding each other close, hiding in the dark while we both cried. Why has this separated us, when those other awful experiences only brought us closer together?

It's not like we've yelled and screamed at each other. There's been no adultery, no violence. Our disagreements have been subtle, quiet ones. But I know I've let him go, little by little. I've taken too much comfort in connection with other people, gone looking for support out there in the world so it wouldn't hurt so much when he didn't quite understand me. When did it start? I remember having my eggs extracted at the Centre, how irrelevant he seemed to it all. And when all the press attention was focussed on me, how I resented him for that.

But when did we stop touching each other? And how could this happen without either of us seeing it coming?

I walk into the kitchen as Sandra comes back inside, shutting the door to the garden behind her. 'Have you had any breakfast, Karen? Would you like me to make you something?'

'Thank you, but I'm not hungry.'

'You should eat something, if you can.'

I ignore her, and head out into the garden. The lawn is crisp under my feet, and everything is silver. Wherever our baby is, I hope he's wrapped up warm.

Rob looks up at me as I approach. His eyes are red-rimmed, his face blank. Despite the thoughts churning in my head, I follow my instincts, reach out to touch him. For a moment it feels like a risk, like a leap into nothingness. But then Rob stands to meet me, and we fall into each other.

His voice is small and choked. 'I'm sorry.'

I stroke his hair. 'I'm sorry too.'

'I've been behaving like a total idiot. A real arsehole.'

'No, no. It's my fault too. It doesn't matter now.'

'I don't want to lose you.'

'Don't be silly. You couldn't. We're in this together. We always have been.'

His arms are around me, clinging on tight, crushing the breath out of my ribs.

I hold on tight.

48

Alex

Now, Sussex

I stumble down the stairs and out of the front door, not stopping to put on my shoes, or shut the door behind me. I make my way down the track, heading for the road. My legs aren't working properly; I'm dragging my socked feet on the gravel, tripping over them as I try to run as fast as I can.

I have to keep going. I mustn't drop X. I mustn't fall.

What am I doing? I should have taken my car, got a decent head start. But there was no time to find my keys, no time to hang about in that house. I just had to get out, just run and keep running. And besides I'm not sure I can remember how to drive.

The trees in the woods are dripping from the recent rain, although the sky is blue and cloudless. I hear the sound of a car engine starting up. It's coming up from behind me, from back near the house.

Who is it? Ted, or Daniel?

I don't hang around to find out, but run headlong off the track and into the sodden woods, tripping over branches, holding X close as I run. My socks are soaked through in seconds, my feet squelching through mud and layers of fallen leaves.

What was it I believed, back at the start of all this? Was this really all just about me, about my ego and my career, the way the papers tell it? Yes, I worked hard for my career; I wanted to do important work. But it was never about the celebrity conference circuit. All I really wanted was to help people: my patients, people like the Freys. I wanted to make the world a better place.

I stumble on through the mud and leaves, the wet trees looming over me, water dripping all around. Yes, I wanted to help people. The strange thing is, I don't care about any of that anymore. I barely care about my own safety.

I hold X close and stumble forward. All I want is for him to survive. He's the focus now, of every desire, every wish or ambition I ever had. Everything has narrowed to this point. My foot snags on some uneven ground; I pull it free and stumble on. I know this won't be my story, not really. X isn't here to make my name, or my career, or anyone else's, any more than he's here to grant Karen Frey's wish, or cure someone's chronic immune disorder, or make billions in profits for Verlaine.

It doesn't even matter now whose eggs were used to make him. All that caring for him, rooting for him, worrying about him, it doesn't matter now. He isn't mine to bestow, like some fairy godmother in a white lab coat. My role was only ever to care for him, and even that, only for a while. It doesn't matter if he never even knows my name.

I'm approaching a road, I can see a break in the trees up ahead, and faintly, in the distance, the sound of a car. Is it the car on the track behind me, or a car on the road ahead? All I want to do is lie down and sleep. But I drag myself on towards the road.

Yes, it is a car. And it's coming towards us.

I climb over a fallen branch and step out onto the tarmac, hoping to God they see us in time to stop, hoping the surface isn't too greasy from all the rain.

I've got to make the car stop. If it drives on past I'm finished, and X too. I'll collapse here on the road and Daniel will be right behind us. I can't risk us not being seen, I can't risk them not stopping. I stagger into the middle of the road, the car speeding towards us. It's close enough now so that I can see the faces of the driver and the passenger, and it occurs to me I must be hallucinating again, because how can that be?

The driver looks just like Dolly.

Blackness floods the edges of my vision, my knees buckle. I fight to keep my eyes open and fail, aware of X in my arms as I fall, holding on to him as tightly as I can, hoping he'll fall safely against my chest.

I hear the screech of brakes, the smell of the tyres against the wet road.

49

Dolly

Afterwards, Brighton General Hospital

Are you okay, Dee?

I don't know. Just about. Are you?

Yeah, I'm all right. D'you think the baby's going to be okay?

God, I hope so.

Poor baby.

Poor little X.

*

Aimee kicks her heels against the grey lino, making a scuffing, squeaking sound. We've been told to sit tight and wait in this hospital corridor until someone comes for us.

This time, we're sitting tight.

There's vomit on Aimee's jeans, and on her jacket, from where she was crouching on the road with Alex. I'd quite like to wipe it away, but I haven't got a tissue. I don't suppose a bit of vomit matters now. When they loaded Alex onto the stretcher and into the back of the ambulance she was very pale, but they said she was still alive. They said it was lucky we found her when we did.

We've haven't seen or heard anything of Alex since then. Or X, or for that matter X's parents. I wish someone would come and tell us what's going on.

*

Are you going to be in trouble with the police?
    I don't know.
    You knew where Alex was, but you didn't tell anyone.
    And then I did tell someone.
    Eventually.
    Whose side are you on anyway?
    Yours. Always yours. You know that, right?

*

I've been trying to piece it all together in my head. I've been trying to work out what the hell has been going on these last few months. Somebody's played me, that's for certain. I feel kind of sick, thinking about it. Sick and stupid and young. I'm not sure if the person who's been stringing me along this whole time is Alex, or maybe Daniel, or maybe someone else altogether. Am I ever going to find out? Is any of this ever going to start making sense?

That's my phone again, going off in my bag. Mum. Again. This time I decide to answer it.

Her voice comes out in a rush. 'Dolly.'

'I'm okay, Mum, it's all okay. I'm at a hospital, in Brighton. I'm not hurt, we're just waiting to find out what happened to Alex.'

I hear the crack in her voice. 'Oh, thank God. I've been so worried.'

'Yeah, I know. You've left like twenty messages on my voicemail today.'

'I can't – I don't know how to –'

'What is it? Mum, are you crying?'

'There's something I need to tell you. A confession I need to make.'

266

'A confession?'

'Those little mice – I –'

'I know that freaked you out, Mum. But you don't need to worry about –'

'No, Dolly. You're not listening to me. It's me who's been sending –'

'What? No way.'

'I didn't kill them. Obviously I didn't. I bought them in a pet shop. Snake food. I've been keeping them in the freezer, underneath the peas.'

'Does Dad know what you've been up to?'

'You don't know what it's like, being a parent. The lengths it drives you to, the madness. I'd have done anything to keep you safe. Anything.'

'But Mum –'

'I just wanted to scare you. When you're young, you think you're invincible. You think nothing can hurt you. Even after that bomb scare –'

'Please don't tell me that was you as well.'

'Of course it wasn't, who do you think I am? But it frightened me. You can't imagine how much. I worried about you night and day. I couldn't sleep for worrying. I just wanted you to take notice, to see that these awful people might target you – you personally. I thought if I got through to you, maybe you'd walk away from that place, walk away from all the danger. It was stupid of me. I should know better than anyone how stubborn you are.'

'Oh, Mum.'

'When you were born you were so fragile, so vulnerable. I was so very afraid. You were just a little tiny thing, like a tiny little mouse. My Samantha.'

'Shush, it's all right. It's all over now. Come on, Mum. Please don't cry.'

*

Dee, I've been thinking.

What about?

I want to have a baby.

You – hang on, you what now?

I want to have a baby. I mean, not right now. But not too far into the future either. I don't want to leave it till I'm – you know – till I'm old.

Are you serious, Aimee? All of this mad shit happens, and that's how you react?

Don't ask me to make sense of it. I've thought about it lots of times before, I always thought I'd like to. But now I know for certain.

It's a weird topic to bring up, right at this moment. That's all I'm saying.

Look, I understand that, Dee. But the thing is –

The thing is what?

The thing is, I want to have a baby with you.

Oh.

And I don't mind how we do all that other stuff, you know, whether we use a sperm donor, or whatever. We can work that out later on. But I do know I want to carry it. The baby. I don't want it grown in a box in a lab. I want to do it the old fashioned way.

Yeah. You're an old fashioned girl, aren't you?

I am. I'm an old fashioned girl.

50

Karen

Ten months later, Market Harborough

I put my baby down for the night in his crib, heavy with milk and sleep. I can't help marvel at the size of him, his rolling thighs, the deep folds at his wrists, as if with a gentle twist you could unscrew his little hands. Sometimes, when I look at him, I think to myself, *I did that*. I mean, all those nights – setting the alarm, the electric breast pump, not to mention the hormones. And yes, I do feel proud.

A few months back I started him on solids. His favourite are dried apricots, boiled and pureed, served in a bright yellow plastic bowl with a sucker on the bottom, to stop it sliding around. He sticks his fat fingers into the orange mush and smears it all over his face. We still manage a nice long boob feed every morning and again every evening, before he crashes out for the night. Claire says he needs to learn to go to sleep on his own, but I reckon there's time for that. Anyway, I'm not quite ready to give up breastfeeding yet, and he isn't either. And it's not like I'm going to have another baby.

After we got him back, allegations were made against the drug company. People said they'd planned to use IVG to supply stem cells all along, alongside human eggs, to develop new treatments. They'd tested something on him, they said, which started up a whole new round of rumours about his health.

You'd think I'd be worried, but I can't shake the feeling that he's doing fine. "Thriving" the health visitor says.

One day a journalist contacted me; Helen Blunt her name was. You'd think I'd've had my fill of journalists, but funnily enough, I liked this one. As we talked on the phone and she told me what she'd been researching, I decided I could trust her.

Helen said that if egg donation was left up to companies like Verlaine, there was a risk to women's health. If it was all about profit, they'd push for overuse of hormones and dangerous extraction techniques. It made me think about Stacie, and I remembered the pain in her face, the day we met on St Pancras Station. Helen said commercial egg harvesting for fertility medicine was "just the tip of the iceberg" when you considered the risk to large numbers of very poor women in the developing world selling their eggs to supply stem cell treatments for rich westerners.

But it doesn't have to be that way, she said. We can make decisions about the way these technologies develop. We have a choice.

'All right,' I said. 'I'll help.'

Helen made some phone calls, and I agreed to do something I thought I'd never do: appear on a television show. The programme's researchers had done their homework. On the sofa next to me was an American woman whose daughter had died of ovarian cancer. The mother felt sure this was connected to the many cycles of commercial egg donation the girl had undergone in the States. She'd been trying to get some coverage of her daughter's death for years, but no one had been interested. But, just as Helen had predicted, our case brought the story to the attention of the television producers.

I can hardly remember the day of the interview. I was

so nervous about saying something silly, the whole thing was a blur. Rob had our baby at the side of the studio, neither of them took their eyes off me the whole time. The producer had wanted the baby sitting on my knee, but I'd said no. And maybe it was something about the way I said it, but she listened, and didn't try to boss me around.

An interviewer in a cream suit sat to the left of me. She smiled as she introduced me and asked me questions. I told her how grateful we were, Rob and I, to the anonymous woman who'd donated her eggs to the Centre. It was such important work, I said, we wouldn't have our baby if it wasn't for her. I'd feel grateful to her, I said, every single day for the rest of my life.

And then I said, considering how important it is that women come forward to donate their eggs, it's also really important that we look after the donors properly. People aren't things, I said.

The item achieved record viewing figures and afterwards there were lots of calls to the programme's hotline. And afterwards, follow up articles in the press, and, needless to say, a lot of people talking on Twitter.

Helen's asked me to be a patron of their campaign. I've told them I'll think about it. I'm busy enough right now, just being a mum. But maybe in a while, maybe I would like to get more involved.

They're lobbying for better information for egg donors, and proper research into the long-term impact of egg donation on women's health. There's a push to investigate safer ways of gathering eggs, like "natural" IVF, where a woman can donate just one egg, at the proper moment in her cycle, so she doesn't need to take as many hormones and won't risk over-stimulating her ovaries. And they want governments to fund research into artificial ova, and other alternatives, so stem cell medicine can progress without over-reliance on eggs. You can Google the campaign if you want to find out more.

I'm not sure I'll go back to my old job. I'm a different person now. I've changed. I mean, I'm a mother now, of course, but also, all those horrible things people said about me online, it's like that somehow cured me of caring so much about what other people think. But I don't know, maybe a life in the media spotlight isn't really what I want either. My old boss, the Head teacher says I needn't go back full time, and the local nursery here is lovely, if our visit last week is anything to go by. I'm sure Little Tyler would be pleased to see me. But then I think, these early years are precious. They go by so quickly, and you can't get them back. We'll just have to see.

Sometimes I catch Rob looking at me, like I'm not the woman he was expecting to find here, in his house. It's a nice look, though. Maybe he's even a bit proud of me, at the way I've come through all this.

My sleeping baby is lying on his back, feet pulled up, fat little legs crossed at the ankle. He's got both arms raised above his head, his face turned to the side. An action pose, as if he's about to blast off into space. I'm astonished he can sleep like that, and wonder what he's dreaming about.

I switch on the lamp at the side of his crib, and the barrel turns slowly, throwing out soft shapes of coloured light that brush the walls gently as they move, all around the little room.

51

Alex

Two years later, Brighton

The police had a watertight case against me, so it was a surprise when the Crown Prosecution Service deemed my trial "not in the public interest". Too messy, apparently, the job of untangling my mental state from my drugging, at the time the offence occurred. And as my solicitor explained, the CPS wanted my help to build a more significant case against Daniel Hall. He's serving time now, at a minimum security facility in the West Midlands. He'll be out in a year or so. Verlaine denied all knowledge of his actions, and successfully deflected the scandal. A lot of people had their suspicions that Daniel wasn't working alone. Not least me, but what can you do?

The public lost whatever appetite they once had for IVG, and the regulator responded by scaling back experimental fertility research. There's been a public inquiry, long-winded, and, in my opinion, not terribly illuminating. Meanwhile, as research languishes in the UK, developments continue abroad. There's a team in India who've just announced that three years from now they'll be ready to launch a – what are they calling it? – an *Ectogenesis Gestation Centre*, to be run commercially, out of Bangalore.

It's not my business anymore. But I'll be watching anyway. I want to see what happens.

Then, a few months ago, I was coming out of the

Westminster Committee rooms – I'd been giving evidence to the inquiry – and I saw a familiar shape lurking on the stone steps. I'd recognise the shape of him anywhere. Ted.

We went around the corner to this tiny Italian coffee place. We caught up. He was still having physio on his shoulder after his run in with Daniel, but for the most part he was doing okay. I told him about my new job, teaching and research at a newer university in the South of England. I might have complained about it, there are times when it gets me down: how junior it is, given my background. How I'm not allowed unsupervised contact with patients. And oh yes, they aren't paying me much.

But I don't know, I might have spoken of the upsides too. How I've surprised myself by enjoying teaching, when I never had much time for students before. How my students love me, worship me, in fact. The notoriety is a major draw for them, my lectures are always packed. But it's more than that. Maybe I was having one of my more optimistic moments that day in the café with Ted. Maybe I told him I knew I'd bounce back, that the scientific community hadn't seen the last of Alex Mansfield.

I remember he sat opposite me and nodded, told me about the woman he'd been seeing. And how he'd been working as a tree surgeon, and was thinking about setting up his own business, which made me chuckle.

I think we both wanted some sort of – what do they call it? Closure. A grim and faintly ludicrous word. Still there was no doubt the old attraction was still there, and after finishing our coffees we went to a hotel. The plan was to get up the following morning, go our separate ways: he'd get his train north and I'd get mine south. We'd swap numbers but not discuss staying in touch, just kiss goodbye in the entrance to the Tube.

It didn't happen that way. We spent most of the next

day together in London, walking along the riverbank, talking, holding hands. And even that wasn't the end of it. He split up with his girlfriend. We've been talking on the phone, taking it slow. Next month he's coming down for another long weekend.

I don't know. Maybe I'm crazy. Maybe too much has happened between us for this to work. We've both got our baggage: he screwed me over, I hit him with a frying pan.

Sometimes I fantasise about us making a go of it. Perhaps we could even start a family together. There you go again, crazy thinking. I mean, would I even be able to get pregnant? I'm already forty-one, I'd be an elderly *primigravida*. I've seen enough women in my clinic over the years to know that my chances aren't good.

And what if I did manage to get pregnant? That's when the old anxieties crowd in. Would I be a good-enough mother? What would my child think of me, of my past actions and decisions? Would I be able to protect him or her from the horrors of the world?

The media have been remarkably restrained towards X and his family in recent years. Perhaps because they already have their hate figure in me. Maybe I've taken some of the heat off them. Under the circumstances, it's the least I could do. But yeah, okay, I'll tell you what I know.

One morning, after Daniel's trial, but before the public inquiry came to an end, I was getting out of the shower when I heard the letterbox clatter. I went downstairs to find a white, handwritten envelope on the mat, addressed to Dr Alex Mansfield, care of the Centre for Reproductive Medicine.

Karen.

Her handwriting was small and rounded, on plain white notepaper. She would rather I didn't contact them, she said. She hoped I would understand. They needed to let go of all of that now, put everything behind them. But she wanted me to know she had no hard feelings towards me; she thought of me often, and hoped I was doing okay.

She enclosed three photographs. Time had passed – it was just after his first birthday – but I recognised him immediately, his crumpled, bloodied, newborn features coming back to me vividly. I sat down in the hallway of my flat, damp in my dressing gown, my wet hair unbrushed, dripping down my back. I read the letter three times over. And many more times in the weeks and months that followed.

Another letter arrived recently, another selection of photos. Karen doesn't say much about Rob or herself; they don't make it into the photographs. Like all parents, they seem to have receded into the background. But reading between the lines, they seem happy.

And so my boy is two. His eyes have remained as blue as they were on the day he was born, and his hair is still fair, like that of his biological mother. He is tall for his age, as I was. Ninety-fourth centile, Karen reports, and skinny as a French bean.

Although otherwise strong and healthy, they've noticed a tendency towards allergies. His skin is somewhat eczematous and Karen is careful with dairy. He comes out in hives on contact with a cat. She worried about bee stings for a while, but they had him tested and that's all okay. It occurs to me that this could be the result of tampering with his immune system *in utero*. But then again, it might simply be a case of bad luck, since allergies are among the epidemics of the modern age. Either way, I'll probably never know.

But yes, I wonder. Old habits die hard.

Predictably enough for a boy of his age, he likes

dinosaurs, construction vehicles, hammer-head sharks. I don't know why I cherish these details, why I clutch them to my heart, when they are so commonplace. He sleeps with a grubby, frayed bear by the name of Lucky. He's a long way off independent reading, but he loves snuggling with a picture book, and he has a children's encyclopaedia which he studies with avid concentration.

Coming upon such details, I indulge my fantasies. Maybe he'll be clever, like me. Maybe he'll develop an interest in science. Maybe he's got a great career ahead of him.

I know it isn't any of my business.

He is happiest, Karen reports, when dashing about on a bit of waste ground behind their estate, playing with sticks and dirt and string, building dens with his father who adores him.

One day he will start school. There he'll paint, and cut felt, I'm certain of it. He'll learn his letters and his numbers, and in time, he'll come to understand the world and his unique place in it. He'll make and lose friends, play sport, learn about history and science. Perhaps he will excel, perhaps he will struggle, and perhaps he will simply be ordinary.

One day he will have his heart broken, by a girl, or maybe by a boy. He'll grow beyond the influence of his parents and learn to be himself. He'll work out who he is, and then perhaps he'll have to work it out all over again. One day, he might even have children of his own.

This isn't my story, not really. I'll never be a major player in his life. Although I still hang on to my fantasy of him turning up on my door (he'll be eighteen and shockingly handsome), in search of his anonymous egg donor, I concede it might never happen. Maybe it wasn't my egg after all. Sometimes these days I wonder if I read that number wrong, if I saw what I wanted to see. I bet I could find out. I could know for certain, once and for all.

The point is, I don't want to know. Whatever X is to me, I reserve my right to take an interest, from a distance. No one would deny me that.

I was there at the beginning, remember? I oversaw his conception, I supervised his gestation, I rolled up my sleeves at his birth. In more ways than one, I brought him into the world.

My memories don't fade. Even years later, they are as intense and vivid as ever, tender to the touch, like a deep bruise which refuses to heal. I remember his tiny wrinkled hands, moving and grasping for purchase on the world. His fingernails, long and faintly purple. I remember the soft, creped texture of his skin, and the way he turned his head towards me, his mouth open like a baby bird, his eyes wide, deep pools of darkest blue. I remember his smell, sour-sweet, like buttermilk, overlaid with the metallic tang of fresh blood.

Acknowledgements

Most special thanks to Teika Bellamy who saw enough potential in a rough draft of this book to take a risk on it, and has been unswerving in her commitment to it ever since. Those running small presses work tirelessly for very little reward and are essential to ensuring that a diverse range of books get published and a diverse range of voices get heard, something for which authors – and readers – should be immensely grateful.

I am indebted to Professor Donna Dickenson's book *Property in the Body* for my thinking on egg donation and the potential for exploitation through fertility medicine. Of course, any scientific errors are my own.

Thanks to early readers Sonia Guinnessy, Dominique Corlett, Jamie Smith, Georgina Aboud, Neil McIntosh and Julie Corbin for advice, pointers and encouragement. Thanks too to Fay, for invaluable professional advice, moral support and plenty of gin.

Very special thanks to Charley Maitland and Pauline Smith, without whom I'm sure I'd never write a word.

And most of all thanks to Dexter and Euan Maitland. Don't believe any of that nonsense about the pram in the hall, boys; how would I have known any of this without you?

Mother's Milk Books

is an independent press, founded and managed by
at-home mother, Dr Teika Bellamy.

The aim of the press is to celebrate femininity
and empathy through images and words,
with a view to normalizing breastfeeding.
The annual Mother's Milk Books Writing Prize, which
welcomes poetry and prose from both adults and children,
runs from September to mid-January.
Mother's Milk Books also produces and sells art
and poetry prints, as well as greetings cards.
For more information about the press, and to make purchases
from the online store,
please visit: www.mothersmilkbooks.com